INSIDE

INS🔑DE

A HOWARD HAMILTON RIDE-ALONG

J.C. DE LADURANTEY

iUniverse®

INSIDE
A HOWARD HAMILTON RIDE-ALONG

iUniverse books may be ordered through booksellers or by contacting:

iUniverse
1663 Liberty Drive
Bloomington, IN 47403
www.iuniverse.com
844-349-9409

ISBN: 978-1-6632-6192-2 (sc)
ISBN: 978-1-6632-6193-9 (hc)
ISBN: 978-1-6632-6191-5 (e)

Library of Congress Control Number: 2024907180

Print information available on the last page.

iUniverse rev. date: 04/23/2024

1

Officer Howard Hamilton of the Orchard Hill Police Department sat in a large booth with his old partner, Donny Simpkins, and John Tenery, a former USMC captain with three years on OHPD. To his left was Michael Alcazar, Hamilton's former trainee. All three wore the typical off-duty cop garb of unbloused Tommy Bahama or Untuckit shirts to hide their weapons. They were waiting on one more to join them, Johnny "Red" Walker, a homicide detective at OHPD.

It was six o'clock on a Friday night at Home Plate. Those with families waiting at home who'd just gotten off the day watch were having one for the road. For some, it meant a long, ugly drive in commuter traffic, whether south to Orange County or north to the San Fernando Valley. Not many coppers lived close to work. The drizzle outside meant it would be slow getting home for many.

A few of the San Pedro longshoremen, those who loaded and unloaded colossal cargo ships from China and other foreign countries at the ports of Long Beach and Los Angeles, stopped by for beers to hear the war stories from those who patrolled the streets of the surrounding communities. Home Plate, or HP, was the watering hole for LAPD, Orchard Hill PD, Garden City PD, and LA Port Police. It was their home away from home, at least until the traffic died down.

The remodel of Home Plate was almost complete. The new owner, Gary Laurenti, had purchased the somewhat hidden bar along the San Pedro boardwalk, among those who lived on board, locally owned fish markets, bait and tackle shops, and trinket stores. He'd knocked out a wall of the empty storage shed that a previous owner had vacated and added booths, two pool tables, and a jukebox. The walls were covered with shiplap rough-sawn wood painted enamel white, with a soft beige trim. Tasteful paintings and other artwork depicted cityscapes.

Laurenti knew how to attract the off-duty cop, one who also carried a sidearm under the shirt or suit jacket. He'd located a copy of Abel Reynoso's famous wall painting that adorned the hallowed wall at the LAPD Police Academy gymnasium. It depicted a historic collage of uniformed officers from the early 1800s to the modern day, including helicopters, police dogs, and changes to the armament and police cars. The artist was also a reserve officer for the department—instant security for Home Plate.

Laurenti brought in live entertainment on occasion. Generally, someone with a guitar could quietly provide background music to conversations centered on everything from family issues to girlfriend or boyfriend problems and a few cop stories embellished a bit for those listening intently.

Rumor had it Laurenti had been a police officer in the NYPD or LAPD, but the information stopped there. No one knew—or maybe no one cared—as long as he took care of his clientele. He'd kept the name HP, affiliated with baseball, to ensure familiarity with the old bar would continue. Laurenti knew how to attract the right clientele, combining baseball and cop themes.

Hamilton often reflected on the dichotomy of his closest friends. Donny was a soft-spoken, Pillsbury-looking guy who specialized in locating stolen cars, many times with the culprits still driving them. Yet he had never had to resort to the use of force in any of his arrests.

On the other hand, Walker had been involved in way too many shootings. It was as if he had a death wish, because he seemed to place himself in positions where he had no choice but to shoot. Howard knew it was a combination of poor tactics, a lust for a gunfight, and a death wish. The powers of OHPD had seen their dilemma, taken him out of uniform, and, because he was a great cop, given him the prestigious assignment of a homicide detective after he worked briefly on the burglary table. There had never been an OHPD detective involved in a shooting, and he had been forewarned that he was not to be the first. Howard tried to surround himself with the good guys.

Home Plate had been their respite just about every Friday night since Hamilton's wife, Clare, had been killed by an illegal street racer in Long Beach. It had been eighteen months to the day, but Howard—or HH, as many called him—was not about to share that information. If they did know, no one would mention it.

Tenery—or Cappy, the nickname assigned to him after he completed his one-year probation—was regaling the booth, along with others who were eavesdropping, with the story of his latest escapade. Tenery was about six foot two and 220 pounds of mean Marine turned OHPD cop. He'd spent four years in the Corps, but those who assigned the nicknames did not want to give him the name Captain, for fear of the wrath of the four captains of OHPD. Cappy it would be. He had a military bearing that oozed respect. The fact that he was black just accented his demeanor and command presence.

He told of receiving a radio call of a man with a machete threatening to attack bystanders at a local strip mall.

"I rolled up to a small strip mall and immediately saw the guy waving the machete at shoppers. He was moving it around like a samurai but not approaching anyone. He was obviously just a 5150," he joked, referring to the health and safety code section for someone with mental problems. "Well, I just stood there smiling at him as backup arrived. I waved at them to stand by while I tried to deal with the guy." He was now talking with his hands and using gestures to amplify his story. "Then I saw something familiar on his rather worn and beat-up jacket. The Marine Corps emblem—looked like he had sewn it on himself. That was when I had an idea."

Now cynosure was evident, as Tenery had everyone's attention within earshot. The noise level dropped a few decibels.

"I asked him if he was a Marine. He responded with 'E-4 corporal, serial number 2086230.' That was when I knew I had his attention. I summoned my best drill instructor voice and shouted, 'Captain John Tenery, US Marine Corps! Corporal, atten-hut!'"

Tenery had given the command that every Marine knew meant to assume the position of attention. No one in the bar was talking; they were only listening now.

A voice from a booth filled with longshoremen shouted, "Did you shoot him?"

No one responded to the idiot.

"Then I gave him another order: 'Hand salute,'" Tenery said in his booming drill instructor voice, which bounced off the walls of Home Plate. "Well," he said, realizing he had overdone his dramatization, "I'll be damned if he didn't drop the machete to the ground and assume the position of attention with his hands down to his sides, his heels together, and his feet at a forty-five-degree angle, with his heels clicking. He looked straight ahead."

Everyone was still spellbound, waiting to see what would happen next.

Tenery continued. "My next command was 'Forward march.' I wanted to get him as far away from the weapon as possible. I had him walking straight at me. When he was about ten feet from me and over twenty feet from the machete, I commanded, 'Detail, halt.' He followed instructions just like a good Marine would. I signaled my backups to get the weapon and handcuff him as we both stayed in a state of military bearing. We were eyeball to eyeball. He was not going to move until I gave him the command.

"Before they handcuffed him, I called out, 'Parade rest.' He immediately moved his feet out thirty inches and placed his hands in the small of his back with his thumbs intertwined, like a good Marine."

"I have to ask, Cappy. What did you book him for?" Hamilton tried to make it a natural follow-up question to the story.

"I didn't book him for anything, HH. I got approval from the watch commander to take him to a VA housing unit I know about. Some Marine Corps buddies run it in Inglewood. WC approved it. I had no real victims because he swung it in the wind and not directly at someone. Well, maybe me, but I don't count."

There was a smattering of applause as he sat back and took a long draw of his 805 IPA beer.

Tenery was in his glory. He had gotten the attention of just about everyone within earshot. But not Laurenti, who kept tending bar, acting as if he had not heard it.

2
CHAPTER

As things started returning to the routine conversation, several non-PD types came by to shake Tenery's hand. It was a level of respect no one else in the booth expected. Hell, it was just routine police work.

As the conversations settled into normalcy, Walker finally showed up. His slacks, suit jacket, and open-collar dress shirt, sans the tie, ensured everyone knew he had just left the station.

"Hey, Red, where've you been? You missed all the fun." Howard tried to catch him off guard.

Walker slid into the booth as everyone shuffled to make room. Now it was tight with five.

"I don't think so, HH. I guess you haven't heard. Well, truth be told, no one else has, except a few of us who caught wind of something happening as we left the station. We had a late investigation, so we didn't leave until after five thirty."

"OK, so what did we miss?" Donny said, sipping his beer and munching on tortilla chips.

"Well, I'll give it to you as straight as possible. The Chief is gone."

Four voices simultaneously responded, "What do you mean *gone*?"

"He's no longer our Chief. He was either fired or quit. No one knows right now."

"Fuck me," Donny said on behalf of everyone. "Fuck me."

The OHPD booth sat in silence for a moment. Everyone stared at the bottom of his beer glass.

"OK." Howard finally broke the mood. "What else do you know?"

"I can tell you what the dolphins say, but I don't want to speculate."

OHPD had adopted the *dolphin* term after one of the guys visited SeaWorld with his family and was told that dolphins passed on information to other dolphins. It was as if they gossiped with one another. No one knew how they'd discovered their communication method, but it hadn't taken long for the term to be used endearingly throughout the PD.

"Because I work in detectives, and we have that big squad bay. We hear a lot of shit about what's happening. I mean inside stuff. You don't, HH, because you're in that supersleuth unit with closed doors."

"Come on, John. Out with it." Howard was getting impatient.

"All I know is that Lieutenant Hospian and the POA had something to do with it. Hospian thinks the Chief is the one who set up an investigation into his stepson being a drug dealer. Weed, I guess. The POA has been doing some digging and found out he may have been the one to arrange the investigation on the two city councilmen. You remember they were investigated for running a swap meet someplace and dealing in counterfeit and stolen goods. The POA had backed both for election against the mayor. And they lost. I also found out two POA guys were reprimanded for working the swap meet without work permits."

Walker asked the waitress for an 805. "Not only that, but the chief also assigned Hospian to audit our evidence room after one of the community service officers was found to have embezzled some of the funds. Hospian cc'd the city manager on his audit and told him the chief should have run the evidence room better. And you gotta know they did not like that he came from LAPD. A lot of strikes against him. That's all I know right now."

Walker took a deep breath as the beer he ordered showed up. It went down fast.

"That's enough," Simpkins said on behalf of everyone. "You know, he got in trouble when Hotel Hyatt and your boot here"—he nudged Alcazar with a friendly bump—"stopped some douchebags in an alley at three in the morning, detained them for almost forty-five minutes, and had to cut them loose. There's no doubt they were going to burglarize a business there. The city had to pay out over two hundred fifty thousand dollars to those idiots. And the chief was home in bed."

There was not much more to be said. Alcazar shook his head.

"I'm going home," Hamilton said in disgust.

Everyone agreed. The wind had been knocked out of their sails.

Like a good confidential employee, Hamilton was not going to say shit. He would not tell anyone that he had given the information on Hospian's stepson to the chief. He'd found out from his daughter, who had unknowingly been at a party where the kid was selling weed. And Jesus, his investigation had discovered the city council people selling stolen items at the swap meet.

Am I responsible for the Chief losing his job?

His head was spinning, and he felt sick to his stomach.

3

Howard pulled up to the home he and Clare had bought when they first moved to Orchard Hill. Geoff was home from Arizona State for the holidays, and Marcia was on a break from the community college. He could not believe it would be the third Christmas without Clare. He could see the kids acclimating to her absence: walking by her picture without looking, getting their meals, and picking up the household chores that used to be hers. Nothing got easier.

It was the weekend, and he did not have to return to work until Tuesday. A lot could happen, but Howard would not let himself get caught up in the intrigue that had overtaken OHPD.

Howard wanted an update on ASU from Geoff, so he suggested early morning coffee at Peet's.

"That would be great, Dad," Geoff responded. "There's no Peet's Coffee in Zona. Maybe I could get a Keurig and order the pods to my dorm."

Marcia opted to tag along and listen to Geoff's stories.

They arrived at their destination, and Howard was relieved not to see any black-and-whites poaching his coffee spot. The rain had stopped, but the wind and chill in the air called for jackets. While he knew some of the guys had found Peet's, he did not want to hear any drama about what was happening at the PD. At least not today.

Peet's holiday blend was on full display with the red packaging. Shoppers were dressed for the holidays and getting their early caffeine fix for the day—many double espressos to go. All the customers seemed to be in holiday spirits.

They ordered and took a booth out on the covered patio area and away from the ambient noise. They got settled, and Geoff started the conversation.

"I love ASU and the Sun Devils, Dad. I've not had the chance to tell you how much I appreciate your letting me go out of state for school. It's been good for me."

"I didn't know we had a choice," Howard said with a smile.

"Well, I know you could have put up a fight, but the experience has been great—no fraternities or anything like that but good, clean social activities. Everyone I've met is a serious student. It's nice."

Marcia chimed in. "Should I consider going there?"

There was a moment of silence because neither knew whom she was asking, Geoff or Dad. Howard saw in Geoff's body language that he was deferring to him.

"Marcia, I think that's totally up to you. I love having you home, but we don't have to cross that bridge just yet," Howard finally said. "You guys know you can go to any college you want. Well, not USC or some other private college with the tuition off the map, but you know what I mean."

He wouldn't say it, but the clear implication was that Clare's life insurance assured their education. The thought of losing Clare to an illegal street-racing accident still haunted the family.

"So let me tell you all about ASU," Geoff said as he returned with their orders. And he did.

"Can I ask a question before Dad does, Geoff?"

"Of course."

"Do you have a girlfriend?"

"If you must know, I have a friend who is a girl."

"That was not my question."

"I know. Just poking the bear a little. As a matter of fact, yes, and we hang out together quite a bit."

"Serious?" Marcia continued the interrogation.

Howard was enjoying it.

"Serious as friends can be, but we see other people."

"Does this girl have a name?" Marcia asked.

"Martha, but she goes by Marty."

There was more to learn, but it could wait. Howard was thinking about whether the relationship was friends with benefits. *Maybe I should have that talk again.*

"What are we doing for the holidays?" Marcia asked the table.

9

Geoff deferred to Dad again.

Howard finished the last of a savory scone before responding. "I thought we'd celebrate them, but I have some suggestions. Last year was a blur; I'm not sure I'll work a uniform shift, as I did last year. I think I'm done with the street for a while."

"I guess we'd better plan something then." Marcia laughed. "Any ideas?"

"Yeah," Howard said quietly with a quirky smile, "something we've never done before. Game?"

"I'm in."

"I'm in too."

4
CHAPTER

The Hamilton household spent the weekend decorating for the Christmas holiday, inside and outside. But they didn't overdo it, as they had in years past. It was not to distance themselves from the consummate home decorator, Mom, but for a different reason. They weren't going to be home for the holidays this year.

After Saturday night Mass at Saint Elizabeth's and Sunday brunch at the Cheesecake Factory, the family tree and some modicum of decorations completed the plan. Now it was up to Lieutenant Rikelman and Sergeant Barber if he could take time off from Christmas Eve to after New Year's. Geoff didn't need to return to ASU until the second week in January of the new year, so Howard was confident their plans would work out. He would know for sure on Tuesday.

Everyone grabbed a quick breakfast on Monday morning, when a monkey wrench was thrown into the Hamilton plans. *Ping!* The text on Howard's phone read, "All hands on deck Tuesday at 9:00 a.m. Be in the office a little early, but plan on spending the morning in meetings. Lt. R."

Was there some big operation planned he was unaware of? Was it going to require canceling the cabin in Big Bear? Was he reading too much into this? Now he was worried. He walked around the house, trying to think of every way the job could screw up his plans. He quickly grabbed an English muffin from the toaster, gulped his coffee, and went to his computer. He was not going to let the job interfere with his holiday plans.

But what if he had no choice? The family had never been in the snow. There was much to look forward to. He even had ensured the place was pet friendly so they could bring Bentley, their golden retriever. Would he lose his deposit?

Throughout his patrol time, he had been a bit envious. The Narcotics

11

and Vice Unit, or N&V, always took off during that time of year to burn up their overtime. Did that include him too? He didn't know. For sure, he was not going to call Rikelman on the weekend. That was a one-way street of communication only.

He hadn't contacted the cabin owner yet. He wasn't going to tell the kids either. But there was someone he could reach.

His email was quick and to the point: "Sergeant Barber, I hate to bother you on the weekend, but …"

In two minutes, he had his answer. Everyone in the unit would be off until after the holidays. It was tradition. Nothing was going to change it, not even dope dealers. Barber did not discuss the happenings in the department or the meeting, and Hamilton would not ask about them.

"Thanks for the info. See you Tuesday, Sarge." He sat back in his chair with an immense sense of relief.

Phew, I dodged a bullet there.

5

Howard looked at the agenda. It was neatly typed with bullet points. There was even a line for questions. It was Tuesday, nine o'clock on the button. Lieutenant Rikelman would not waste anyone's time.

"Not like him," Howard muttered. He wondered what was going on. "OK, it looks like we have one hundred percent attendance today. I wonder why."

Rikelman did not indicate that he heard Howard, but he smirked as only Norman Bates could have. He was two people, two personalities. One was the casual but stern leader everyone wanted. The other was out of the movie *Psycho*, an old Alfred Hitchcock thriller that depicted a deranged and dangerous motel manager. That was Norman Bates.

Thus, the question of the day was always "Is he Norman or Rikelman?" Rikelman could be either, depending upon his mood, the subject matter, and whom he had to deal with. He intimidated everybody, even other lieutenants, the captains, and, some believed, the previous Chief. But not this Chief. The Chief who wasn't there any longer was on the agenda but was the last item.

Hamilton looked around the room and counted heads. Five teams of two narcs made ten, plus Joanie, the administrative assistant, who knew where all the bodies were buried, and Sergeant Barber. Counting Rikelman, HH was fourteen. It was a tight fit in a room that held six comfortably.

"First on the agenda"—Rikelman nodded to Joanie—"this is a new form we developed just for this unit. You can see it's titled 'Confidential Employee Agreement.' IA—or the Professional Standards Unit, as we now call it—also has to fill it out."

Joanie passed them around, with Howard being the last to receive one. It was two pages long.

"You must complete it and give it to Barber for approval. No ifs, ands, or buts. Let's talk about this for a minute."

Rikelman stood to go into lecture mode. "As for the Chief, I'll get to that moment. Our strategic planning unit copied this from some other agency—I think LAPD, not sure—and made it ours." He walked around the tight quarters in the small conference room behind everyone, ensuring they were all looking at the form—another Norman Bates tactic. "Everyone in here must sign it. Before you do, I want to instill in you that we"—he waved his hands around the room as he returned to the head of the table—"are all confidential employees. What does that mean? It means what I said it means." He looked again at everyone for eye contact, and he got it.

There was silence as he paused to let his words sink in.

"What you see, hear, smell, or taste does not leave this unit. Understood? We get in situations and handle cases that nobody should know about. Not your wife, detectives, patrol buddies, or even your girlfriend."

All nodded in agreement.

"Smell? Did someone say smell?" Morgan could not help himself.

"Not me," said the Everlys together.

Everybody had a good laugh.

"Start filling it out right now. It should be self-explanatory. You are out of this unit if you violate its conditions. No questions asked. But not before I have your ass. Got it?"

Again, the silence was a tacit understanding that Bates was alive and well.

Howard took the opportunity to get a cup of coffee from their new Keurig. He needed his caffeine fix this morning. He'd brought Peet's Major Dickason pods and introduced everyone to a better cup of coffee.

6
CHAPTER

"Any questions? I want to remind you that we have changed all the locks in our office. All of you have secure, lockable desks and lockers, and we even built a vault for our renowned intel officer to live in."

Rikelman referred to the relatively spacious office built for Hamilton, who had been working out of a closet. He'd convinced the Chief to remove a wall to take space from the downsized traffic division and create a secure location for Hamilton and his three computer screens. Most of what Hamilton had was stored digitally and in hard copy in file cabinets.

"Item two, vice complaints. Yes, the name of our unit is narcotics and vice." Rikelman placed a strong emphasis on *vice*. "As you know, we only investigate these issues if we determine we have a valid commercial complaint, there is vigorish involved, or it's conspicuous." He counted the infamous three Cs of vice enforcement on his fingers: commercial, complained of, and conspicuous.

"We know the drill, sir. What do we have?" Bobby "BB" Bowers said, trying to be sarcastic without disrespect.

"Well, I must keep reminding you because it's been a while since we've had any complaints in our city. Are you volunteering to take one of these investigations, BB?" Rikelman was challenging him in a way only Norman Bates could have.

"No, sir, it's not Disney's and my turn," he said, referring to his partner, Al Disney Garcia. "It's the Everlys'."

"That's what the board says, BB, but do not tempt me," Rikelman said, pointing to the old-fashioned sign-out board posted to let everyone know the status of each team. It showed that the Everlys—Don and Phil—were up. A red star indicated the next team up for a vice complaint investigation.

"I've got two here. Don, do you guys want both or just one?"

"Do we get to pick?" Phil asked on behalf of both.

"Nope. All or one only, and I get to pick which one. But before I talk about these complaints, one more class lesson."

"Aw, jeez, Lieutenant, another one?" BB responded. Bowers had been the senior member of the unit for seven years and running. He was making it a career-ender with only three more to go for his retirement.

Rikelman didn't have to say anything. He just gave Bowers the Bates stare and let the silence shout.

"Moving on, I want to see some creativity in these investigations. You can work on them this week, look at the landscape, and come back after the holidays ready to do some problem-oriented policing. I want the problem solved. And not with just arrests. That's too easy."

Phil reached out for the complaint forms Rikelman was holding. "We'll take both of them, Lieutenant, and show these assholes how it's done." He passed one to Don, read the one-page complaint, and said, "This is a 647a PC complaint for lewd conduct at the Orchard Park restroom just west of the Little League field. That's way up in the back part of the park. Pretty secluded. Males are soliciting and committing lewd acts on other males in the bathroom. It says the action occurs after the baseball field has wrapped up play but just before dark and into twilight. Sounds like a perfect lovers' lane." Phil chuckled to himself.

Others caught the joke and decided to laugh with him.

Don spoke up next. "Here's mine—647b activity along Albion Boulevard. Streetwalkers are hitting on lone males in cars. Who's hitting on who here? Prostitution? In Orchard Hill? Come on, Lieutenant."

Rikelman looked at him with a snarl. "The pandemic has caused a lot of people to lose their jobs. It looks like some of the housewives have had to find other work. It's right on the border with LA, so we may be getting some spillover. Take a look, and keep us updated."

"One more question, Lieutenant. Well, two more. How creative can we be on these complaints?" Phil asked with a straight face.

"As creative as the law permits. What's your second question?"

"Can we take the kid with us?" he asked, referring to Hamilton.

7

"OK, here we go." Rikelman became the serious manager. "Remember the form you signed at the beginning of the meeting?"

Everyone in the room, including Joanie, nodded.

"The Chief—our Chief. Well, for most of us. Well, anyway, you know what I mean." He stumbled for the right words. "I will say this, but it does not leave this room. Your POA and a specific management level in this department wanted him gone. They and the new city council. Watson got his cronies in on this last election with the help of the POA. And your dues money. They now control the majority of the council. The Chief's last day was Friday; many wish him well. But not all." He looked at the back wall for divine guidance, hoping he could choose his words carefully.

"You have to remember," he said somberly, "we have been isolated from policing turmoil in the last few years. Orchard Hill is like an island, with a strong community and political support. People made it known at council meetings that their support for us was unwavering. The bullshit reporting on 'Hands up; don't shoot' on Canfield Avenue in Ferguson, Missouri, led to even more community support here. Nothing changed when the incident occurred on Thirty-Eighth Street and Chicago Avenue in Minneapolis. They watched as Minneapolis burned, and the community standards eroded overnight. Once again, the OH community stood for proactive enforcement and not passive patrol to keep their city safe."

It was one of the longest speeches anyone had heard from him.

"I'll finish with this. The sense of community support encouraged the Chief to push for our assertive enforcement and strong community outreach. He defended us, and so did the community. I think he knew what true community policing was all about."

Hamilton's phone went off unexpectedly. He glanced at it to see it was

Flowers. "Sorry, sir. Forgot to silence it." The sound of the phone broke the stillness in the room.

"Anyway, here's the unofficial list of issues that sent him packing, *confidential* employees." Rikelman's emphasis was intended. "First, those two city councilmen were convinced the chief orchestrated the investigation against them by the motion picture industry investigators. Number two, Hospian's stepson was never arrested, but somebody put enough pressure on him to send the boy out of state to a military school. The kid was tied to a local drug dealer. He was just a low-level supplier to the school kids around here."

More silence engulfed the room.

"Number three, the Chief initially agreed to move into Orchard Hill from his home in Orange County. That was according to initial reports when he was selected. It never happened. Number four." He held up four fingers to make the point that there were many issues, none of which were more important than the others. "They found out he was still on the board of directors of a youth program in his old city, LA. *They* did not like that either," he said, using air quotes to emphasize *they*. "Add the Hyatt lawsuit and our evidence room scandal, and it was over for him. The six items would not be enough individually, but they piled up. That was enough for the city council and the POA to pressure the city manager. He had no choice."

Howard was not feeling well. He squirmed in his seat, took a deep breath, and took another gulp of coffee to calm his nerves. Two of the issues were directly related to his investigations. *Fuck me!*

Wilton was first with a question. "So who is our new Chief?"

"Shit, buddy," Bowers responded, "the body's not even cold yet, and you're asking who's next up?"

"Yes, dickhead, I am."

Everyone but Rikelman and Hamilton laughed at the banter.

"If you must know, that becomes a little complicated," Rikelman said in his quiet, more analytical voice. "The city manager has two choices. First, we need to bring in an outside interim chief. That is a no-go with the council and the POA. His only other choice is to appoint one of our captains as interim and then go through the worldwide search and testing process again."

Wilton seemed to dominate the questions. "Let's see. Do we get the Bible thumper, the attorney on his way to the DA's office, or the one ready to have a heart attack?"

Bowers couldn't resist. "Hey, now who's the dickhead?"

Rikelman relaxed his command presence and smiled along with everyone else. "Now you're thinking like an administrator. By process of elimination, who do we have?"

There was a momentary silence, and then Scotty spoke up. "Rod Tustin."

"You got it, Guitar Man."

Newly appointed Captain Rodney Tustin was the next fair-haired golden boy after Lieutenant Blair Rydell. Everyone knew the Chief had been grooming Tustin as his eventual replacement, but no one had counted on this recent series of events.

Rikelman had to add a piece of information that not everyone knew. "You know, guys, his wife is Rose Tustin."

"Who's Rose Tustin?" Wolford asked on behalf of everyone.

"I thought everyone knew." Rikelman smiled sinisterly, as if he were the Cheshire cat, with information no one else had. "She's the police chief of our neighboring city, Redondo."

Hamilton decided to break the void of silence. "Wow, we are an incestuous bunch, aren't we?"

Morgan didn't have a question, but he added his two cents. "So we could have Rod Tustin as our new Chief, and his wife is right next door in Redondo. That is some serious coin coming into the Tustin household. I think they only have one daughter."

There were collective nods all around.

Disney Garcia chimed in with a sarcastic "Hey, we got no Hispanics around here?"

Graham countered, "Not till you put your nose in a book and get your head out of your ass."

The best and worst part of a small unit was the banter. One could be irreverent, even obscene, but it stayed in the room, and no one took offense. That was N&V, and everyone knew it. They had to accept it or else.

"Here's the rub with that little item," Rikelman, always the source of crucial information, added. "He's at the esteemed FBI Academy in Quantico, Virginia. That's where all new captains go for indoctrination into the management skills necessary to handle you assholes."

8
CHAPTER

The Bates smile came from nowhere. "Item three."

No one could figure out what item three on the agenda was all about. *Roundtable?*

"Gotta ask," Scotty Moore said. "What is *roundtable?*"

"Glad you asked. I want us to go around the room and let everyone know our holiday plans. It's that simple. We're a tight group here, but we don't know much about what happens away from the shop. And I'll start. This does not leave this room until it happens. Remember, you are confidential employees." Rikelman tried to laugh at his attempt at humor.

He stared into the distance and then came back to earth. "I'm getting engaged on Christmas Eve." Rikelman sat back.

Everyone was in shock. Even the person who should have known, Joanie, had her mouth open.

Thirteen of the fourteen voices were heard saying, "What?"

Rikelman let it all sink in.

"I think I know who," Hamilton quietly muttered.

"Oh, you do, smart-ass?"

"Well, sir, I am the intelligence officer here." He chuckled. "I saw this coming a mile away. Even two years ago. Vivian Hayes, sir. Am I right?"

"Your intel must be good, HH."

"Just a good observer of human nature, sir."

Vivian Hayes was the widow of Charlie Gabby Hayes. A few years back, Hayes had had a heart attack in court and passed away before paramedics arrived. Only a few people knew that Rikelman and Vivian had been engaged years before she'd married Charlie. She had opted for Charlie over Rikelman for who knew what reasons.

Maybe she saw his Norman Bates side.

"Congratulations, sir" was the unanimous reply in many different forms.

"Well, it hasn't happened yet," Rikelman said, "but I think she knows it's coming. We're too old to pussyfoot around on this kind of stuff." He did the distant stare on the back wall again. "OK, next up are the Everlys. What's each of you doing? I hope it's not together."

Don spoke first. "God, no! I see enough of this turd here. We are having a few kids and our grandkids over on Christmas Eve. They'll make a U-turn on Christmas Day and return for dinner. Then the wife and I'll kick back, and I get to do the old honey-dos for the next few weeks."

Phil chimed in. "Same. But not with his family—mine. Kids, grandkids, and work around the house on maintenance I haven't been doing. Looking forward to it."

Don and Phil might not have been real brothers, but they were kindred spirits.

Next up was Scotty "Guitar Man" Moore. His nickname came from his real name. Elvis's original lead guitar had been Scotty Moore, which had made his name a foregone conclusion.

"I know you won't believe it, but a quiet Christmas Eve and Day, and the next day, the wife and I are going to Graceland."

The laughter took almost a minute to subside.

Moore's partner, Billy "Blackie" White, finally jumped in. "We have to go back east for my grandfather's funeral. He just passed away. It'll be during the week after Christmas. Sorry. I didn't want it to be a downer."

Condolences of various sorts came after the laughter had been exchanged for reality.

Tony "Shotgun" Morgan, the second most senior and the only black officer in the unit, jumped in to save the day. "I'm barbecuing ribs on Christmas Eve, attending midnight Mass at Saint Elizabeth's, and spending quality time with my boys. Going to see a lot of cousins and make it another Morgan family thing."

Scotty jumped in. "I'm going to his house on Christmas Eve. Changed my mind."

More laughs came, even from Blackie.

Morgan's partner was the newest member of the unit. Pat "Don't call me Patricia" Wolford, or the Wolf, was married to Donny Simpkins,

Howard's best friend. "Donny and I are staying in. It's our first Christmas together as a married couple, so we have much to do in our new house in Cerritos."

Hamilton had been the best man at their wedding, but no one knew about it. They had just slipped away, and Howard had tagged along to witness the quiet nuptials. Donny had been Wolford's training officer. In the OHPD weight room, HH had caught Pat giving Donny a head job at four o'clock in the morning. It was a match made in heaven.

Next up was Johnnie "T-bone" Wilton. Nobody knew Wilton except for his steady work habits. He was always in the office or the field with his partner, Louie Graham, who was called Louie Louie after the early '60s song. Someone had suggested calling Graham Cracker, and even though it was a term that might offend, most did. He was the only one with two nicknames. Some settled for the initials *GC*. Those in the know knew what it meant, and no one was offended—yet.

"Gonna spend some nice downtime at home. Maybe visit the parents and catch some *z*'s," Wilton said in almost a whisper.

Rumor had it there was a street called Wilton Place in the ritzy Hancock Park Wilshire district. It was named after the Wilton family and was part of the long history of old LA. He might have come from wealth but was still T-bone to everyone.

"Boring," the Everlys and a few others said.

Wilton extended a middle finger for all to see. "Sorry, Pat."

Graham wanted to be quick, as he and his partner had things to do that day. "No kids and no family. Sherrie and I are going to the beach and walking along the sand."

Garcia jumped in to move the agenda along. "We have huge family gatherings. We may go to my uncle's restaurant in East LA on Christmas Eve and do the menudo-and-tamale thing on Christmas Day. Shotgun, I cannot do midnight Mass, but I will be at the nine o'clock morning service if anybody wants to join me and my brood."

Bowers decided to chime in. "Based on the size of his family, there would not be any more room in the pew. Hell, in the church."

Everybody had loosened up with the roundtable. Was Rikelman changing, or was this how he would be from now on? Who knew?

One by one, everyone went to the coffee counter and box of pastries brought in by the Wolf.

Bowers's statement put a damper on the merriment. "On December 26, I'm going in for an angioplasty heart surgery," he said matter-of-factly. "Maybe a stent or two, but they've got to clean out the pipes a bit."

Rikelman brought it back. "Well, our prayers will be with you, BB. Could you keep us posted?"

All nodded and seemed to tuck their tails between their legs quietly. "Howard?"

HH was the last to share. He wanted to get to the next item on the agenda: the chief.

"As you know, this is year two without Clare. Our third Christmas." He paused, not for sympathy but to take a breath. "I've rented a cabin in Big Bear. Geoff is home from ASU, and Marcia is on winter break, so we're headed to the mountains with Bentley and, hopefully, some snow. What's the next item on the agenda, Lieutenant?"

Rikelman spoke like an attorney making a closing argument. "Let's wrap this up so Hamilton can get to his phone call. I will emphasize it again," he said, holding up a hand to start his infamous finger counting. "One, you are all confidential employees. Two, we have some vice investigations to get our teeth into. Three, we know what everyone is doing on holiday break. Four, we lost a good man, and five, we have no idea who will run this fuckin' ship."

9
CHAPTER

Hamilton headed to his new office to return the call from Efin Flowers.

"Hey, HH." Phil Everly caught him just as he unlocked his office door. "If you can, come in a little later tomorrow, and plan to go out with Don and me to scout out our new investigations. Should be EOW by nine or ten."

"Sounds good, Phil. That'll give me some time at home to pack for our trip."

HH liked the ability to work whatever hours he chose as long as the work got done. Hell, even if he worked OT most of the time, he never put in for it because it allowed him to come and go without worrying about punching the clock—unless one of those long shifts went fifteen or twenty hours.

Hamilton was settling into his position. For the last two years, he had immersed himself in learning everything he could about open-source intelligence. He'd met with the Chief, who'd tried to convince him he should study for sergeant and move up the ladder in the department. Howard had convinced him he would rather become a subject matter expert in his new assignment and not get into the weeds of the department. The Chief finally had relented and wished him well.

In a short time, he had worked with his former intelligence class instructor and mentor, Dennis Packer of DEA, and learned from others. He'd found that Packer had a mentor named Mike Bazzell. Hamilton had contacted Bazzell and had become the prodigy of both of them.

It wasn't just the sources he developed. He was developing the skill to investigate hacking cases, data removal, high-tech criminal investigations, online child solicitation, abduction, kidnapping, and cold-case homicides—anything that used technology. He was in his element as he expanded into understanding terrorist databases and other high-level intrusions in a world he had never known existed.

What does Flowers want?

Hamilton had been partially responsible for recruiting Melanie "Mel" Flowers. She had walked into the station one night while he was sitting at the front desk. She'd asked for some recruitment literature and confided that her father was an LAPD deputy chief. While she had been interested in law enforcement, she had not wanted to work in the LAPD, for obvious reasons.

She had laughingly told him, "LAPD isn't like New York and other back-east agencies, where being a relative is a shoo-in for getting on the job. Here on the West Coast, you have to earn it."

Hamilton had been gun-shy about talking her into coming to the OHPD. The primary reason had nothing to do with her father. He had seen she was dressed in jeans, a sweatshirt, and running shoes, but there was more. She was a knockout—a nine or ten on a ten scale. She had blonde hair to her shoulders and was five foot nine or ten, lean, and athletic looking. She was the poster girl for anything but a police department.

Regardless, Mel "Efin" Flowers had come on the job, excelled in the Police Academy, and made her probation easily, even though Hamilton had never gotten a chance to be her field training officer, or FTO. Now, with almost four years on the job, she was an FTO training others.

No one knew who had given Flowers her nickname. It had just come out as Efin. The story went that she was named after a character in acclaimed author John Sanford's novels. While his main protagonist was Lucas Davenport, Virgil "Fuckin'" Flowers handled tough cases. The character had become so popular that Sanford had spun him off for books about Virgil Fuckin' Flowers, an investigator for the Minnesota Department of Criminal Apprehension.

One had to be selective when using her nickname, but she knew it and loved it. The alias made her feel accepted, as the name Wolf did with Pat Wolford and as Chili did with Anita Hernandez in detectives. It just came with the territory of being OHPD. It was part of the culture.

The department had received accolades from everyone initially. He had tweaked a good culture into one more focused on the community. The department was more involved with schools, businesses, and service organizations, such as the Rotary, Kiwanis, and the YMCA. He ensured that someone was represented at their meetings and worked toward becoming a board member. His emphasis on technological advances, from computer-aided dispatch to Howard's position, showed he was a visionary. Would all change with a new chief?

He hit Recents to call Flowers back. She was not in his favorites, at least not yet.

10

"Mel, to what do I owe this pleasure?"

"Hello, HH. How's it going in the inner sanctum?"

"Going great. How are the boots? Have they blossomed yet?" Howard laughed at his joke. Would she get it?

"That's a great one. No one has ever said that to me, but I like it."

"That's why they pay me the big bucks—to be a little caustic but truthful."

"I need a favor. A big one," she said, speaking quietly, as if someone else were around. "I'm on a call right now with my trainee. Can I come into your office and talk sometime today? Maybe at my EOW at four?"

"Sure, see you then." *What's that all about?*

The time moved fast. Howard did some cleanup on a child porn investigation he was working on with detectives. He missed code seven again but had some caramel candy to keep feeding his sweet tooth until he filled the void later at an early dinner date.

The knock on the door told him it must've been four o'clock.

Efin was now the poster girl for everything right about OHPD. She was even striking in full uniform with forty pounds of safety equipment, including a full Sam Browne with a bulletproof vest, double ammo pouches, and a camera hanging from the middle of her chest. Another great hire by the Chief.

They hugged as much as possible, with all her equipment hiding her best parts. Even after a long shift, her slightly perfumed scent left no doubt she was one beautiful woman. Howard closed the door and offered her a seat.

"The room is soundproof, if what you have to discuss is that important."

Hamilton had been a mentor to her, even if they never had been partners. She was as close to a sister as he had; he hoped she felt the same.

"I'll get right to the point, HH. I need a date." She let that hang out there for the audience of one.

"I see. Are you asking me out?"

"I am."

"What's the catch? Is there one?"

"Yes." She paused. "My dad is friends with a family here in Orchard Hill. Well, it's almost in Sparrow Hill, so you know where I'm talking about."

"Oh, the under-two-million-dollar homes we have just before you enter Sparrow Hill, with their ghetto homes that go for two mil."

"You got it. Well, my dad's friend passed away about a year ago. He was a bit older. My mom and I are still close with my dad's friend's wife. She's having a holiday party on the twentieth. We're all invited, and I think there'll be at least twenty people or more."

"OK, this is hard to follow, but go ahead."

"My parents want me to attend and bring a date."

"And aren't you seeing someone? I have no idea who you would be dating, but I know you're not gay or anything like that, right?"

"No, it's worse." There was more silence as she searched for the right words. "I told my parents I was dating you. I should have told you, but I never figured I would be in this predicament."

"Why would you do that?"

There was another pregnant pause.

"I'm seeing a man who is, well, married."

"I see, said the blind man. Ouch." Howard's face scrunched.

"Can you help?"

"Of course. That's what friends are for, to quote a famous song."

They locked eyes, and Howard could see and feel her pain.

"I got myself into this mess, and I'll figure out what to do, but you're the only one I would ever ask. You keep things to yourself, and under other circumstances, well ..." She let the phrase hang out on the cliff of conversation.

"I can do the twentieth," he said, looking at his calendar. "That's next Tuesday. I'm leaving on Friday, so it's doable."

"I can't tell you how much I appreciate it. I owe you again." She reached out and placed a hand on top of his.

"It's good to be owed. What time do I pick you up, and what's the attire?"

11

Howard's dinner date had turned out all right. She just was not his type. *Friends keep fixing me up, and I wish I could just say no.*

It was Wednesday of a wind-down week before a few weeks off, and Howard was enjoying the holiday time with Geoff and Marcia. Now there was this dinner party with Mel.

The alternative work schedule gave him a chance to do some home projects. The English garden he and Clare had cultivated needed some TLC. He decided to go in at noon to do some catch-ups.

Hamilton had become the computer guru of the South Bay. At Packer's urging, he had built secure protocols and downloaded almost every type of free software on the market. His desk now contained three screens, with a backup hard drive and small boxes with USB ports and multiple thumb drives. His private office was his home for cybercrime investigations of all sorts. Everyone within the department approached him with specific requests, and the surrounding agencies hounded him.

His ability to access data anywhere from his tutorials with Mike Bazzell and his sources at Inteltechniques.com over the last eighteen months of learning had become legendary. He created custom USB drives that contained hundreds of files. It was all public-domain information but needed to be compiled individually. While most data was accessible, some had to be purchased through OHPD's vast budgetary resources. That was thanks to the chief's efforts to establish the department as a modern, technologically driven law enforcement agency.

No good deed ...

His expertise had developed in many areas. He was deeply involved in the location of missing children and investigating human trafficking, as many of those perpetrators relied on social media in their criminal activities. He could search for social media content posted by children as long as it was related to an ongoing investigation. He was putting together a lesson plan to go around to parent groups to assist them in monitoring the online content of their underage children. He was adept at analyzing threats involving the workplace throughout the South Bay business community and even aided background investigations being conducted by his and other departments.

With his access to custom search tools created by similar tech investigators, Hamilton's resource repository was second to none.

Howard knew he was developing his skills to a level he would never have dreamed of. But he also knew he must be vigilant in their use and protect his systems from the wandering eyes of others. He was always cautious about sharing too much with his fellow officers but would help get what they needed to complete an investigation—on his terms.

HH was a Microsoft guy, not an Apple guy. He used their antivirus software and Malwarebytes for his Windows applications. He used CCleaner to sweep and clean his unused software weekly. These recommendations came from both mentors, so he was confident he was doing it right.

He stayed away from Google, Edge, and Explorer. His preferred search engines were Firefox and Chrome. The strength of the systems he used meant they could withstand the more sophisticated interfaces he would require as he developed his entire software library.

12

He went into the office early to update the security protocols on his computer system. When everyone started showing up, the noise level increased.

He overheard that the lieutenant was not going to be there that day. Sergeant Barber would do a brief roll call and turn it over to Don and Phil to discuss their vice investigations. Barber coordinated the timekeeping to determine who would use actual vacation time versus using their OT bank.

All members of the unit were in attendance. Don stepped to the whiteboard to go into lecture mode. He wore a dress shirt and slacks and could have passed for a college professor, especially with the beard and goatee. It was lecture time.

"We're going to deal with the *a*'s first," he said, referring to the lewd conduct complaint. "I'll contact the reporting person and get as much detail as possible. Some of you—" He looked around the room. "Most of you have not conducted one of these capers, so I'm going to go slow so you can ask some questions."

Everyone nodded.

He wrote California Penal Code statute 647(a) on the board. "I'm not going to break it down, but here it is in writing," he said, handing out a one-pager from the penal code. "The type of guys we are dealing with at the Orchard Park restroom are typical of the male-to-male pickup. Sometimes they act inside the restroom if they can get a lookout and not be disturbed. Other times, they'll go out in the bushes if the restroom has too much traffic."

"What kinds of acts, may I ask?" the Wolf asked.

"The typical head jobs, blow jobs, or sodomy."

"Thanks for making that clear, Don." Wolf smiled with a relatively innocent look.

Hamilton knew better.

"There are other ways they violate the law as well." He wrote *head job* and *sodomy* on the board. "Number three is the direct solicitation. Let's say you're operating outside the restroom and see a lone male approach. He may walk up to you, asking an innocuous question like 'Come here often?' Then he might say, 'Can I suck your dick inside here?' That's a violation. You're in a public place. And there does not have to be any discussion of money unless they bring it up. Then you can negotiate. That would make it a solicitation for prostitution. Sex for money." He wrote the number four on the board. "The city attorney does not like to file the verbal solicitation cases for the 647(a). It gets into he-said, he-said."

"Does it matter who starts the conversation?" Bowers asked.

"Again, the city attorney would like everything initiated by the suspect, OK?"

"Yup."

Don sat up straight, as if his back were bothering him. He carried too much weight, so sitting was likely not his favorite position. "The next one is pretty straightforward. When you do a bathroom check, sometimes they will just be standing at the urinal, jacking off to get a hard-on or at least to get themselves semiflaccid. This is enough for a violation, but let them get more than enough strokes, so their defense isn't that they were shaking it to get the last drop. They may even ask you to go down on them, so you have a violation either way."

"Aw, jeez, Don, this is gross," Wilton said with a straight face.

"It is, but this is a different world than narcotics investigations."

"I think I'll stick to dope."

"Number five is the touchiest. And pun intended here. Sometimes suspects will coax you into the restroom, urging you to follow. They can get pretty bold. They may reach out to you, touch your arm, and then reach down and try to grope you by the nuts. To see if you have a hard-on yet."

"Are you fucking kidding me? I ain't goin' to let any fag grope me." Morgan was livid.

"Good." Don chuckled. "Here's the thing with that: pay close attention to what I am saying." His statement was unnecessary because he already had everyone's attention. "I mean, he has *almost* touched you. Just as he gets close to your crotch, within an inch or so, you knock his hand or hands away. Come up with some lame excuse, like 'Not here' or 'I'm not ready.'"

Morgan again chimed in. "No fucking way is he even going to get that close to my dick. Sorry." He shrieked with a sound that had everyone laughing at him.

"Then you don't have a violation, Shotgun."

Morgan had gotten his nickname from his last training officer while getting off probation. He didn't like to drive, so he called shotgun every time he started a shift. He enjoyed keeping the books and leaving the driving to his partner.

"That's OK by me. Let him grope my partner—well, that won't work. Will it, Pat?"

There was another round of laughter.

"Well, a few more things. So far, I'm the only one in the South Bay area qualified in court as an erection expert."

Scotty jumped on that statement. "A what?"

"Yes, sir, erection expert. The only one I know of. I had to explain in court that I knew the difference between a flaccid, semiflaccid, and erect penis." Don smiled as if he were proud of it.

"Did you have to demonstrate?" Pat joked.

"I hope no one here has to go that far to get a conviction. You have to know if it gets to court, you have a serious situation going. Someone could lose their job or become a public laughingstock. You don't have to worry as long as you do your job. Can I go on to the next-to-the-last item?"

Everyone agreed to move along.

"Now, this gets a little sensitive. You will need to make eye contact if you are approached and they try to engage in a conversation. It's their way of communicating. Let me give you an example. If you see a pretty girl and think you can initiate a conversation, you make eye contact, right?"

He demonstrated on Pat. It was the "You're OK to talk to me" look.

"With these guys, it's a different look. You connect eyeballs like you're in love but in a solemn mode. He will nod an acceptance that he is, well, you know. You then need to give him a look and a nod back." He demonstrated with Hamilton. "HH, you are a natural."

"Oh, Howard," Pat said in a sexy voice, laughing with everyone.

"Any other questions from the peanut gallery? If none, I'll move on to the arrest process."

There was tacit approval, as no one jumped up after Don's incredible lecture.

13

Don was in his element but turned it over to Phil for the next part. Phil decided to stay seated. He threw out the overhead question to see if anyone would bite on it.

"The arrest tactics are critical here. This goes for the *a*'s and the *b*'s, which we'll discuss later. Rule number one is never ID yourself when you are alone. Always have a partner within eyesight and preferably very close by. Anyone know why?"

Hamilton bit. "Officer safety issue, Phil. Always good to take someone down with two."

"You got it, HH," Phil said in approval. "But there's more to this. Let me explain. You don't know who these guys are. They come from all walks of life. And they can become violent. Don and I have conducted these investigative complaints but not for a few years. Something is happening here to reopen this location to this type of activity. We don't know what yet. Don and I have arrested family men, salesmen, other cops, and even a priest and schoolteacher."

Phil looked around the room to see that he had everyone's continued attention. He did.

"When you say the magic words 'You are under arrest,' many things go through their minds. They may fight, they may cry, or they may run. Some couldn't care less, as that's their lifestyle, but others are in the closet, and being revealed in an arrest report will cause them to panic." His voice was loud and commanding now. "You don't know, so always make the arrest with at least two of you. Use good arrest tactics, and control their environment. A hand on their bicep to see if they are tense. Get them in cuffs as quickly as you can. Got it?"

A collective "Got it" was voiced by all.

Next, Phil brought up a Google Earth map on the big screen. "This is a view of the park. I'll zoom in to the baseball field just north of the restroom, the lot where the parents park, and the bleacher area." He pointed to the bleachers and diamond area. "And here is the restroom. As you can see, it's a beat-up piece of shit. It is made of wood. It could be a log cabin for as old as it is. The urinals are beaten up, and the toilets are older than any of us in the room. Most of the time, parks and rec keep it clean, but it's old. Everything is wood. Even the partitions between the urinals and the stalls. I guess they haven't replaced anything since our last complaint."

"Maybe as part of our problem-solving, we can get them to upgrade it and, in the process, make it more difficult to conduct lewd business," Wolf said.

"Good idea," Don said. "Maybe I can give you that part of the investigation, my dear."

"I'll take it if you promise never to call me your dear again, Don. By the way, what is my role in this, while I have the floor?"

Don jumped in. "Sorry, Pat, but I should have covered that. You'll be a part of the arrest teams. We know you can handle yourself, but these restrooms are not gender neutral. We have just one team operating at a time, so the arrest teams will be critical. You may have a calming effect when the magic words are spoken."

"Or not," she joked.

"OK," Phil said, "moving on to the next item. It's an FRC—you know, field release from custody. It's essentially a citation with a promise to appear. We no longer book these guys into our jail system. We'll do want and warrant checks, verify their identification, complete the cite, and kick those who qualify. We'll set up a mini–command post on the other side of the baseball field, away from the restroom. We'll use a big sedan and put them in the backseat while they are processed. We'll have a black-and-white transport team to bring those in with warrants for booking. One of our teams will be assigned to coordinate that duty." He looked to Wilton and Graham to tell them they were the designated transport team.

Hamilton was in shock. "All this for lousy misdemeanors for which they will never do jail time?"

"Yup," Phil said. "And now I'll turn you over to Sergeant Barber for some key information you'll not want to miss."

Barber stepped right up. "I'll go into the *why* of all this later, but I want to talk about officer safety first. Surveillance of our operators is going to be critical. Many of you have developed some signaling strategy to communicate with your partners without talking. For this type of operation, I want to standardize our signals."

Barber stood to make his next point. "It goes for everyone here: your safety is essential in this operation. As was said, these guys can get violent. They see their whole life changing because of the arrest. But keep in mind one thing: they do this for a reason. It's part of the thrill they get, thinking they are getting away with something. Most of them get a hard-on doing things in public places, as you will see tomorrow."

Barber walked to a file cabinet and opened a drawer. "These are all the arrest files for that location, going back years. We may see repeaters, but I think these new people somehow found out about this location. It's popular in the gay community. Remember that guy from the musical group Wham?"

Wolford, the youngest member of the group, raised a hand. "What's a Wham?"

Most of the group laughed.

"Way before your time, Wolf." Barber smiled. "That was not his first time at that location but his first arrest there. I don't think we have to dig too far, but sometimes we find out more than we want to know during the arrest process. Some of these guys will tell you they are construction workers or salespeople. Don said it could be a senator or teacher from another jurisdiction."

He closed the file drawer and resumed his seat. "I want to review our hand signals so everyone knows them." He rubbed his nose. "What does that mean? Don, Phil, don't answer."

Graham jumped up. "I know, Sarge. It means your nose itches."

Again, there was laughter.

"It means 'I think I have something going. Just give me some time.' Just think, *I smell something cooking*; maybe that will remind you. Well, at this spot, your smell will be challenged anyway. OK, next one." He pulled on his ear.

"All right, I'm going to get serious here," Garcia said. "Too much levity. It sends a message to your partner that you need to talk."

"Thanks, Disney, and you're right."

Al Garcia had been in the unit for a few years and was mature beyond his years. He was a solid narc and conducted in-depth but creative investigations. His wife worked at Disney Studios in Burbank. He was accustomed to dressing up or down in costume for his undercover escapades. He had access to makeup artists to make him look like an old man, complete with gray hair and stuffing to make him look heavier than he was. He was double-jointed, so he could wrap his leg behind him and go as a one-legged cripple on crutches or get props like a zippered cast to make him look injured—anything for the cause.

"All right, one more here." Barber demonstrated by patting the back and top of his head with one hand. "To get rid of the suspense, this is the signal for 'I have a violation, and we need to make the moves to close in and arrest.'"

Wolf jumped in again because Howard would not bite on this one. "What if your head itches?"

Her comment brought down the house.

15

Barber looked around the room. "I can see we overdid this part. We won't do any operating or arresting today, even though we know it's probably going on as we speak."

They were having too much grab-ass to break the boredom, so Barber pushed his hands down on the table to tell them to keep it down. "I want to stress one issue that Hamilton raised. Why all this planning and detail for misdemeanors no one cares about? Today's male gay community has a hell of a network, not just with the VIPs but also at the operational level. They have the ear of the press, so whatever we do will get scrutinized in detail. Maybe even in the media. Who knows? So why are we doing it?"

No one would make an idiot out of him- or herself by answering this question.

Barber stood again. "We're doing it for the father who was brave enough to make the complaint. We're doing it for the Little Leaguers and parents who have to use that restroom during games. We're doing it because that bathroom is public, and lewd conduct is against the law. You and I have to abide by a bunch of rules that these weirdos do not. Don't push it or perjure yourself for a lousy infraction if you don't have a violation. You'd be jeopardizing your entire career. Even if you know he stroked his mule or spanked his monkey more times than he needed to shake it off. Make sure you're right at every step. These operations are heavier than any narco case I've ever dealt with. Done!"

Barber looked down at his notes. "Whoops, one more thing. Most vice-related crimes are misdemeanors. So you're a misdemeanor cop with a gun, conducting an investigation and making arrests. Unless your life is threatened, your weapon does not come into play. Got it? Use your head and mouth to get yourself out of any problem. It's not worth it."

It took thirty seconds for everyone to make eye contact without saying a word. It was a silent oath that everyone took to heart.

Barber broke the mood. "Let's take fifteen minutes or so for a head call and maybe some coffee. Be back here by three thirty."

Hamilton and Graham made a dash for the restroom. They got to their intended destination simultaneously, and two spots were available. Thank goodness for several urinals. The relief was immediate.

Graham was the jokester of the unit, so he could not resist. "I want you to know, HH, I'm not spanking the monkey or stroking my mule. I am merely draining the lizard."

They were laughing, when the unmistakable sound of a gunshot resonated throughout the building.

*　*　*

The restroom was directly adjacent to the stairwell from the first-floor basement, where the briefing rooms, lockers, and a few other offices were housed. The second floor was for all investigative units, and the third was for administrative offices and dispatch. There was no doubt the shot heard came from the stairwell, because the echo was unmistakable.

Hamilton and Graham were the closest to the doorway and ran from their separate urinals directly to the solid metal door leading to the stairwell. There was a small window in the door, but Hamilton could see nothing. He signaled to Graham, and they both drew their weapons, not knowing what to expect. Graham grabbed the door latch and swung it open, directing Hamilton to enter first and go to the right. He would cover the left side.

In three seconds, it was over. They knew exactly what they had. Howard's tension turned to anger and frustration as reality told him everything he needed to know. A dead officer in uniform brought back memories of others he had witnessed but did nothing to deaden the pain of the loss of another fellow officer.

"I'll go check on him, and you bar the door. Don't let anyone in. And, oh, Louie, your fly is open." He didn't mean for the comment to be funny, just necessary.

Howard rushed to the side of a uniformed officer spread-eagled on the landing between the first and second floors. The gun was beside him, still in his right hand but hanging loosely. Hamilton felt for a pulse but knew better, as he saw the back of his head blown off and blood draining from the back of what was left of his skull. His eyes were open and glazed, staring at no one. The blood spattered against the wall and the fact that they were first on the scene right after the shot was heard made it clear what they had.

Touch nothing; do nothing. Stand up, and do not let anyone near the body until the right people show up.

He glanced at the name tag: Morrison. Then Howard looked down and zipped his pants back up.

16

I t felt like an hour, but it was less than a minute before everything was being handled as it should have been.

Suicide is such a giant "Fuck you" to the world.

Hamilton's thoughts were all over the map. He felt composed and organized as he talked with the detective supervisor while standing over the body. He had not moved since checking for a pulse. He told the supervisor what he had done and not done and asked to be relieved from the scene. He was advised he may need to give a more detailed statement later. He walked away with a combination of prayers and anger. He took a moment to compose himself before leaving the stairwell. Deep breaths to slow the heart rate and calm his nerves seemed the only formula.

He saw Sergeant Kip Bennett in the hallway.

"You find him?" Kip asked.

Hamilton nodded.

"He showed up to work today. I saw him in the locker room, changing into his uniform. I started briefing and realized he wasn't in the lineup. I asked him why he was showing up on a day off. He smiled at me and walked out of the roll call room."

"That doesn't make any sense, Kip."

"It does now. I put him back in the lineup as a U-boat."

The U-boat was a one-man unit that took reports to free up the patrol guys to handle more calls. Hamilton reflected on A. J. "Foyt" Anderson as the last time a person assigned to such a detail had died. The entire scene flashed before him.

What a curse.

"Are you OK?" Kip stared into his eyes and could see the sorrow.

"No."

The investigative system of OHPD was kicking into full gear.

They don't need me, so I'll just go back to my cubbyhole office.

He overheard a comment from one of the sergeants: "Somebody should notify the chief."

Then someone else chimed in. "Hey, we don't have a chief right now."

"Hamilton!" Kip called down the hallway. "Come see me before your end of watch."

As Howard walked down the hallway, he almost bumped into Father Mike. He caught his eye to acknowledge him. It seemed Father Mike was always around when needed. As the department chaplain, he had his own parish to minister but liked to hang out inside the halls and as a ride-along.

How does he know he needs to be here? Another thing the Chief did right. Is he an angel who just appears? Things will all work out now.

He passed the coffee lounge and saw Graham sitting quietly, staring at the floor. "You OK? Come on; we'll shake this out together. Let's get back to the office." It was Howard's turn to hold someone up.

They returned to the squad room to see if anyone else had made it back for the next go-around on the meeting, which was now taking on less significance. That was when it hit him.

Bud Morrison was the officer he'd confronted a few years back. Morrison and his partner, Pistol Pete Laidlaw, had transported his homicide suspect to the station for questioning regarding the satanic cult killing of Ginny Karsdon on Kensington Road. They'd searched him but missed a wooden flute the guy had stuck inside his boot. While simmering in an interview room, the guy had started playing his flute, and no one had known where the music was coming from.

Hamilton had chewed a little ass, but both officers had been thankful he didn't report them to a supervisor. Hamilton had figured he needed their backup more than he needed to get them in trouble for conducting a lousy search.

17
CHAPTER

Barber reconvened the meeting after a half-hour break so they could collect their thoughts. He acknowledged the efforts of Graham and Hamilton but did not make a big deal about it. He made a few brief remarks about the tragedy but kept it nonsecular with a moment of silence, even though more was necessary. Barber then turned the meeting back over to the Everlys.

Don jumped right in as if nothing had happened. "Any questions on the hand signaling?"

Morgan broke the ice. "If we get a groper, can I just grab my crotch to let you know I have a violation?"

The levity was back.

"Unless there are any other questions, here's how we'll use the rest of this fucked-up day. Before it gets too dark and the dragons and witches come out, I'd like to have us meet at the location so you get an idea of the layout. Seeing it on Google is not the same as being there. I don't think anyone other than Phil and Barber has been up there. It takes a while to find it."

Morgan jumped in again. "We're not idiots, Don. We can find it."

Don shuffled off the comment. "I want you to work in your teams; one team will walk through the restroom at a time, inspect the interior, and view the various paths leading up to it. Other teams meet at the proposed staging area on the other side of the baseball field. There may be some potential subjects there, so use your judgment, and try not to make any arrests unless it's obvious. I want to wait until tomorrow to go fishing in the pond." He looked directly at Morgan for the last comment.

"Any questions?" Phil asked.

They were like the Everly Brothers. They took turns and knew when to come in with their solo and how to quickly back out of a situation.

"Hamilton, you can ride with me." Barber wanted to see if Howard needed any debriefing after the shooting incident, but he wouldn't say anything directly. He knew Graham could handle it, but he did not get a good read on HH.

* * *

Hamilton and Barber surveyed the restroom location first. Morgan and Wolford had not shown up yet.

Parks and Rec appeared to be doing minimal maintenance. The place was a mess, with trash thrown all over the floor. Wooden partitions between the urinals and toilet stalls had graffiti from gang members outside Orchard Hill. Hamilton recognized some of the older scripts. But it wasn't the graffiti that was the most bothersome. Two other items stood out: the odor and the mess.

"This place stinks," Barber said, holding his nose and walking in and out to take a breath. "Urine, feces, and who knows what else. We have to get Parks and Rec to clean this fuckin' place up a bit."

Toilet paper was strewn about. Used condoms were piled in a corner, along with empty bottles of amyl nitrate, a lubricant Hamilton knew was used by the gay community. He remembered seeing the same lubricant at a gay bathhouse in Rampart Division when investigating a murder-suicide a few years back. That investigation helped him understand the situation regarding restroom antics.

The most interesting aspect of their inspection was the mutilation of the partitions between the toilet stalls. Someone had taken significant precautions to ensure easy access to stranger-to-stranger oral sex. Holes had been drilled waist-high, about three inches wide, with soft rubber grommets installed. Each partition had at least three holes suitable for inserting something without fear of getting splinters.

Barber's earpiece radio monitor told him Wolford and Morgan had finally shown up.

Garcia interceded on the simplex channel: "When is it our turn, Sarge?"

After everyone had taken a turn to review the restroom, staging area, parking lot, and various pathways into and out of the relatively secluded baseball field, the banter on Morgan and Wolford was relentless.

"GPS not working, Shotgun? Stop by for a quickie? Car trouble?"

It went on and on until Barber finally called a halt.

"Go back to the office, clean up your desks, and then go EOW. I'll see you all there," Barber said dismissively.

18

Hamilton and Barber stopped for In-N-Out. Howard introduced Barber to the protein animal-style Double Double. They ordered one each and a chocolate shake and got it to go. No unit members had eaten since reporting for duty, but each team was responsible for code seven.

Hamilton quickly devoured his lunch/dinner without making a mess of his desk. He checked emails and phone calls. His most intriguing call was about an old case from a few years back involving his former partner, John Bresani. The caller was Nicole Getty, Bresani's girlfriend. Bresani had gone to the dark side and started dealing drugs. Hamilton had used him as an informant in a significant cartel drug-smuggling investigation. Eventually, Bresani had been arrested and terminated, but the district attorney had not filed criminal charges. Bresani had been shot and killed by a SWAT team during the takedown in a warehouse in Irwindale.

Nicole Getty had not been explicitly involved in the drug dealing, but Bresani had supplied her with his products. They'd lived together in Irvine, and Hamilton had met with her at the residence to follow up on the investigation and make the death notification.

He was getting ready to call her back, when there was a knock. It was Kip Bennett, the on-duty watch commander.

"Mr. Intelligence, got a minute?"

"Sure, Sarge. Anytime for you."

A mutual respect and friendship between Howard and Kip transcended rank.

"I wanted to fill you in on Morrison. You deal with a lot of people here, so you've gotta have the straight scoop." Bennett still had a touch of his Brooklyn accent and New York slang. "Some assholes here will twist and turn this damn thing, but those with some creds around here need to speak up when and if it becomes necessary."

"Understand."

"Morrison came to me last Thanksgiving. Not this Thanksgiving but the prior year." Kip jiggled the handle of the door to make sure it was closed. "It was actually Thanksgiving Eve. I will never forget it. He advised me he had been bleeding through his ass for over a fuckin' week. He hid it from his wife by buying new underwear and tossing the bloody ones." He looked around to ensure no one else would hear him, not realizing Hamilton's office was soundproof.

"No worries; my office is soundproof. No one can hear what goes on."

"OK." He started whispering anyway, which emphasized his New York accent even more. "I got him to an emergency room; the bottom line was that he had the same thing I had—colon cancer. Long story short, he went through surgery and chemo, and it looked like they got it. Nine months later, he came back to light duty, but you know the good guys; they want to be in the street. He'd been back on the street, but I saw things were still not right. I asked him, and he shined it on."

Kip squirmed in his seat, trying to get comfortable. "I saw in his eyes the exact look I had. You think the C is comin' back. You have some symptoms. But they're phantom symptoms, and I tried to tell him that. He wouldn't listen, ya know. On a day off, he showed up today, walked into the briefing, and was laughed at when I told him he was not on the schedule. I saw the same look in his eye when he got up and left the room. Five minutes later—you know the rest."

They both sat back in their chairs to take a breather.

"Father Mike, Captain Pierson, and I just got back from making the notification to the missus. He's got two young boys. I think the wife knew his state of mind. The bottom line is, I made it look like he was scheduled to work. His widow needs his pension. Maybe we can classify this as an on-duty incident. I don't know, but we'll try."

Hamilton sat back in his squeaky chair. "We sure could have used our Chief for this one. You went over and above the line of duty."

"Oh, and another thing. The fuckin city manager, your buddy, made Captain 'Bible-Thumping' Pierson acting chief until he can find somebody else. He made him swear he was not going to apply for the job. I think the CM just wanted someone with a bit of spirituality to calm all this shit down. But he didn't want a Bible-carrying chief on his hands."

After staring off into space momentarily, Kip added, "One other thing. I know you're good with these damn computers. If I give you a phone number, can you get me a printout of the incoming and outgoing?"

"Piece of cake, but why?"

"Rumors are flying that Morrison did it over a girlfriend dumping him because of his sickness. I talked to Laidlaw, and he adamantly denied Bud had a girlfriend. And if anyone knew, it would be his partner. I want to nip this in the bud before the wife gets wind of it. No pun intended. If he did, let the chips fall where they may, but if not, I gotta stop the dolphins. So get me the numbers, and I'll do the rest."

"You know, Kip, you should be our Chief," Howard said solemnly.

"That, my friend, is a story for another day."

"Perhaps at Home Plate?"

"Never."

19

"What a shit fuckin' shift this has been," Kip mumbled as he left the office.

"Agreed," Howard responded.

Hamilton turned and stared at the wall, letting everything that had happened replay in his mind. He ensured that Kip had closed the door, returned to his desk, picked up the phone, and dialed.

"Nicole Getty, this is Detective Howard Hamilton of the Orchard Hill PD returning your call. You may have been transferred to my office, so let me give you my direct number." He left a message.

Nicole had worked at the Orchard Hill Mercedes-Benz dealership. He figured she must've been busy that time of year if she still worked at her previous employment.

He scanned his emails and saw one from Anita Hernandez. The subject line was "Human trafficking." She was the department's best long-distance runner, doing marathons and leading the charge at the annual run sponsored and created by the LAPD from Baker High School in the Mojave Desert to downtown Las Vegas. It took more than twenty hours to complete the run over 120 miles of mountain, desert, and treacherous terrain. More than one hundred law enforcement agencies from all over the country participated.

Who would do that? Anita Hernandez and nineteen other crazy OHPD members. I'll get to her tomorrow.

He was thinking about LAPD, and it hit him. *I should call my old friend Detective Patterson at Rampart. He might know something about Gary Laurenti, the new owner of Home Plate.*

Several things about Laurenti bothered Hamilton. He was too young to have retired with a pension. That meant he'd left before he was vested and had been terminated or quit.

Why had he been terminated, or why had he quit? He didn't appear friendly with the other cops, so Howard was missing something, and his prying mind needed to know. If Laurenti was catering to cops, Howard needed to learn more about the guy.

"Patterson here. I mean Detective Patterson. May I help you?"

"Yes, you may, Len. Howard Hamilton from Orchard Hill PD."

They both laughed at Patterson's almost slur as he answered the phone. *It must have been a long lunch.*

They exchanged pleasantries, and Patterson asked, "What do you want now? Another chief? You assholes dumped the best one you'll ever see."

"I know," Howard said, "but that's not why I called."

They talked briefly about the Chief, but Hamilton could tell Patterson wanted to go home or somewhere else.

"I want to run a name by you: Gary Laurenti."

There was silence for a moment.

"Why?"

Howard filled him in regarding Laurenti's buying the cop hangout in San Pedro and the rumors that Laurenti had been a former LAPD or NYPD officer.

"Yeah, he worked here in Rampart. Here's what I know, but you didn't hear it from me."

Patterson filled him in on the details of what he knew. They wished each other a merry Christmas and New Year.

"The offer is still open to meet at Home Plate someday."

"I may take you up on that, Howard, but not right now."

There would be no Home Plate that night. He'd go home, kick back with a glass of wine, and chat with the kids. With Geoff home for winter break, he looked forward to their week in Big Bear.

CHAPTER

Hamilton was leaving the station, when his cell phone rang. He looked at the screen and said, "Hi, Nicole. What can I do for you?"

"Detective Hamilton, I don't know if you remember me, but—"

"Of course I do. You're John Bresani's old girlfriend."

"Well, for me, that was a long time ago. If you know what I mean. I'm no longer that person."

"OK" was Howard's one-word reply to keep her talking. He sat in his car in the parking lot with Nicole on speaker.

"I don't know if you remember what I used to do, but I still work here at the Orchard Hill Mercedes dealership on car sales row on Albion Boulevard. I'm now the manager of the Sprinter division for the dealership, and that's why I called."

"That's great, Nicole. I'm happy for you. Congratulations."

Howard remembered that he and a regional drug task force member had gone to Irvine to notify her that Bresani had been killed in a warehouse where they transported a large quantity of drugs, money, and weapons. Bresani had been Howard's informant on the case, but a SWAT team had taken him out in a shooting when they served the search warrant. He'd suspected Nicole was a drug user, and Bresani had supplied her with cocaine. As he reflected on the meeting in Irvine, he let silence fill the airwaves for a moment.

"I didn't call to sell you a car, Detective." She laughed at the notion, and so did Hamilton.

"I couldn't afford one of yours anyway."

"Well, some people can, and they buy in great numbers, which is why I called. I feel a bit uncomfortable talking on the phone. My general manager and I have discussed this, so I am calling on behalf of the dealership. Can we meet to discuss this in person?"

"Can you give me a hint as to the topic?"

"I'll be as straightforward as I can. Remember the people Johnnie was doing business with?"

"Of course."

"Well, somehow, they started calling me for more cars. Johnnie told them where he got his Sprinter and a few other vehicles. They started coming to me, and I did great business, selling them just about every model we make, primarily Sprinters. You know, the big vans. They tried to work with us to customize the interiors—to hide their product, if you know what I mean."

"All right, Nicole, I think I get the idea. When do you want to meet?"

"Tomorrow if possible. These guys are preparing to order more of our cars and vans, so something must be happening. And, Detective, I don't engage or work in these circles. I live here and am a member of Rotary and other civic groups, and I don't want to do anything to jeopardize my position. That's not who Nicole Getty was or will be, and I want to ensure you understand." She was clearly making every attempt to get her point across.

Howard watched the black-and-whites as they came in for a shift change. He longed to be back in uniform. "I do, Nicole. What time, and where?"

After arranging to meet for lunch at a local restaurant, Hamilton started the drive home and immediately called Barber.

After Hamilton explained his phone call, Barber became very direct.

"Howard, no matter what, you are not to meet this person alone. You'll need someone to go with you or at least shadow you. I wouldn't classify her as a citizen informant—too much baggage now. It's your first CI, so we need to go over the rules. We may want to wire you up for this. I feel it could be another big case like Bresani's was. Meet me tomorrow."

Damn. I hope this does not screw with my holiday plans.

"What time, and where?"

21
CHAPTER

Hamilton met Barber at the appointed time.

"You generate a lot of shit, don't you, HH? I don't think I've seen anyone else who finds cases that blossom to the big time like you."

"It's just my clean living, sir. They're drawn to me like fucking magnets."

"Wasn't going to say it, but you are a shit magnet. Tell me what you know about this person who called you."

Hamilton gave a rundown on Nicole Getty's relationship with Bresani, his visit to her place in Irvine, and how she'd gotten involved with him, including that Bresani had been providing her with cocaine for her personal use.

"I think she has conflicting motivations, sir. She sold a ton of cars to these guys while she was with Johnnie, and now, I guess, it's started up again. And she gets a great commission for each transaction. Not sure why she wants to get rid of the golden egg."

"Here's how we handle this, Howard. You record everything. We'll treat this like a CI with unknown motives. I want you to find out what those motives are and dig as deeply as possible. Got it?"

Howard nodded and focused on everything Barber was saying.

Barber was back in lecture mode and wanted to ensure Hamilton did everything by the book. "Run her criminal record, and see what we have. Get her photo from DMV files, and do an intel card with everything you know about her: addresses, phone numbers, physical description, occupation, and what kind of car she drives, along with a detailed description. All the info you would need if you were going to book her. And give her an identification code to use when we're unsure who listens. Make one up, and put it on her i-card."

Hamilton pulled up the i-card form on his computer and left it open.

"I can grab somebody coming in today to go with you as your shadow. I cannot stress this enough. Never meet a CI alone. It's a fuckin' recipe for disaster. Especially if it's a female and she's decent looking. I don't care if she's a tweaker, hype, street whore, or housewife. Never meet them alone." Barber looked him directly in the eye to ensure his words sank in.

"Got it." He was getting a little flustered with the constant lecturing. *I get it, Sarge. Really, I do.*

"Keep this one at arm's length. There is no friendship, just business. I don't mean to sound cold, but look at it this way. Informants are our tools. You are the mechanic. When tools work, they work. When they don't, you get rid of them and get a new one. You're the plumber, and she's the pipe wrench. Got it?"

"Of course, sir. Oh, I already set up the location for the meeting. It's at the mall."

"Great. And, Howard, the lieutenant or I must know whenever you meet with her. You can take anyone available as a partner here, but we need to know when you will meet. Log every contact in your daily log and on the i-card. Do not share her with anyone else unless we are OK with it. I know I'm throwing a lot of shit at you, but it's because this is your first merry-go-round with CIs."

"Sarge, I need all the help you can give me here."
Maybe patronizing him will work!

"Your first meeting sets the ground rules. You're in charge of her and the investigation. Do not let her direct it. You direct her. Always pick up the check if you're meeting at a place to eat or drink. They do not pay."

Their eyes met, with almost a Norman Bates look coming from Barber.

"Think about everything we discussed. Every move is on your terms. Ensure she's not talking to any other law enforcement agency, city, county, state, or the feds. If you're unsure, tell her you'll get back to her, and we'll powwow."

Just as Barber was trying to wrap up, in walked the Wolf.

"Pat, got a minute?"

22

Barber briefed Wolford on her assignment to shadow Hamilton. He reviewed the guidelines for what he wanted her to do and turned them loose.

Howard gave her a look up and down. Wolford wore combat boots, jeans, and a red flannel lumberjack shirt. "You're not going dressed like that, are you?"

"God, no. I have several changes here at the station. While we're there, let's go shopping for clothes at the mall, OK?"

"Sounds good."

"HH, we finally get to work together. Wow, wait till I tell Donny."

"Yeah, he'll have a cow. Hey, Pat, I have something to do before we go out there. We'll head out to the Barrio Queen restaurant at the mall at one. I need about an hour to take care of some business. Make yourself useful for a while."

"Got it."

Hamilton went to his office and locked the door. He called Kip and obtained the information he needed. He now had Morrison's two email addresses and his personal and department-issued cell phone numbers. He then went to work. He had no idea what he was looking for but would recognize it immediately if it stood out.

The robust system in his series of computer software permitted him to check all of Morrison's personal and department-related emails. His modified software package of serviceobjects.com/developers/lookups/geophone-plus allowed him to view the contents of emails and the list of phone numbers side by side. He tied it to Morrison's two cell phones and obtained all incoming and outgoing phone calls for the last thirty days.

He looked at emails generated to addresses more than three times on

57

both systems and determined they were job-related or tied to home and friends. Nothing appeared to stand out. He then cross-referenced his two phone numbers and hit the jackpot.

Did Morrison have a girlfriend? Suicide leaves so much unfinished business.

He did a caller ID search using calleridservices.com. He'd used the site before, registering for its service with a PD account at twelve cents a query, up to twenty-five. He found a number that had been called more frequently than any other. The number had made and received calls at least two times per day, sometimes on both phones.

He realized that if this were a criminal investigation, he would probably need a search warrant to obtain all he saw on his three screens. The only people who would know about his efforts on this little investigation were himself and Kip—hopefully.

He used the number to tie into one of his premium sources, opencnam. com, and sat staring at the screen.

Now I feel like a dumb shit.

It was for the Southern California Cancer Research Center.

23

Howard notified Kip of his findings on the Morrison matter.

Looking at his watch, he saw he had thirty minutes before his meeting, just enough time to follow up on a few messages. He decided he should probably make notes the old-fashioned way, maybe on Post-its or something, as he could not rely on his memory. It was getting too filled up with technical mumbo-jumbo.

He called Anita Hernandez's inside line to see if she was in the station.

"Detective Hernandez. May I help you?"

"Hey, Chili, you called me?"

There was silence on the other end.

"Howard." There was another long pause. "Howard, I would appreciate it if you would no longer call me Chili." It was a stern Anita Hernandez on the other line.

"What do you mean? That's the nickname you've gone by for almost ten years."

"I know, but it doesn't work for me now. Understand?"

Now it came to him. She had not taken offense at the name for years—maybe to get along. Anita was a strong woman in many ways, and now she was asserting what she believed to be an offensive term to her.

"Hey, I haven't seen you in forever, so I didn't get that memo. Sorry."

"I need to spend some time with you on a case I'm working on. Is now a good time?"

"No, it's not. I am just getting ready to go out on an investigation for a few hours. How about if I call you when I get back?"

"Sounds good, HH."

Obviously, nothing else needed to be said about the matter.

Well, at least one of us gets to keep their nickname.

He sat back and thought for a moment. He'd attended all those classes regarding sexual harassment and cultural awareness, but he felt it should not matter to the in-house goings-on at OHPD. Perhaps he was wrong. Maybe he could get some insight from Wolford.

He walked out of his cubbyhole and saw Pat at her desk. She wore a blue blouse, which was untucked to cover her on-duty weapon; black slacks; and classy running shoes, just in case.

"Hey, Wolf, how about if you go out with me to the meeting location, and I can just drop you off near it and make it look like I came alone? You can walk in later."

"Sounds good, HH."

"I have to check out a tape recorder. I mean a digital recorder. I guess I am a little out of date."

She looked at him with a "What's up with you?" look.

Hamilton signed out the pen recorder from the 007 room and grabbed his keys.

Boy, do I need fine-tuning on a few things.

CHAPTER

They jumped into the undercover car and headed to the mall to meet with Nicole Getty. There was no rain forecast for the next few days, but it was windy, and a chill was in the air.

"Pat, can I ask you a question?" He told her about the conversation with Hernandez.

"Howard, it's a changing world, and I think some people here want some of our old customs updated."

"Do you mind being called Wolf once in a while?"

"Hell no. I wear that as a badge of honor. It means someone strong, cunning, and maybe even a bit dangerous. I'm good with it. Hey, think about this," she said as she turned in the passenger seat to face Howard as he drove. "*HH* could have some Nazi meaning, like 'Heil Hitler.' Does that offend you?"

"I never even thought of that. I brought the nickname with me. I was named after a disc jockey from the fifties. I've been called that since I was a baby, but Hitler? I never."

They arrived at the mall. The Barrio Queen had been a stand-alone sit-down eatery, and the mall had been built around it. It served good old-fashioned, traditional Mexican food that one could not get from any of the fast food places in town. Another positive was that they did not have to share their parking area with mall attendees.

Wolford jumped out of the car, and Hamilton drove into the parking lot, walked in, and saw someone he thought might be Nicole sitting in a booth toward the back of the restaurant. He was met by the hostess and pointed in Nicole's direction.

He would go by the numbers on this one, particularly after the lesson on informants from Barber. He was comfortable that Wolford would come in and get a seat where she could observe their interaction. He activated his recorder with the date and time and with whom he was meeting.

As he got closer, he recognized Nicole right away. He only saw her from the waist up, as she didn't get up. She was well dressed, and her hair was in a tight ponytail, pulled back to reveal a clear complexion and a bright smile. Her white high-collar blouse, with the two top buttons open to show a small diamond necklace surrounding the distinguished Mercedes emblem, ensured no cleavage but little doubt of her status in life. Her fashionable gray blazer sported a brooch pinned to the lapel, with a softer logo of her employer. Clearly, there was something different about her. She didn't have a skanky look anymore.

She extended a soft hand to him, reaching across the table, and Howard could see her jeweled bracelets and a diamond ring on her right hand.

Hmm. There is a lot of bling but nothing on the left hand.

"Good to see you, Nicole. It's been a long time. Thanks for picking a table inside. It's too cool this time of year to be eating on the outside patio. Things look like they're going well for you."

"They are, Detective Hamilton."

He would not let her try to be any more familiar than she was right now. Howard quickly reflected on their first and only meeting.

"So, Nicole, to what do I owe this pleasure?" He tried to be as casual as possible. Open-ended questions always allowed the latitude to see how the void of conversation could be filled. It didn't take long.

"I'm glad you asked, Detective. That's why I reached out."

The wait server stopped by as if on cue to take their drink orders and drop off some of the restaurant's famous tortilla chips. White wine for the lady and an Arnold Palmer for Howard started the luncheon.

"I'm now the regional manager for OHMB, Sprinter division. Whoops, that's Orchard Hill Mercedes-Benz." She laughed, and Howard joined in.

"I figured out what those initials were, Nicole. I do have some investigative skills."

They both laughed again.

"That's terrific, Nicole, but I don't do vans."

"I know, but call me if your department ever needs a Sprinter to buy or a loaner to do a onetime undercover case." She passed her business card proudly, sliding it across the table and touching Hamilton's hand briefly.

Oh shit. Was that an accident, or did she do that on purpose?

25

Howard quickly moved his hand away from hers, trying to be casual but purposeful.

"But that's not why I called."

"I didn't think so." Hamilton looked over to make sure Wolford had them in sight. He was glad the booth next to them was empty. "That could have been done over the phone or email."

They gave their orders to the waiter. Hamilton opted for the luncheon enchilada plate with beans and rice. She was having two tacos à la carte. The chips were already half gone.

"Remember back a few years with Johnnie? I think he told you I was providing some cars to some of his business partners." She animated *business partners* with finger quotes. "They were paying the MSRP, the manufacturer's suggested retail price, sometimes with cashier's checks or some phony business front check. They also tried to pay with cash, but we couldn't accept it due to the amounts. I never offered a deal, and they never asked."

"I think that's where Johnnie obtained the licenses, either temp or plates, to give us so we could track them."

"Right. Back then, there were only a few cars. Our E class and a few AMGs, with a Sprinter or two thrown in. They wanted us to customize the vans, but I pushed them to a third-party vendor because I didn't want to know what they were doing."

"OK, Nicole, I think I know all about it, so is it still going on now?"

She sat up straight, arching her back against the booth. Her high-collar white blouse and blazer jacket made her out to be a classy young lady. Howard would not react to anything, regardless of how she moved her body.

"Some new people have been coming to see me. Johnnie and his friends referred all of them and are not shy about dropping names. I've never met a lot of these people before and, quite frankly, do not want to do business with them. They're a bit creepy."

"I have to ask: How much does your boss know? About your past dealings and this recent activity?"

"After everything calmed down and I moved back to Orchard Hill, I sat down with Mr. Dryer, our general manager, and explained everything. Well, almost everything, if you know what I mean."

She probably didn't share her drug problem.

"I think I do. What about now?"

"He asked me to contact you—well, your department—to see if you're interested in any follow-up with these people. He doesn't want to get our company in trouble and particularly not bring a blemish to the Mercedes name. Are you interested?"

"Maybe. Tell me more." He would play coy as long as possible.

"That's good because we have an excellent standing in the community and don't want it tarnished. They didn't want to go to the third-party vendor for modifications to the Sprinters. But we've insisted that we not do the work they want."

"What kind of work is that?"

"I'll give you the list. They want four Sprinters. Two with bulletproof siding and lead-lined boxes under the floorboard of the camper-type vans. On the other two, they also want bulletproof siding and glass but bench seating to hold at least twenty passengers. Why would they want these vans so fortified, Detective?"

"I can only speculate, Nicole. What's in this for you?"

"Mr. Dryer would like to continue selling cars, of course, but wanted me to discuss it with you. We continue to sell them cars, and I get my commissions."

She moved around to eat her tacos and sip the wine. "Here's the offer. We'll turn over all documentation, including copies of invoices for all cars and vans, their credit references, FICA information, driver's licenses, and all their banking information that we become privy to. I will go so far as to copy down all license plates on the cars they arrive in at our dealership. We believe this to be an exemplary citizen commitment. We are not bound by any confidentiality agreements or privileged communication issues."

"I can't approve that, but I can run it by my bosses."

"I understand. You do that and get back to me. Here's our good-faith preliminary effort." She opened a briefcase that Hamilton had not seen on the seat beside her.

Is she recording me? Whose side is she on? Is she trying to set me up?

26

She selected a folder and put it on the table to the left of Hamilton, which was not visible from the aisle.

"This is all the information from the business transactions from a few years ago. When Johnnie was involved. I don't know if any of it is still good, but we wanted to show you we want to cooperate. There's much more where that came from."

"That's my next question, Nicole. Are you perhaps talking to anybody else?"

"Like who?" was her slightly innocent reply.

"Like the sheriffs, LAPD, the feds, DEA, FBI, or anybody else."

The emphatic negative reply assured Hamilton he was on safe ground. He was not going to go through the paperwork now. He would accept it and change the tenor of the conversation.

"I had to ask. We don't want to butt heads with other agencies. I'll get back to you after the holidays." He was going to ask for her approval but realized then she would've been directing things.

She nodded a tacit acceptance. Barber's directions seemed to be working.

"Any plans for the holidays, Nicole?"

"This is the hottest sales time of year for us—year-end sales and trade-ins. I'll be swamped and take off later in January. And you?"

"Just going out of town for a few days. Nothing special." He would not share personal information, at least not at this first meeting.

She slid two more business cards over to him with a casual brush of his hand—this time with a smile that meant more than it should have. He looked over to Wolford, who was devouring a taco and not paying attention.

"You never stop selling, do you, Nicole? You already gave me your card."

"I know. Here are two more for your bosses. And I called you, so I'll get the check." She started to reach for the check.

"Well, we have a policy that we can't do that. I've got it." He gently took the bill from her hand. "The city pays for it anyway."

He knew Barber would ask that question, and he wanted to have the correct answer. He had the cash to take care of the bill, so getting reimbursed would not be a problem as long as he had the receipt.

"I like that. And, Detective, no, I never stop selling."

She smiled again, looking as if she were telling Hamilton more than he wanted to know or think about. Now he knew why Barber had said never to meet with an informant alone.

27

They parted company. Howard watched her leave the restaurant area and ensured that no one was following him or her. He watched her climb into a new white two-seater Mercedes S550 with a white interior. He waited until she left the parking lot.

He looked around for Wolford and saw her standing beside their Dodge Charger parked behind the restaurant. He unlocked the doors with his remote, and they both sat there momentarily.

"That looked interesting, Howard."

"What do you mean by that?"

"From where I sat, it looked like she was coming on to you."

"If you must know, it was sort of like that, but she handed me this packet." He referenced the folder Nicole had given him. "She tried twice to touch my hand, but I moved it away, just like we were taught in the class yesterday."

"Nicole looks damn hot. Are you sure nothing was going on?"

"Hey, hold it here. Why the fuck are you so accusatory?"

Hamilton jumped into the driver's seat as Wolford entered the passenger side.

She turned and smiled coyly. "Well, Donny and I have been talking about you. We never hear of you dating. You always come alone to our house. Are you ever going to move on from Clare?"

"Hey, Pat, you can tell Donny that I date, but there's nothing to talk about. No one more than once or twice. I'm just not interested right now. Listen, this situation with Nicole is as an informant. She gave me some information I have to work on, and that's it. I'll report everything to Barber and let him know she tried to come on to me. Will that satisfy you?"

"Lighten up, Howard. Donny and I are just concerned about you.

That's all. Donny says you never talk about dating, and he's your best bud. I didn't mean to come down hard on this. We want you to be happy. Right now, we don't see a happy Howard Hamilton."

"I'm OK, Pat. I really am."

"Just watch yourself, OK?"

"What do you mean by that?"

"OK, I'm going to play Lieutenant." She held up five fingers. "Number one, you are a catch for some very lovely girl. But there are a lot of charlatans out there, like Nicole. Number two, you are a catch because—and don't think I'm crazy—you bathe daily. Number three, you do not shove shit up your nose. Number four, you have a steady job, one with benefits, and you make good money. And number five, you aren't a bad-looking guy." She made a fist after closing her hand one finger at a time, just as Rikelman did.

Howard concentrated on the road but was thinking about everything Pat had said. "I guess I understand, Pat, but as for that thing that just happened with Nicole, you can be assured I'm not going to cross the line and screw up a career. Just not me. And you know that. I know I should probably move on from my attachment to the memory of Clare, but I also have two kids to think about."

He pulled the two-door Dodge Charger back into the station parking lot. It was just before the shift change, so there was not a lot of activity in the lot.

"Let's continue this for another time, HH. We love you, you know."

"I know, Pat, and thanks."

"Hope so. And, HH, here is my receipt for lunch. I want to be reimbursed too."

"I'll turn them both in when I meet to give an update."

28
CHAPTER

He went to the office, but there was no one there. He got on the radio and asked for a location for NV-20, Barber's radio designation.

"A few of us are at the complained-of location for *a*'s. You and Wolford can join us, but enter from the other side of the target location. That's where we're set up while Don and Phil operate."

Howard acknowledged and advised Wolford.

"Well, I guess we partner for a while longer. Let me change my clothes again, and we'll go out there."

Hamilton had to consult his GPS to find the location. He had gone there with Barber but ignored how he got there. He had worked the streets for almost thirteen years and had not even known the place existed. Hamilton took a winding road off a tree-lined residential street and kept looking down at his screen to ensure he was going in the right direction. Off to his right, he spotted the outfield of the baseball field. He could see no other cars, indicating Barber and the teams weren't even there.

Then it miraculously opened up to a blacktop parking lot. He spotted a black-and-white patrol car and three other undercover cars. They finally arrived to see Wolford's partners, Shotgun, Bowers, and Garcia. Barber was in his car, making notes on his iPad, and Morgan had what looked like two arrestees in the back of a black-and-white.

The tree-lined parkway did not offer a look at the restroom in question. Wolford and Hamilton walked up to Morgan with their arms open as if to ask, "What's going on here?"

"We got here, and it was hopping already."

Morgan came away from the uniforms and bodies in the backseat. "Don walked in on these two. One had his dick sticking through the shitter partition, and the other dude was sucking like there was no tomorrow. I've never seen anything like this."

Hamilton said, "I've been in the restroom, but Barber and I came in from a different direction. Where is it? I can't see anything from here."

Morgan led him to an opening between two tall cypress trees blending into each other. He raised a hand and pointed. "Look through the trees. You'll see two lights on the building, like porch lights. They can't see us, but we can see the entrance well from here. That's the restroom, and it's only fifty feet away."

Hamilton went to Barber's car and sat in the front passenger seat. He gave him an update on his meeting with Getty, what the folder contained, and how they would meet again after the holidays.

"Here's our next move, Howard. I don't want you to meet with her until we get a letter from her general manager indicating they want to cooperate. I'm unsure if I trust she's not trying to string us along. Everything sounds good, but let's take this slow. You analyze what she gave you when you get back, and we'll see what we have. Got it?"

"Yes, sir. Sounds good." Hamilton looked around. "What do we have going on here?"

"I've got Don and Phil operating, Disney and BB are the arrest team when they come out, and one of the Everlys gives us the violation sign. Morgan and Wolf are standing by with the two bodies we have right now, but more will be coming."

"What can I do out here, sir? I feel like a fifth wheel. I'm not sure I want to operate with no partner."

"No worries, Howard. I always have things for you to do. This is such an obscure place. Something is going on. We don't know what. Interview each of these guys, and find out who they are and why they came here."

"I can do that, sir."

Hamilton exited Barber's car and walked over to the black-and-white. The two young officers had some idea of what was going on. He introduced himself, took down their names, and filled them in as much as possible.

"Have you run these guys for wants or warrants?"

The more senior officer, Stone, advised they had, and there was nothing in the system for either. "One is out of state, but the other is local."

Hamilton walked one arrestee back to his car and sat him in the front seat, still cuffed behind his back. Hamilton introduced himself, and immediately, the guy started crying uncontrollably.

"What's going to happen to me? Am I going to jail? To prison? Oh God, what if my wife finds out?" He continued to sob until there was not much left of his emotion.

"Here's what's going to happen, sir. We checked, and you don't have any warrants, so you'll get a notice to appear before a court. It's like a ticket. You can then plead guilty or not guilty. You'll be released shortly. Now, I want you to calm down. I have some questions for you. OK?"

There was a moment of silence.

The arrestee took a deep breath and tried to lean back, but the cuffs would not give him any comfort. "Can you take off these fuckin' cuffs?"

"No, sir. They're for your protection and mine. Not negotiable. Now, tell me a little about yourself. You mentioned you were married. Do you live around here?"

"No, I'm from Chicago. Out here on business." He was calming down, but something in his eyes told Hamilton to be cautious and not get sucked into his changing demeanor.

"Why did you come here to this particular location? Don't you see the ball fields? Kids are around here."

"It's on the app. I have an app telling me where I can meet up."

Hamilton asked Stone for the arrestee's phone. "Show me where it is on your phone."

The arrestee guided him to the second page of his apps. "See the one named Nearme?"

The man tried to nod, but Howard saw it immediately.

"I just got off the plane at LAX and was on my way downtown. It was a tough flight, so I needed some release. I looked up places to go, and this is a hot spot. It tells you it's near a baseball field but also shows what time the games are over, so you can be assured no one else is around. It connects to a directional map, and I found it pretty easy."

"So from Chicago, you get off the plane; rent a car, I assume; check out this app; come here; get a head job; and think you'll just go about your business?"

"The app also tells you if any arrests have been made. This place was clean, so I figured you wouldn't know about it. But I would rather do it out here than in a hotel. It's more exciting. Maybe get a threesome or—"

72

"That's enough about that, sir." Howard was not going to get into the weeds on this guy. "You mentioned a wife."

"Back in Chicago. Home."

"Kids?"

"Two."

"Why?"

"You married, Officer?"

"No."

"Then you wouldn't understand."

"I guess not."

Howard was done taking notes, when Morgan and Pat showed up with two more arrestees.

29

CHAPTER

At six arrests, Barber called it a night. "We have enough bodies to process here. Make sure we have good IDs and no warrants. Don and Phil, you do the FRCs on them, as it's your investigation. Do we have anyone we have to take to the station?"

Phil responded. "I think only one. I have some issues with twinkle toes over there," he said, pointing to arrestee number four.

Hamilton spoke up. "I'll take him in if someone will ride with me. I haven't talked to him yet."

Barber spoke up. "I have a better idea. Howard, you go back to the station and set up the interview room. I'll have Wolf and Shotgun transport after we finish up here. We'll get the paperwork and release them after we take them back to their cars on the other side of the park."

"Much more efficient, sir. I guess that's why you get the big bucks." Hamilton smiled.

"Your time will come, Hamilton. Your time will come."

*   *   *

Hamilton arrived at the office and set up the interview room to accommodate video and audio taping. He had no idea what awaited him.

His thoughts rambled as he reflected on the one arrestee from Chicago who'd told him about an underground network involved with the gay community. He remembered the case of Broderick Mason, a cross-dresser who'd committed suicide in a storage warehouse locker. They eventually had determined Mason had killed a lover in Rampart Division at an S&M bathhouse and become despondent and offed himself. Then there was the Ginny Karsdon case. Some satanic cult group had murdered her.

Both cases had opened his eyes to a world he could not fully grasp. What was he going to learn tonight?

They must have caravanned to the station, because everyone arrived at the same time. Barber went immediately to his office, and Wolford walked the lone arrestee to the interview room and closed the door.

Don and Phil walked in carrying a large banker's box, while the other teams scattered to their respective desks.

"Look what we have here," Phil proclaimed as he laid various items on the conference table. "This was in numbnuts's backseat."

There were the expected sex toys, but they also found photos of arrestee number four in various nude poses with other males, some of whom looked close to being underage.

Hamilton spoke up. "Who has this guy's ID?"

Wolf showed Howard a wallet. She pulled out an identification card from a school district. "I took it off him after he gave us his driver's license to help us fill out the FRC. We stopped the FRC when we found this," she said, pointing to the school district card.

It read, "Los Angeles County Unified School District."

"Yup. This dipshit works in a school district and has access to all sorts of potential partners. I'll bet he drools every time he goes to work. Asshole. Need to dig into this guy." Phil was never one to spare a word.

"Give me a shot at him, Phil. I would love to find something more." Howard could not wait to delve into Mr. Damian Sparks's background.

30
CHAPTER

"How come I didn't get released at the park?" It was a demanding voice, not one bit conciliatory.

"I'll ask the questions here, Mr. ..." Hamilton caught his eye and continued with the bad-cop routine as he tossed his notebook onto the small aluminum table and stared directly into his eyes.

"Damian. Damian Sparks." His response was much softer now.

Hamilton knew he had the upper hand. "We just have a few questions for you, Mr. Sparks. More than likely, we'll release you from here. We brought your car back to the station, so if you cooperate, perhaps you'll leave here in a little while."

Sparks sat back in the metal chair, which was not designed for comfort. His right arm was handcuffed to the chair arm, but his body language said, "Take your best shot."

"What were you doing in the park this late in the day?"

"That's where I go when I want some activity. To meet up."

"Do you always come here?"

"No, I have other places. But my app said this was an active pickup spot."

"What app?"

"Nearme."

There it was again. Howard had interviewed all six arrestees, and all but one was using Nearme.

"You've been arrested for lewd conduct, and I see you have some prior arrests but only convictions for disturbing the peace."

"That's what I got to plead to so I didn't have to register as a sex offender. I didn't know that the person I tried to touch was a police officer. Don't you guys have to tell us before we do something?"

"That's a myth floating out there, Mr. Sparks. No, we do not. What was it you had in the backseat of your car? It is your car, isn't it? It's registered to you." Howard wanted to ensure he established ownership so Sparks could not later deny the car was his.

"It's my car."

"What's with all the toys?"

"Toys?"

"Mr. Sparks, do not be coy with me. I know the types of items found in your car and what they're used for—for whatever you do with them with other people."

"To my knowledge, Detective, it's not a crime to possess them."

"You are right, Mr. Sparks; it is not. But what about the photos?"

"That's my business."

"Mr. Sparks, you are employed at a high school in Los Angeles County, correct?"

"I am."

"In what capacity?"

"What does this have to do with what I did here today?" His attitude was approaching obstinance.

"Well, those boys you were posing with seem pretty young. You have not answered my question. What's your position at the high school?"

"I'm a senior administrative analyst."

"What does that entail?"

"It's pretty much a human relations position. I oversee the hiring of teachers and staff."

"Have you ever been in the classroom as an instructor?"

"No."

"So who are the boys in the photos?"

"I don't think that is any of your business, Detective. Consenting adults. I can vouch for the fact they are all over eighteen."

"Three more questions, and we are done, Mr. Sparks. Have you ever had to register as a sex offender?"

"No."

"Is your employer, the principal, the school district, or anyone aware of your attraction to young boys?"

"Not that I am aware, no. And they're young men, not boys. And your last question, Detective?"

"Are any of the young men depicted in the photographs we found in your car students or former students of your school?"

"I am not going to answer that question. We are done, aren't we, Detective?"

It wasn't a question.

31
CHAPTER

Hamilton walked out of the interview room, frustrated. *What kind of world is this? Is it real? We let freaks like this work in our schools? This had better not happen in Orchard Hill, but I don't care what school it is. This guy is done!*

He met with Barber to give him an update. "Can I spend tomorrow on this case, Sarge? It's my last day before vacation, but I want to dive into this. I have some ideas."

"Hey, HH, it's only a simple infraction we have this guy on. What do you think you'll find?"

"I don't know, but give me a few hours, and I'll tell you if I come up with anything."

The Wolf hugged him and made her exit. "We'll talk during the holidays, HH."

The other teams wrapped up their paperwork, shut down their computers, locked their desks, and wished everyone a merry Christmas and happy New Year.

But Howard barely heard them, as he was thinking about Sparks. The familiar voice of Sergeant Kip Bennett broke his thought process.

"Hey, Detective," Kip said in his sarcastic tone. "Just wanted to let you know there are a lot of people who owe you a debt of gratitude, but they will never know it was you."

"What are you talking about, Sarge?"

The office was empty except for him and Kip.

"The info on Morrison. I put the dolphins to bed and assured the family there were no other motives than his fear the cancer was returning. It helped that I went through what he did, thinking it was coming back, not realizing it was faux pain. It was just a normal reaction to what he was

79

experiencing. He didn't see it that way, obviously. I wish I'd jumped on him sooner."

"Getting the information was easy, Kip. Give me a hard one."

"Next time, brother from a different mother. Next time."

"Hey, Kip—I mean Sarge—you're not working the holidays, are you?"

"Yup, all of them. It keeps my mind clear of a lot of garbage. You'll probably be off like the rest of these goofballs for a couple of weeks, huh?"

"Yeah, I am. Rented a cabin in Big Bear and taking Geoff and Marcia. Oh, and Bentley."

"That's great, HH. You deserve it. Hey, merry whatever to you and your family."

"Back at you, sir. I didn't do cards this year, so maybe you'll get a call on Christmas Eve to say hi. I do have your number."

"You certainly do, HH. I'll look forward to it."

32

Hamilton couldn't wait to get back to the office in the morning. Before doing that, he needed to take care of the home base. He promised Geoff and Marcia dinner at their favorite restaurant, the Cheesecake Factory, and there was no Cheesecake Factory in Big Bear.

He jumped out of bed, showered, had a quick breakfast, said goodbye to the kids, and raced to the station. He had been thinking about Sparks all night. There was something sinister about him, and Hamilton would get to the bottom of it.

He walked into the station, which was busy on a Friday morning. Not his problem. He unlocked the N&V office door, started Peet's coffee, and opened his computer. He had the FRC information. He did some searching on open system sites for Sparks. Nothing.

Time for a deep dive.

Digital photograph uploads were extremely common among social network users, thanks to cameras on every cellular data phone. The various images used could create an entirely new element to the art and science of open-source intelligence analysis.

Howard knew he needed to tap into the metadata after entering the make, model, and serial number from Sparks's phone; his school address and home address; and the various sites used to take, store, and transmit photos. If people only had known how much information could be gleaned from their phones, they would have seriously questioned if online photos should stay online.

Before Sparks had been released last night, Hamilton had copied all photos taken from the backseat of his car and pages from his old-fashioned address book, which listed not only phone numbers but also some URLs and websites. He noticed that Sparks made no use of Google or Bing.

Sparks obviously knew he could filter search results from both sites by date, size, color, type, and license type. He had done the homework to ensure a routine hacker could not use his data and photos.

Hamilton knew that going into Google or Bing to do reverse imaging would be futile. The same applied to other relatively unknown search engines, such as TinEye, Yandex, and Baidu. Those sites were similar to the more popular ones, requiring more specialized input data that Howard did not have. He had to do each site to ensure Sparks did not use them. It only took a few minutes. Then he would move on to the more specific tools in his war chest.

He decided to go to the website Nearme. It was not very interesting. If one looked at it innocently, it appeared to be a dating site or alternative to Google Maps. One could not tell the nature of its contents without a username and password, which Hamilton did not have. Could he figure out Sparks's username and password? It was worth the investigation.

His next step was to put Sparks's personal information into the Instagram application programming interface (API), a public source that led to other portals that were not public. He used a proprietary source code he'd learned in his latest intelligence class that could amplify the search in a friendlier way. The key was not in the name and search information obtained but in the source code attached to the name. Using this code, he could link all photos of Sparks, pictures of his friends, and general information not revealed on his Instagram page.

Howard was studying Sparks's Instagram account, when he saw what he thought could be his username or password for Nearme. He saw his email was sparks@sparks.com. Could he have been stupid or audacious enough to use his last name as a password? Or maybe even *nearme*? He would try every combination.

Bingo.

He was into the Nearme website, which provided detailed information on where to go and how to meet partners in public displays of lewd activities. But they had rules. The screen read,

Welcome to Nearme. Here are the rules to follow when using our site:

Never use your real name.

Never agree to meet another user of our services.

Please do not use our message board for discussions of illegal activities.

We are not responsible for our content, as our users provide it.

The mapping was straightforward, with directions to pinpoint each location and notations regarding whether law enforcement routinely patrolled the area. It even tallied arrests within the last year.

Interesting.

He verified that Sparks used a geolocation setting. By entering a few more tidbits of information, along with the source code, Hamilton could identify, through Google Maps, the location where the photos were posted. The API view gave him a chronological picture of all recent images, with the newest on top.

Now I'm getting somewhere.

With source codes provided by his instructor, Hamilton could enter the GPS latitude and longitude of Sparks's school and home. He expanded it to include the distance between Sparks's residence and the school.

Bingo again!

His next step was to identify the people Sparks was following on Instagram and those following him.

The search located the source of the photos, with the most explicit image linked to his place of employment, a local high school in the Los Angeles County School District. He entered several images, and the exact address popped up. Sparks accessed a classroom and used those coordinates for his lurid activities.

Howard then tied in Flickr Map and Exif Data sites to obtain the photos' metadata. Most people did not realize that each picture had a specific fingerprint. The metadata of each image was not visible when viewing the item.

He used Echosec, a Canadian firm that covered Twitter, Panoramio, Foursquare, Instagram, and Flickr, to ensure he was only dealing with a local issue. He didn't think Sparks would have been stupid enough to use a popular site, such as Twitter, so Echosec provided the easiest way to tie up loose ends.

Now that I have the information, what the hell do I do about it? Hmm. I think I know.

33

Howard looked at the clock. It was just past two in the afternoon.

Good grief, have I been shut in my office since about eight? Yup.

He took some time to walk around the office. His body was stiff from all the concentration. Only a few of the team members were around. He decided he needed to clean the cobwebs from his brain. He went to the weight room, pushed some iron, and did some ab work and squats to loosen up his body, which had tensed during the last few hours. He had to think this through.

There was no doubt Sparks took his photos at the school. But who were the kids? Before he went too far on this, he needed to powwow with Barber.

"Hey, Sarge, got a minute?" Howard brought him up to date on his search results.

Barber thought for a moment. "We need to determine if any kids were underage and whether they went to that particular school. Do you know how to locate photos of the boys?"

"Not really. They didn't teach us anything about that."

"You mean I have a one-up on Mr. Intelligence, Detective Howard Hamilton?"

"I guess so" was the rather shy reply.

"Try classmates.com. I used it in detectives many times. Easy to use. Compare our photos to the school's annual pictures. They're all posted on that website. As long as you have the year and school, it's a piece of cake."

"I'm a bit embarrassed about not knowing that site."

"Well, HH, we can still teach you something here. You're doing an incredible job, but I like that you're not afraid to ask. I still think you know more than we would ever know about that world."

Howard anxiously returned to his office to work on his latest project. In another hour, he had all he needed. He printed everything out and set up a case folder under Sparks's name.

"Hey, Sarge." He once again approached Barber.

"Hamilton, I know you have a lot of information to review with me, but I don't have time right now to discuss it. Can it wait until we get back in January?"

"You got it, sir. Merry Christmas and happy New Year to you and your family." He wasn't about to piss off Barber over this thing. "I'll wrap everything up and see you after the holidays. And you don't have to tell me twice, sir. I'm out of here!"

Hamilton walked out of the station, trying to leave all the baggage of this case, the case with Nicole Getty, and what would be waiting for him when he returned from vacation. But it wouldn't be easy. With everything going on in the unit and inside the department, he took all of this too seriously.

I almost forgot. Anita Hernandez called, and we're playing phone tag. What did she want? Was it something to do with my current investigation?

He sat in his car and thought about the events that had transpired.

Captain Pierson as acting chief of police? Good grief. Rikelman is getting married, wow. Bowers is having an angioplasty, Donny and the Wolf are celebrating their first Christmas together, and Scotty Moore is going to Graceland. And the Morrison family without their dad this holiday.

It was all a bit too much to digest. Maybe a couple of beers at Home Plate would help, he thought.

34

I t was four o'clock on Friday, and the parking lot was already full.

There must be many early outs, not just for the coppers.

Laurenti was in his usual spot, and the place was buzzing. Longshoremen, some police groupies, and what looked like half of Orchard Hill's detectives were taking up most of the booths and barstools. Hamilton saw that new photos had been added to the walls—pictures of Kent McCord and Marty Milner in LAPD uniforms, standing next to a black-and-white. And they were personally autographed to Laurenti. *Adam-12* might've been on reruns, but they had a premier showing at Home Plate. Another autographed photo of Ty Welliver, or Harry Bosch, was affixed in a place of prominence. This guy was obviously connected.

One barstool was left near the cocktail waitress's order station. He took it. He knew most of the regulars, but there was no Donny, Red Walker, or Tenery to engage with.

He studied Laurenti while he worked at the bar. He could not make eye contact, so there was no "How you doing?" or any possibility of a conversation. He just watched the man Len Patterson had told him about.

Patterson had spared no detail regarding Laurenti. He had been one of Rampart's golden boys. He was a little over six feet and had blond hair, blue eyes, and a smile that sucked you in. He worked in community relations, and the public loved him. In a predominately Hispanic community, he spoke Spanish and quickly made friends. He even had married a local girl, and he bought or rented a home right there in Rampart—Patterson did not know which.

Where is all of that now?

When a golden boy crashed and burned, it was likely a significant incident or series of incidents. In Laurenti's case, a series of little things added up. The little things were money from a discretionary community relations fund that no one had thought to audit. His overtime submissions often had been forged with his supervisor's name because the supervisor either didn't care or was incompetent. The administrative assistant at Rampart, who processed overtime slips, had started to see a pattern and brought it to the captain's attention. An investigation had begun, and the amounts of funds from the community relations account and overtime had been staggering. It could not, or would not, be ignored, no matter who it was.

The investigation had revealed that Laurenti was feeding his wife's gambling habit. She routinely spent her nights at the Crazy Horseshoe in Gardenia, a poker club that catered to addicted gamblers. They gladly had taken her money provided by Laurenti from his abuse of overtime and station funds for two years. There had been a quiet resignation because Laurenti had not had twenty years on the job and had not been vested in the LAPD pension fund. But there had been no prosecution.

At first, Howard stared at the man who had once had it all together, lost it all, and somehow rebuilt his life. Was he still married to his wife? How had he found this place? Where had he gotten the money to open it, remodel, and decorate? There were too many questions, and he was done investigating anything for two weeks.

Not my problem. At least not tonight.

He continued to look around to see a friendly face but decided to concentrate on his beer. A soft guitar played in the background, but he could not see anyone playing. Was it piped into the speakers? No, it appeared to be live. He moved his stool slightly and saw a head at the other end of the bar. A seat was now open at that end, so he packed up and moved closer to the music on the other end of the bar.

On his way to the other corner, he spotted her sitting against the wall, where the acoustics worked to her advantage. She had a headset microphone, with a small Fender amplifier at her feet. Her hair was short and blonde, and her brown eyes stared into space while her fingers moved effortlessly among the frets. The guitar music complemented her voice. It was soft, with a touch of melancholy. It was a Joni Mitchell song he remembered from the late '60s, "Both Sides Now." She was perhaps in her late twenties. The innocence that might have been there years ago had faded, and a more determined look told Howard more than he wanted to know.

A tip jar no one had been feeding was off to the side. He reached down and moved it to a chair seat that was more visible to the customers. He dropped a five, a ten, and some singles into the jar to chum the room for more. It did the trick. In about twenty minutes, others walked by to show appreciation by filling the jar.

One more beer, and he would be ready to hit the road. Chips, salsa, and some salty beer nuts filled the void and soaked up some alcohol. He wasn't paying attention and didn't hear the music stop, and the tap on his shoulder made him jump a bit. He turned in his stool to face Laurenti, who still would not make eye contact again.

"Thanks for moving the tip jar. I didn't think of that."

Hamilton spun around, and his off-duty gun belted to his hip nudged against something soft. "What—"

"I didn't mean to startle you, Officer. Are you OK?"

She didn't have her guitar, but he was caught off guard. And that didn't happen.

"I guess I'd better watch my back, Miss ..." Howard fumbled to ask her name.

"It's Sam. Samantha. Yours?"

"Howard, but my friends call me HH."

"OK, Howard."

"How did you know I was an officer, a cop?"

"Most everyone in here is, and I brushed up against your gun." She tapped the side of his belt line.

35

Pixie haircut. Short. Maybe five foot two at the most. Is she gay? Who can tell these days?

Donny would have said she was a potato chip away, but he always liked his ladies on the thin side. There was no other place to sit, so Howard offered her his stool. He remembered calling the kids on his way there and telling them he would be home by six thirty. He looked at his watch.

"I'm leaving, so the stool is yours."

"Thanks."

He saw her glance at the wedding ring he always wore. "I'm going out of town for the holidays. Will you still be here after the first?"

"You'd have to ask Gary." She pointed to Laurenti, who never seemed to leave the bar area.

"Do you live around here?" Howard tried to make conversation, which seemed more challenging than he thought it should have been.

"Yes, as a matter of fact, I live on Gary's boat here in the marina. But you ask a lot of questions for a married man." She glanced at his wedding ring.

"Well, I am a detective, and that is what we do," he said, laughing to keep the conversation light. "You live on his boat?"

"Yup. What department do you work for? LA?"

"No, Orchard Hill. Just up the freeway," he said, pointing in a northerly direction. "I think that's north," he added, laughing and pointing to a wall with photos of bygone days.

He called Laurenti over to ring up his tab. He placed a twenty on the bar and, without any conversation, left the remainder as a tip.

"Maybe I'll see you after the New Year, Samantha."

"Perhaps. Perhaps not."

"Well, if I don't see you, you have a very nice singing voice. It's a bit haunting, but I like it."

"Thanks. Maybe I'll be here when you get back. Maybe."

The parking lot started to clear as home beckoned for many that preholiday weekend. Howard walked past a few cops he knew were LA and saw some OHPD guys but not those he knew well enough to chat with. The night air was chilly, and he was glad he'd worn a lightweight jacket.

While waiting to get on the freeway ramp one car at a time, he reviewed his day and the tasks ahead.

Should I go in for a few hours on Monday? I could pack over the weekend. I have some work to do on the Sparks matter. That demon will not get away with his evil ways. The case with Nicole Getty needs work, and I can't forget the evening with Mel Flowers on Tuesday night.

And what about Sam? Is this something I should follow up on? Maybe.

The trip to Big Bear with the kids seemed far away.

He glanced at his left hand routinely at the ten o'clock position on the steering wheel. Sam had reminded him he was a married man. He always wore the wedding ring. It was his shield from the real world, perhaps like Sam's guitar was hers. He hadn't seen if she wore rings, but didn't everyone have some hand jewelry today?

Why am I afraid to say I am a widower? Everybody at work knows, but I guess I've been hiding it from the rest of the world. Why?

36

The weekend passed quickly. The Hamilton family discovered that preparing to leave home for two weeks was more difficult than anticipated. The consensus was that they would buy it in Big Bear if they forgot or needed something. It made all the decisions that much easier. But it was not December 23 yet, and Howard had much on his mind.

He had been reluctant to admit it, but the phantom had him by the throat. He could not get work out of his head. When he was in patrol, removing the uniform, putting it in his locker, and walking away from the station until the next shift were much more manageable. There was always someone to relieve him. The intel job was not that way. He could lock his office door but would bring everything with him, regardless of where he went. No one was taking his place now. It was all up to him—no one else.

He often reflected on his and Clare's favorite Broadway play, *The Phantom of the Opera*. He interpreted the phantom differently than it was portrayed. He saw the drive Christine, the female lead, had to perfect her singing. The phantom wanted her to take it to the next level of perfection. However, she could only accomplish that if she left her relationship with Raoul, her boyfriend. She had to give up everything and go with the Phantom to practice and perform.

For Howard, the Phantom was a metaphor for the drive and commitment needed to reach that next level of perfection. He'd hoped he would never get so involved in his work that he lost perspective and balance. But it was happening right before his eyes.

Maybe I could sneak into the office on Monday and clean up a few things to settle my mind. Is there medication for this?

Except for the packing, the weekend was routine.

* * *

Like the Mamas and the Papas song, he could never trust Mondays. He was determined to leave as much behind in his inner sanctum as possible this time. He wasn't surprised to find himself alone in the N&V office. The lieutenant was busy making engagement and wedding plans, and Barber was doing whatever.

But his plan for Sparks was taking shape. First, he had to obtain Sparks's email and IP address. His toy to do that would be blasze.tk. Blaze gave him Sparks's IP address, access to his emails, and the websites he visited. He could generate a unique internet identifier address requiring Sparks to open a proprietary Google link to a site he trusted and ensure he opened the innocuous emails Hamilton sent. That was step one.

The Google link goo.gl/ created a path for all Sparks's emails to be forwarded to the Blaze account Howard set up. HH could then see when Sparks opened his messages, but they would not show as coming from any computer Howard was working on. They would show another computer with a fake IP address.

Howard typed the following message to Sparks: "Hi, Damian. You do not know me, but the project you have been working on has been leaked. Many people are reviewing it, so I hope you are excited about it. Take a look at goo.gl/."

Howard decided to let that message resonate with Sparks to see if he bit on the message. He would give it an hour.

Meanwhile, he retrieved the folder Nicole had given him and reviewed the bill-of-sale records. Her transactions made OHMB a lot of money, and there was no doubt her commissions were hefty. He set up a spreadsheet to enter as much data as possible from the records. He had names but was not sure they were legitimate. There was license plate information, both temporary plates and the plates from vehicles they drove into the lot to make their purchases. Nicole knew what she was doing.

He examined the financial records and hit pay dirt. Bank accounts, checking accounts, and credit information were right before him. He noted that while several of the purchases used the same banking information, after a few times, new accounts emerged. He would dive into the banking files to trace their source when he returned from vacation. This was a fucking gold mine.

He needed to tell Nicole about Barber's insistence on getting a letter and formal approval from the general manager of OHMB, Jeff Dryer. He left a voice mail on her cell to advise her of the requirement.

He returned to his emails to find that Blasze had notified him Sparks had read the anonymous email. Step two was complete.

Was the Phantom lurking?

37

CHAPTER

Step three would be the easy part. He went to the Los Angeles County School District website and reviewed the board of education's members. He selected two at random and dug deeper for their county email addresses. Then he went to the individual school Sparks was working for and located the principal's name and email address.

The fourth step would be a bit more challenging. After accessing Sparks's files, he searched Sparks's emails to locate photos he had shared with his online buddies. He wanted to make sure there were no photos of the items they had seized from his car. All those photos had been returned to him when he was released, so Sparks knew which ones Hamilton had seen.

He found two images with different backgrounds that more than likely had been taken at the school. They portrayed lewd acts being committed with Sparks or with others. He identified at least five students in the images who, based on the high school's annual photos, had attended the school within the last year.

Hamilton knew he was treading into dangerous territory now. He had to ensure he had built a wall between his computer and the targets he was going after. It would not be an easy task. If someone tried to point the finger of guilt at him or the unit, he had to ensure that none of the images they had seized during Sparks's detention would be used and that the source for any emails could not be identified.

Step five would be to use two of his anonymous source emails, ones that could not be traced, to send to the board of education and the school. He would test them first. He sent himself two emails from the anonymous emails. As he had hoped, he was notified that the IP address did not exist. The first email used returned a blank page showing an error. The second link led to an online forum about cars, but it was unavailable. Such links were designed to make the target believe whatever was on the pages was unavailable.

When the recipient clicked on the sent email, the system would notify Hamilton that the target email address had been opened. But it was the Christmas holiday, and his intended targets probably were not at work.

Someone needed to stop Sparks and his antics with students. Hamilton had convinced himself that what he was doing was honorable. It was not something he would share with anyone, including Rikelman and Barber. Absolutely no one. He knew what he was doing could be viewed differently than his intent. He had never ventured into this area of the greater good, but this seemed fitting. Before, his actions had been straightforward. Now purpose overrode reason.

Am I going to the dark side and abandoning my principles for this idiot? Perhaps. Is it worth it, and will it work? If it works, maybe it was the morally right thing to do.

It was as simple as that. He wanted to be judged not by his actions but by his noble intentions. Howard formulated his email and hit Send.

He thought he was done for the day, when his cell phone rang.

38

He didn't recognize the number. "This is Hamilton."

"HH, this is a voice from your past: Bonnie Carvin, Whittier PD. Remember me from the LADUECE squad?"

Carvin had been involved with the Bresani investigation after the case had been turned over to the regional drug task force, fondly named Los Angeles Drug Undercover and Elimination of Cartel Effort, or LADUECE.

"I do, Bonnie. It's been a few years. What's up with you?"

"First, I have to say how sorry I am about Clare. I don't know if you remember, but we were all at the service. Our entire unit." She paused to let it sink in on both sides of the line. "How are you doing? It's been a while."

"We're doing good. Family is surviving and …" Hamilton drifted off from his wandering thoughts.

"I called because I'm on a new county task force on human trafficking. We have a pretty dumb name, HURT, which means 'Human Undercover Response Trafficking.' I heard you are the go-to guy in LA County for intel."

It came off as her bragging about his expertise being known throughout the county.

She said, "I would love to hear about how you developed those skills. But I need you to help us right now."

"I can do that if I get the OK from Barber, but I'm going on vacation for a few weeks. Actually, I'm on it now but jumped into the office to do some catch-up."

"That's OK. We're going to be off too. The bad guys will have to wait. Those are some of the perks of these task forces. Listen, I have some data I'd like to forward to you, but maybe we'll wait until we all get back to work. Can I call you then?"

"Sure, that'll give me time to get the approval to work on it. Sounds interesting."

"Hey, with what's happening now, we all have job security. Have a great Christmas and New Year, HH, and I'm so sorry about Clare."

"Bonnie, it was great to hear from you. Happy holidays and all that shit. All the best to you and your family."

"Talk to you next year."

He put her new number in his contacts for later. Now he was going home. Then his message chime went off. It was from Flowers: "HH, see you on Tuesday night. I'll come by your place to pick you up. It's an early event. Look sharp! Flowers."

Hamilton sat back in his chair and stared at the computer screen shutting down for two weeks.

I have too many women in my life right now. I need some male bonding.

He also had a family to consider.

On his way out of the station, Hamilton called home. Geoff answered.

"Hey, Geoff, is Marcia there?"

"No, Dad, I think she's out with some girlfriends."

"Great. How about you and me catching an early dinner?"

"Sounds good. Can I pick the spot?"

"Of course. See you in about twenty-three minutes."

He was almost in his car, when Donny caught him in the parking lot. "Hey, HH, Pat sure likes working with you. Said you make a good team."

"She's good, knows her job, and gets along with everybody."

"Can I ask you a favor?"

"Donny, you know I'd jump off a cliff for you. Of course."

"Well, maybe not after you hear what it is."

Howard let the silence allow him to go on.

"I'd like you to start training her for your position. The intel position."

Howard opened his car door and stood with one arm on top of the doorjamb. "She'd be good at that, Donny, but it's not my call. Rikelman and the chief originally came up with the position and chose me. I can't pick who I train. And I think I'm going to be here for a while. A lot to learn."

"Any ideas?"

Howard thought for a moment. "Why don't you get her to work on Barber and Rikelman as my backup? I'm a one-man show, and it would be good to train somebody else. Maybe they could send her to the intel school. If you have her do that, I'll work on it from my end."

"That I like. Now you're thinking like admin. Jeez, HH, you should take the next supervisor's test."

They both laughed at the notion. Donny reached out for a man hug, and they wished each other a merry Christmas.

"Taking the kids to Big Bear for the holidays—not sure I told you."

"I know that, HH. What department do you think this is?"

"Almost forgot. I guess the dolphins know everything."

They parted ways, laughing at each other's comments.

He was going to give Donny's idea some thought.

With a new chief coming in and all the movement in the department, perhaps it is time to think about the future. My future. Maybe I should consider taking the sergeant's exam. And the dolphins don't know everything.

It was Tuesday—time to think about getting out of town. Dinner with Geoff at the Barrio Queen, his choice, was excellent. Neither wanted to talk about family issues, just old-fashioned bonding about sports, the upcoming college football playoffs, and the NFL road to the Super Bowl.

With the chips and salsa half gone, Geoff started the conversation earnestly. "Dad, just an FYI, but the Super Bowl is in Phoenix this year. If you want to go, I can score a couple of tickets. Some of my buddies are well connected with the stadium people. One of the guys' dads is in charge of something there. He's trying to get me a part-time job to help with all the events they have after football season."

"What's the date of the Super Bowl? Do you know?"

"I think it's in the middle of February, but I'll check. The only thing I know right now is that it's on a Sunday."

They both laughed at the obvious.

"But there is one condition," Geoff said, "and I don't want you to take this wrong. If I can get tickets, I'm going to try for four. I'm planning on bringing Marty, my girlfriend."

The food arrived just as ordered—cheese enchiladas for Geoff and two carne asada tacos with rice and beans for Howard.

"Can I get an 805 IPA?" Howard asked the waitress.

"Sure, and for you, sir?" She looked at Geoff.

"I'll"—Geoff looked at his dad—"have an Arnold Palmer."

Howard smiled at the waitress. "He has one more year to get the privilege of having an 805."

"Seven months, Dad."

All three had a good laugh over the exchange.

"An 805 and an Arnold Palmer are coming right up, but you could have fooled me. I wasn't even going to card you."

For now, Geoff had to settle for the iced water with lemon until his drink arrived.

"Where were we? Oh, if you do get the tickets, bringing Marty is fine. I want to meet her. I'll bring Marcia."

"Marcia could give two hoots about football, Dad. I would like you to bring a date."

"Whoa, what? Are you kidding? I'm not dating or even thinking about it."

Geoff glared at him with a serious look that communicated it was not a joke. "Well, you have two months. I'll work on the tickets, and you work on getting a date."

"Seriously, Geoff, I don't know if I'm ready to do that. Your mom—"

"Mom would understand. You can't be a hermit all your life. Marcia and I have been talking about it for a while. It's been over two years, and we have not seen you really happy. Maybe a fresh start is in order. We both know how much Mom meant to you and you to her. If the tables were turned, we would say the same thing to her."

"Geoff, I—"

"Think about it. We'll discuss it in Big Bear."

41
CHAPTER

The Hamilton household was more than ready to get out of town. No one had misgivings about leaving their holiday-decorated home behind. Howard had not been forthcoming with Geoff and Marcia about Tuesday evening and his plans.

"I have some dinner plans tonight, so I won't be home until probably sometime after nine."

"With who, Dad?" Geoff smirked.

"Well, it's with a girl from work. Mel Flowers."

"I think we heard you talk about her with Mom. Somebody you recruited on the job, right?"

"Yes. Mel's boyfriend can't make this dinner she's been invited to, so she asked me to accompany her. More like an escort than a date."

"Really, Dad? You expect us to believe that?" Marcia was trying to be serious.

"No, it's true. The holiday dinner is at a family friend's house here in Orchard Hill, and she and her parents were invited, but her parents insisted she bring a date. If you don't believe me, then ask her yourself. She's going to pick me up here."

"We believe you, Dad. We're just pulling your leg a bit," Geoff responded.

Marcia reached a hand out to his. "Come on, Dad. I'll help you pick out some nice clothes."

She led him into the bedroom, opened the closet, and went to work. "Tie or no tie, Dad?"

"I don't know, Marsh. Maybe we pick one, and I'll ask Mel when she gets here."

Marcia passed by the black suit her dad had worn at the funeral. She selected a dark blue blazer, a powder-blue dress shirt, dark brown slacks, and several ties to pick from. She laid the clothing items out on the bed for him to see. "I think that's a good look. Don't you, Dad?"

"They're the same clothes I wear to court."

"Well, it's a little late to upgrade your wardrobe now. We should have considered it before five thirty. Maybe Santa will dress you better, but that'll have to wait." Marcia fumbled through the dresser drawers. "Here are some good socks, and you should wear these shoes because they go with this belt."

The doorbell rang precisely at 5:30. Howard heard the commotion as both kids rushed to the door to answer.

"Hi. I'm Mel. You must be Marcia and Geoff. I've heard so much about you." Mel held out a hand for a firm but gentle handshake.

They exchanged pleasantries as Geoff excused himself. "I'll get Dad."

Marcia looked at Geoff and mouthed, "Wow."

Mel stepped into the living room. She wore a soft, form-fitting, knee-length white dress accentuating her slender form. The neck was tasteful but clearly showed her cleavage, tan, and jewelry. There was no bulletproof vest, body-worn camera, or Sam Browne belt to cover her stellar look.

Geoff ran to the kitchen. "Dad," Geoff stuttered, "you didn't prepare us for Mel."

"What do you mean?"

"She's gorgeous. Drop dead. I don't know any other way to put it."

"Well, I know she's good looking, but I've only seen her in a uniform."

They both walked out to the area where Mel and Marcia were talking.

"Dad, you need to wear one of those ties. Mel told me this was a dress-up affair. I mean dinner."

Howard hugged Mel and said, "I'll be right back."

Geoff was right. She was stunning in that outfit. What had he missed?

By the time Howard picked out a tie, struggled with the perfect Windsor knot, and returned to the living room, he could not believe what was going on.

The kids and Mel were engaged in rapid-fire conversations about school, their social lives, and plans for the future. Mel had only spent a few minutes bonding with Geoff and Marcia, as no one had since Clare's passing. Bentley sat beside Mel, near the couch, as if she were part of the furniture.

"Excuse me, but we have to go. Maybe you guys could catch up later."

"Oh, Howard. You look very nice," Mel said, standing and walking over to readjust his tie.

Geoff and Marcia rolled their eyes while Mel's back was turned. Howard caught the look and tried to give them a stern frown.

"You look great, Mel. Shall we go?"

"So what time are you kids going to be home?" Marcia joked.

"Long after you're in bed, young lady." Howard struck right back.

Everyone had a good laugh.

"OK," Mel said as she walked to the door, "I would like to hear more about your plans, so before you return to school, let's make a date to catch up."

Both kids agreed.

"You got it, Mel. You two kids have fun now."

42
CHAPTER

They walked silently to Mel's two-seater Audi sports car, which was silver gray with a tan interior. There was a slight breeze, but the evening chill had yet to set in.

"Nice set of wheels, Mel," Howard said as he opened the driver's door for her. "By the way, you look stunning tonight. With all the commotion with the kids, I didn't get a chance to say that. Are you sure you don't want me to drive?" He walked to the passenger side, slid in, and continued the conversation.

"No, I know where we're going. It's kind of hard to find. Glad you like the wheels. Paid for with overtime." She pulled away from the curb. "Howard, you have done a masterful job with those kids. They are phenomenal. I meant it when I told them I'd like to get together before they go back to school."

"We'll see, Mel. And Clare did all the work."

Mel found her way to Albion Boulevard and headed north toward Sparrow Hill. "Don't sell yourself short on that. They have a lot of your personality and overall demeanor. I see more of Clare's gentleness, but I didn't know her. But maybe I do."

"OK, enough about the family, Mel. Tell me what I am walking into with this party."

"OK, the hostess is Dolores Reynolds. She's friends with my parents. Her husband was Thomas, a real estate mogul who they say built half of the South Bay. We got together frequently as I grew up, because he and my dad went to school together. Dolores is his second wife. The first one ended in divorce. She's quite younger." Mel took a sharp turn up a side street that seemed to climb to the clouds. "She's more the trophy type he wanted, I guess. Closer to my age than his. Also, you need to know that she's close to my mom and me. She and I are more like sisters. I love her to death."

"So what have you told them about me?"

"They know you helped recruit me. We never worked together in a radio car but stayed close friends, and now we're dating."

"Are we serious?"

"No, I didn't share anything more with my parents." She let the last sentence fade away. "There will be about twenty people here, but I don't know anything about them other than they all have money and are a bit snotty. Don't worry. Knowing Dolores, nameplates will be at the tables, so I'll do my best to make introductions and stay close."

"I'm not sure I want to meet any of them with that kind of introduction. What are your parents' names again?"

"Michael and Becky. We're here. It's Rebecca, but she goes by Becky."

The tree-lined street had older retaining walls covered with ivy, which provided privacy for the estates behind them. Mel approached a gate, put in a code, and drove up a long approach to the house. There was no valet but plenty of parking because many guests apparently had walked over. She parked at the end of the horseshoe drive and looked at Howard.

"Are we ready?"

"Let's do it. But wow, Mel, you have some ritzy friends." Howard took in the expansive entrance to the home and shook his head in disbelief.

43

The home was overly decorated for the holidays. He lost count of the number of Christmas trees, all decorated as if they were in a department store. Nutcrackers were spread throughout each room, acting like butlers as one entered or exited. The glitter of small lights reflected off large wall mirrors and made each room look larger than it was.

Howard met Mel's parents. He knew he would have trouble calling her father anything but Chief. He was a deputy chief with the LAPD and looked every bit the part. Mel took after her mother in looks and demeanor. She'd gotten her outgoing personality from her father—a nice person.

He was then introduced to the hostess, Dolores Reynolds. She was striking, with medium-blonde hair, green eyes, and a figure that only Mel topped. Her dress probably had cost more than Howard made in a month, and she showed much more cleavage than Mel. Howard was not ready for that either.

After the introductions, Dolores immediately turned to Mel. "May I take Howard around to meet everyone?"

Without waiting for a reply, she put her arm in his and walked into the next room, where many guests had assembled around a twelve-foot flocked tree with all the trimmings. A bartender strategically placed in the corner served cocktails, wine, and nonalcoholic beverages.

She approached a man in his early sixties and provided introductions. "Howard Hamilton, I would like you to meet my friend Daniel. You and Mel will sit with us near the dining room window. You'll see your nameplate when we go in."

"I'm sorry, Daniel, but I didn't catch your last name." Howard was going to try to remember everyone he met that night.

"It's Carmona, Howard. Daniel Carmona."

"Great to meet you, sir." Before he could engage in a conversation, he was whisked away by his escort to another group of her friends.

He met six other couples and tried to concentrate on remembering the men's names and at least the first names of their wives or girlfriends, whatever they were.

A bell quietly rang, announcing dinner.

He found Mel at the bar and lightly touched her elbow. "Oh my God, this is incredible. I've never been to such a lavish event," he whispered to Mel as they went to the dining room.

"If you hang around with Dolores, this is how she rolls."

The table was set with white linen place mats, silver utensils, and water glasses strategically placed on the plates' right sides. Three candles were spaced tastefully between small bowls of flowers designed so everyone could see one another for easy conversation.

Howard marveled that the table could seat all attendees. Dolores sat at the head, with her friend Daniel to her left. Howard saw that his nameplate was to her right, with Mel to his right. He counted heads and determined there were eighteen people. The others seemed to find their way.

He was even more surprised when Dolores asked one of the guests to say grace. Howard had forgotten the man had been introduced as Reverend Patrick Holmes.

Howard looked around the table to see if he should make the sign of the cross.

"Thank you, Patrick. For those who do not know, Patrick is the new pastor at the Sparrow Hill Presbyterian Church. He and his wife are new to the community. I thought you should all get to know them."

Mr. Flowers welcomed the new community member and asked Dolores, "Where are Dick and Rita?"

"They canceled at the last minute. But their turn will come up again someday. Dick has a big trial coming up." No one knew whether Dolores was kidding.

Michael said, "Well, it's probably one involving my department. I'll say it here, and I don't care if it is repeated: he's not one I would be hanging around, Dolores."

"We'll talk, Michael, but they were Tom's friends, not mine."

"I know. Just the same. We'll talk later, as you said."

Reverend Holmes said quietly, "Shall we pray?"

CHAPTER

Christmas carols were sung, soft holiday music was in the background, and all the TVs showed holiday scenes in every room.

Mr. Flowers pulled Howard aside. "Howard, let's talk for a minute." He ushered him into an unoccupied side room. "I didn't mean to come off that way, but my old friend Tom, rest his soul, had some friends I didn't care for. Dick Anderson is one of those sleazebag attorneys from the National Lawyers Guild. They're a bunch of socialist liberals—and I'm being nice here—who try to beat the judicial system every way they can.

"There's another guy here you should know about because he lives in your city. See the guy with the red bow tie?"

Howard nodded to let him know he understood whom he was indicating. Howard knew the man he was talking about, Lawrence Justice.

"He's a big shot at Disney. Almost single-handedly, he has brought them to their knees due to his woke policies. He's somebody high in HR, and I've been tracking him. You should know about him too."

"I think I know about him, sir. I had a recent project and researched a few people my chief asked me to look at. Now I've put two and two together and see who we're dealing with."

"Your former chief and I are great friends. He is a super guy, and you can be assured he'll land on his feet somewhere. And when he found out you were seeing Mel, he was delighted."

I'd better talk to Mel about this on the way home.

As everyone was starting to leave, Dolores pulled Howard aside. "Howard, can we talk for a moment?" Without waiting for an answer, she ushered him into the same side room Mr. Flowers had used. "I know that you and Mel are not dating. I know all about what is going on in her life, and while I don't condone it, it's her life. We're like sisters more than friends, and I think the world of her. I do not want to see her get hurt. Maybe we can team up to make sure that doesn't happen."

The look in her eye told Howard there was to be more to this conversation.

"I'll do what I can, ma'am. And thanks for the heads-up. I am a little concerned."

"There is one more thing you can do—two things. My name is Dolores, and my friends call me Lori."

"OK, Lori. I didn't want to overstep my bounds here."

"Howard, I don't think you can do that with me." She reached out her left hand, not to shake but to hand him something. "This is my phone number. I like you, and I would like to see you again. I'm a pretty straightforward person, Howard, and I like what I see." She put both hands on his left hand and led him to the entrance to her home.

*   *   *

Everyone but Mel and her parents had left. A few of the guests looked as if they had been overserved, but Howard figured those were the ones who could walk home. Howard walked to the driver's side of Mel's car and asked, "Do I need to drive?"

"No, I'm good," she said, smiling like the Cheshire cat in a tree.

He jumped into the passenger seat, buckled up, and looked directly at Mel. "Do you mind telling me what that was all about?"

"Just a fun holiday party, HH. Why? Did you not have fun?" She started the Audi and moved slowly out of the horseshoe drive.

"I think you know. Your dad was hot under the collar over Anderson and Justice. Are all of your gatherings this contentious?"

She waited for the gate to open. She stared straight ahead. "Most of the time. Especially when Tom was still alive, Lori was on my dad's side. They argued a lot. She didn't like any of them."

"And another thing. Your friend Lori"—Howard used finger quotes when he said *Lori*—"knows about your boyfriend and knows I was just an escort for the evening."

Mel stopped the car outside the gate, which automatically closed after a few moments, and turned to Howard. "I told you we were close friends. She knows it all."

"When do I get to know who this guy is? Is he in the department?"

"No, not OHPD."

"What Department? LA?"

"No. If you must know, he's at Redondo. That's all I'm going to say right now, HH. Please, I'm going through enough with all of this." She was almost pleading now. She turned down the hill toward Howard's home.

"OK, OK. I'll drop it. But some time, we need to talk. Lori is worried about you, and so am I."

Mel tried to change the subject. "Do you like her?"

"Did you put her up to this?" He showed Mel the paper with Lori's phone number on it.

"She asked my permission. Is that a problem? Don't you like her?"

"That's a lot of questions to answer, Mel."

She concentrated on her driving but made sure Howard knew she was listening. "You're a great guy, Howard. You deserve somebody as good as you are, and she is. Look at her. Gorgeous and wealthy—and lonely."

"Who was that guy she was with tonight?"

"Just a guy. There was nothing there, but she needed a date like me. I mean, well, not like that. I like you too. But he was nothing, just a friend. You're more than that to me."

When their conversation wound down, they arrived at Howard's home.

"Mel, come in for a drink, coffee, or something. We can finish this discussion tonight. It's early, and I'm going out of town with the kids on Friday for the holidays."

She took him up on the invitation.

45

The next few days were a blur for Hamilton. He decided to visit Guy Coyle, his retired LAPD lieutenant friend, bringing Peet's coffee for both. He called ahead to make sure he was home. Coyle lived on a street that was all Craftsman homes. He had restored his house to the point anyone could eat off the lawn or the floors.

He and Coyle discussed the Chief's removal, what might happen with the department, and who Coyle thought might be the next Chief.

"Boy, Howard, I don't have a crystal ball, but I think it will be another outsider. I hear rumors but am not sure I should talk with you about it just yet."

Howard could tell he was being a bit evasive. "Why not? I'm a confidential employee, you know."

They both laughed at the humor.

"OK, from my mouth to God's ears. This is what I know. Do you know George Melendrez?"

"No."

"He's the current chief of Gardenia. Now does that click?"

"I guess I've heard the name now that you mention it. I don't keep track of all of that. But Gardenia has less than one hundred officers. He needs to have managed a larger department, I would think."

"Well, there's more. Melendrez is the acting city manager there as well as the chief. He's been talking to your city manager, and I hear they've become close. Being a minority and having city manager experience would put him in the driver's seat."

"Where did you get this information, Guy? This will affect the entire department. I mean, I don't give a shit, because who is chief isn't that important to someone like me way down on the totem pole. But it sounds like you have some good sources. And I can always use good, solid intel." Now he had Howard's full attention.

"I can't tell you that right now, Howard. I've been sworn to secrecy. Sorry, but the source would be highly upset if they knew I was having a conversation with someone from OHPD. I can't burn my snitch right now. You understand? Maybe later."

They talked around the topic for a while, so Howard changed the subject. Howard brought him up to date on what was going on in narcotics and vice.

"No city is immune to those kinds of investigations, Howard. Until the laws change to permit gays to do what they want in public or they legalize prostitution, it's our job to enforce the laws as they stand. You know the three Cs of vice crimes, so dealing with complaints from the public is still a requirement. Remember that if you don't control those petty-ass vice crimes, someday they'll control you. And that, my friend, is not a good thing. End of lecture for today."

"OK, one last question." He had to ask the question that was burning inside him. "Are you seeing anyone?"

Coyle countered. "Are you?"

Hamilton responded quickly, "No." He wasn't going to let him off that easily.

"I can't say that right now." Coyle sat back and stared at Howard.

"Can you tell me a little about her?"

"No, not right now. Maybe later."

Hamilton wasn't done. "When is *later*?"

"Adios, Howard. Stop by after the first of the year with more coffee, and we'll continue this conversation." Coyle stood up, signaling it was time to go.

A man hug ended their visit, and they wished each other happy holidays.

What could Coyle be hiding?

46

For many, two weeks of vacation was not enough. For others, it was too much. For the Hamilton family of three, it was just right. Big Bear had the snow they'd prayed for. The cabin was more than anticipated.

Each of the Hamilton family got something different. For Marcia, it was seeing her father happy again, listening to the stories of his relationship with her mother, watching him return to the family after being consumed by work, and eavesdropping on the banter between her dad and Geoff. She discovered that her dad had a friend who was a girl—not a girlfriend but a friend—in Mel. Priceless.

Geoff felt he finally got his dad back—his best friend and confidant. The gap from Mom's death to today was filled as he saw his loss and rebuilding of the family as four minus one. Geoff got to share his relationship with his girlfriend, Marty, as a friend and perhaps even more. And Dad finally listened to him about everything without being judgmental or critical. He ended the two weeks not knowing who had changed more, himself or his father. He saw Marcia in a completely different light. She seemed more intelligent, poised, and filled with a confidence he had never seen before. Was this the kid sister he'd left when he went away to college?

The three decided there were four again, even with Clare's passing. Bentley had taken to the snow and the fireside chats, even if it was just a gas fireplace made for a family rebonding after their tragic loss.

It was like seeing the fruits of his and Clare's parenting for Howard. She would've been as proud of her children, who had grown into young adults, as he was. Perhaps she did know, as they all mentioned that they felt her presence as they walked in the snow, threw snowballs at one another, and tobogganed down slopes, laughing all the way. Even Bentley seemed more alive and a part of the family as he frolicked in the snow without a leash.

Howard learned Geoff was experiencing his first love in Martha. There seemed to be a mutual level of respect they had as a couple, even though Howard had yet to meet her. He learned that Martha was a second-generation Hispanic from El Salvador, born to migrant parents who had legally come to the United States. Martha came from a similar traditional family. She had been raised Catholic and attended parochial schools until she went to high school in Fremont, California.

If Howard was bothered by any one thing, it was that his children insisted he pursue a more personal relationship with Flowers. Both kids doted on her. Howard had invited her for a nightcap after the dinner party on that auspicious evening at Dolores Reynolds's home. Geoff and Marcia had been dutifully waiting for them.

Howard might as well not have been in the room as they'd bantered back and forth for more than two hours. It had been eleven before Mel left, much to the chagrin of Geoff and Marcia, particularly Marcia. She was captivated by Mel, and Howard saw it firsthand.

As the second week was winding down, New Year's Eve approached. They watched the New York ball drop and gathered to summarize their time together. At midnight on the East Coast, he heard his phone chime with a text. He was not surprised to see who it was: Amanda Johnson.

Amanda had lost her husband, rookie officer Andrew Johnson, or A. J. He had been killed by a fleeing felon several years back. Howard fondly recalled last New Year's Eve, when he and Amanda had bonded as a widow and widower. After his losing Clare more than two years ago, they'd had sympathy sex on the floor of her condo in Lomita.

The text was timely, about one year since their happenstance: "Howard, I was thinking of you this evening as I prepared to watch the ball drop on New Year's Eve at my new home. I have moved to Austin, Texas, since we last talked. I hope all is well with you and your family. I am happy here, but I still miss our time together. Fondly, Amanda J."

He also thought of that evening, but the time with his kids surpassed it as meaningful.

While reflecting on his time with Amanda, he received an email message. He was shocked to see it was from Lieutenant Rikelman and was addressed to the entire unit:

Dear members of the N&V,

With a heavy heart, I let you know we lost a unit member this week. As you remember, Bob "BB" Bowers announced he was going for an angioplasty to fix a heart problem. He, unfortunately, passed away on the operating table. All we know right now is that there was a puncture of the aorta, and he bled out before they could save him. I hope to have more info when we return next week—prayers for the Bowers family.

Lt. R.
What else can happen to OHPD? Are there more surprises?

47

CHAPTER

Walking into the station via the employees' entrance, Howard took his regular tour to ensure everything was where it should've been. He walked through the locker room, went by briefing, and went up to the detective squad bay. He should have known never to underestimate what drama would unfold at OHPD. Walking by the watch commander's office, he spotted Sergeant Kip Bennett sitting at the watch commander's desk. He couldn't remember Kip ever being on days. He was the Dracula of the night shift, never to see the light of day.

The door was propped open on the N&V office. Everyone in the unit was already there, doing something. He wasn't sure what. Rikelman was in his office, Barber was on the phone, and Joanie was unpacking her file cabinets to make way for the new year. The Christmas decorations were a distant memory.

Rikelman walked out to greet him. "HH, I was not expecting you until tomorrow. How was Big Bear?"

"It was great, sir. I had a great time with the family, and getting away was good. Things seem to be going a bit crazy around here. What's all the activity I sense? Is it OK to make this a workday and get right to it?"

"Sure, but I may have something for you to do on the QT in a few hours. Step into my cave."

He followed Rikelman into his office and closed the door.

"The death of BB has caused quite a stir around here. But it got a little more complicated after we left the family. Chief Pierson, the acting chief, and I met with the family. And that's where I may need you."

"I'm not following you, Lieutenant. What would I have to do with it?"

Rikelman motioned for him to sit. "Bowers was the victim of a shoddy piece of surgery. Not sure what for. He went to a heart surgeon who was coming off a license suspension. The doctor had a hand spasm while putting the probe up the aorta to clear some blockage and put in a stent. It punctured something, and he bled out before they could take care of it."

"That sounds like the family may have some recourse."

"And therein lies the problem. I came into the office to look up his home address and family information so I would know his wife's and kids' names." He fumbled through some papers on his desk. "We went to the house to pay my respects and found a different family than he had on record here. The lady there said she was Betty, his wife. She didn't speak very good English but had no clue where Bowers was. There was one two-year-old child there. Our records show his wife's name to be Barbara, with two kids in their early teens."

"Sounds a bit confusing, sir."

"So I came back to the station and went upstairs to Personnel and pulled his records. Sure enough, it listed Barbara as having two kids and a different address. I went to her address in Hawthorne. She was in mourning, so I figured I had the right wife. According to Blair in HR, they audited his medical insurance records, and everyone was listed as family. Betty, her kid, Barbara, and the boys."

"Did he have two wives?"

"That's where I need you, HH. Blair will work it from his end, but I need you to do some sleuthing to find out what was happening in his life."

"What does Disney say about this?" Howard asked, referring to Bowers's partner, Al Garcia.

A frustrated Rikelman responded, "He says he knows nothing more than we do, but I think he does know more. I'm not going there right now until you get me some answers. Hell, right now, we don't know whose hand to hold or who receives the insurance. Here you go." He handed Howard a personnel file.

"I'm not sure I should be looking at this, sir," Howard responded.

"Hamilton"—Rikelman looked him in the eye with the Norman Bates stare—"you are a confidential employee, remember? Oh, and by the way, one more thing."

"Sir?"

"I signed you up for a three-day school on asset forfeiture. We don't have much expertise in that area, so you might as well take that over as well. I'll send you the details. I think it's right after the first of the year."

"Got it, sir." He gave a half-assed salute and backed out of the office with a smile.

He was on the way to his office but was delayed by Don of the Everlys.

"Hey, Hamilton, did you hear what happened?"

"About Bowers? Yes."

"No, we've all heard about that. I mean about the restroom up in the park. We don't have to worry about it anymore."

"Why?" Howard said as he unlocked his private office.

"Because it burned down over the holidays. Right to the fucking ground. Nothing left. I guess it was so remote that it was in ashes by the time Fire got there. The place was a firetrap anyway." Don could not stop grinning as he told Hamilton the story.

"Any idea if it was arson or an electrical shortage?"

"Don't know yet. The only thing was that the cameras on the outside weren't working, so I guess we'll never know."

Barber hung up the phone call he was on. "That was the arson unit. They're calling it an electrical wire problem. No arson. So you guys are in the clear." Barber looked at Don. "Did you or Phil have anything to do with this?"

"No, sir, Sergeant Barber. I called Phil to let him know about it. I joked that maybe he burned it down so he wouldn't have to work the complaint any longer."

"What did he say?" Barber said with a smile. "Never mind. I'll ask him tomorrow."

"He said he didn't, sir," Don said with a return smile, "and I believe him."

"Sounds like you get to close another case with arrests and a fire," Howard joked.

"Problem-oriented policing at work," Garcia said with a forced smile.

Not everyone smiled at that comment.

48

Howard had his priorities regarding his intelligence-gathering investigations. But Rikelman's was the most important to get out of the way first. He opened Bowers's personnel folder and searched for cell phone and address information.

On a hunch, he returned to Joanie's desk and asked, "Joanie, how were your holidays?"

"What do you want, Howard? I'm a bit swamped today."

Recognizing she was a bit testy today, he softened his approach. "Perchance, would you have our call-out files with everyone's home and cell number handy?"

"Help yourself," she said, pointing to a Rolodex on her desk. "I have it on my computer, but the Rolodex is the easiest because it has a history of just about everyone in the unit over the last ten years and all of their old addresses and phone numbers. Will that help?"

"May I borrow it?"

"It's all yours. Remember where you got it, and put it back when done."

"Yes, ma'am." He snapped to attention, did an about-face, returned to his office, and relocked the door.

Without a doubt, Joanie ran the administrative side of the office with an iron fist.

He found several phone numbers for Bowers and several home addresses listed over the years. Bowers had been the most senior unit member, so it made sense he might've changed addresses or cell phone numbers.

He plugged it all into the database truecaller.com, and the site did not fail. He obtained the carrier for each phone number, the billing address, and the credit card used for payment. He next transferred the data received to a proprietary site given to him in the intelligence school, and a wealth of data told him everything he needed to know.

Bowers had been in massive debt. Credit cards were found in Betty's and Barbara's names. They had been all maxed out. Payments had been made to avoid late fees, but little had been done to reduce balances. He printed everything out and went directly to Rikelman's office. But he wasn't there.

"Joanie, do you know where the lieutenant went?"

"No, HH, I do not," she said with a frustrated "Can't you see I'm busy?" attitude. "It's not my turn to watch him. Maybe Sam knows."

"He's upstairs with the captain. I mean chief. Acting Chief Pierson. Is it important?" Sam responded.

"No, just let me know when he returns, please. I'll be in my office," Howard said, trying to be as condescending as possible.

Man, everyone is on edge around here. So much for happy holidays.

49
CHAPTER

Hamilton went back to his office and set the printouts aside. He opened his email and searched for Bonnie Carvin's message. She had called him before the holidays, needing help with a human-trafficking case. Twenty emails later, he found it. He read her note and saw an attachment. The message said to call her after he reviewed the information forwarded.

It was a spreadsheet with names and what appeared to be bank accounts and financial records. Howard whistled softly. Bonnie Carvin's message contained an attachment with bank accounts and financial records. The amounts were in the six-figure range, so it seemed she had a hefty investigation. After getting approval to work on the case, he called her.

"Howard, welcome back. How was your vacation?"

He filled her in, remembering he had shared his plans.

She said, "I think I told you, but I'm on another task force: HURT."

"I remember."

"We've tied these people to a Mexican mafia or cartel working our entire county. We think it may be the Zetas with some new players. They're bringing these people in, setting up call-girl rings, and funneling accounts with their proceeds to places we can't trace. We hear you're good at supersleuthing in this area. We don't have the expertise yet, so can I lean on you? For old times' sake?"

"Where did you hear that?"

"We have our sources," Bonnie said coyly.

"Would one of them be a guy named Dennis Packer?"

"Might be."

"Why not just go to him?"

"He said to give you the information, and if you need him, you can call. I think he was pretty busy himself. So you're our first stop."

"Well, let me get the OK to help, and I'll look at what you have and get back to you. Maybe by tomorrow. Will that work?"

"You bet. Oh, and you might want to check in with your Detective Hernandez. I think her first name is Anita. She has another similar investigation, but I'm unsure if it's related to ours."

"We used to call her Chili, but we'll have to find another nickname. She wasn't too hot about it the last time I called her that. Pun intended."

"It's a different world, HH. Can I still call you that?"

They both laughed and said their goodbyes.

There was a knock on the door. "HH, you wanted to see me?"

It was Rikelman.

50

"**Y**es, sir. Come on in, but close the door, please." Howard never knew who would show up: Lieutenant Rikelman or Norman Bates. He reached for the printouts regarding Bowers. "Before we go over this, can I ask a few questions?"

"Sure, and I hope I can answer them," Rikelman responded.

"First, sir, how was Christmas Eve? You know, the proposal."

"It went really well, Howard. We're going to tie the knot on Valentine's Day. Thanks for asking."

"That's great, sir. I'm happy for you both. She's a nice lady. One more item. I spent some time on vacation thinking a lot about this job. I mean OHPD and this intel assignment."

"OK." Rikelman stared intently at Hamilton, unsure what was coming next.

Howard decided to let it all hang out. "I think it might be time for me to train a backup for this position," he said, referencing the room and his computers. "I'm thinking about taking the next sergeant's exam. I don't want to be left behind with everything happening here: retirements, promotions, and even deaths. I think I have much to offer, and it may be time to start planning ahead." He took a deep breath.

"That's some good thinking, HH. I agree. Wolford talked to me about this very matter this morning. She didn't come in but called to ask if she could shadow you. I hadn't given it much thought, but I will now."

Howard felt a sense of relief. Wolford had done her part. "Thank you, sir. I'll, of course, need some help preparing for the exam. Is it still a written and oral board?"

"As far as I know. With an acting chief right now, I don't foresee many changes. Hopefully, we will have one permanently soon."

"What do you hear?" Hamilton did not want to divulge the information he had heard about the Gardenia chief.

"We hear it could be soon and that the Gardenia chief is in the running. Can't think of his name."

"Melendrez. George Melendrez," Howard responded a little too quickly.

"Did you already know this, HH?"

"Just a dolphin or two talking, sir. Nothing official."

"And did you know Wolford talked to me?"

"To be honest, no, sir. We just talked about her looking over my shoulder. I didn't know she was going to talk to you."

"Well, Barber and I think it's a good idea, regardless of whose it was. We all need to be planning around here. What do you have for me about Bowers?"

"Before I get into this," he said, referring to his desk full of papers, "I have a question, sir. Are you going to take the next captain's exam?"

"No. And why do you ask?"

"Well, you've been around here quite a while as a lieutenant. It seems you would be a natural for a promotion to captain."

Rikelman gave him the Norman Bates stare once again. "Howard, kind of you to say, but then who would keep all those assholes," he said, pointing to the ceiling but referring to the third floor, "on the straight and narrow? They don't get involved in police work or deal with all of this," he added, referring to the N&V office. "They're paper shufflers. I like what I'm doing just fine. If a new chief decides to move me, I'll consider it. But not right now. Understand?"

"I think I do, but …" Hamilton took advantage of the change of topic and handed Rikelman the printouts.

Rikelman reviewed everything he'd found in just a few minutes. Howard sat back in his chair and allowed Rikelman to ponder the information.

"You know, BB may be better off where he is," Howard said, trying not to smile and acting more businesslike. "Do you see what I see?"

"I think you're right."

"May I make a recommendation, sir?"

"Of course. You've been spot-on regarding everything so far."

"Before this goes too far, I think you should sit down with his partner, Garcia. I think he knows more about what's happening than he leads you to believe." Hamilton collected the printouts, put them in a folder, and handed them to Rikelman. "Let's hope Bowers didn't go to the dark side and get in bed with someone he shouldn't have."

"Agreed, Howard. Thanks, but I'm one step ahead of you."

51

CHAPTER

Well, that's one more thing off my plate.

Hamilton sat back and stared at his screen. His thoughts went from Morrison to Bowers and all the past deaths that seemed to plague the department. The Chief was gone, so he might as well have been dead. The department was in limbo, with no authentic leadership to speak of. The lieutenants and sergeants were in charge of keeping the ship from sinking. It was equivalent to a sailboat steered by the wind with no one at the helm. They could tread water for a while, but who knew how long it would take to get everyone back on course?

He decided to take a walk to clear his head. Walking into the coffee break room, he saw Kip and several other sergeants huddled in a corner. He was already carrying his third cup of Peet's, so he read the bulletin board rather than interrupting Kip. There were condos for rent in Palm Springs, someone was selling a five-year-old car, and there were reminders from personnel to update beneficiaries.

I wonder who the beneficiaries for Bowers were.

He went back to the list of rentals and cars for sale. The five-year-old Toyota Highlander was listed for $15,000 or the best offer. The name was listed as BB in N&V. Hamilton looked at the number. It was not one he'd found on any of Bowers's records.

Hmm.

Kip called him to the corner table where the supervisors were huddled. "HH, sit down and join the conversation. You'll be a supervisor soon, so you might as well add your two cents to the conversation."

"Don't rush me, Sarge. I have a pretty good thing going."

"We were just taking stock of the state of the department. I'm sure you know this guy Melendrez from Gardenia is the front-runner for chief.

From everything we can find, he's a dickhead. His POA hates him, and everybody thinks the CM is just picking him because he's Hispanic. What are your thoughts?"

"Well, I think he might have the quals, but he's only commanded a hundred-man department. OHPD is a much bigger ship. I heard he's acting city manager over there, so he must have something on the ball. But why would it matter to you guys?" He swept his hands to acknowledge the other supervisors.

"What do you mean?"

Hamilton had a smile on his face. "It shouldn't matter, because you guys run this place anyway."

"True, but we need somebody else to blame when things go to shit." Kip was now poking the bear. "You know, HH. Get your ass into the books, and help us out."

"I think I'll do you one better, sir. I'll take the lieutenant's test and skip you guys."

Kip gave a sarcastic laugh. "Until that day comes—and I'm sure it will—what are your thoughts? Before you answer, here is our position." He raised one hand as if to hold court. "We want someone from the inside. Somebody who knows us. We think that guy is Rod Tustin. He's a new captain, but he was a great lieutenant, if such a thing exists. He returns from the FBI Academy next month, so that's where we're leaning. We've all worked for him, and I think we can get behind him to do much good for the department. Maybe carry on what our last chief was doing."

Howard thought for a moment. "I can go for that. Do you want me to pass that along to the city manager? I'll be meeting with him later today."

There was stone silence for a long moment.

"Ha, got you guys for once." Hamilton laughed as he departed the coffee room. It felt good. He couldn't often yank a group of sergeants' chains and see how they reacted.

CHAPTER

He had a hunch about the phone number Bowers had posted for the sale of his car. He was right. It was Betty's number, and she answered. Without identifying himself, he inquired about the Toyota Highlander and was advised it had been sold. She was challenging to understand with her broken English. Was she Chinese? Vietnamese? He wasn't sure.

It was apparent to Howard that Bowers had been liquidating to pay some bills and make sure at least one of the wives was getting her debt reduced. His suspicions were confirmed when he reran Bowers's credit cards to find out. Bowers had been working on getting them within normal limits, at least for Betty and her child. The system must have taken a while to update payments.

He checked with Lieutenant Rydell in Personnel—or HR or whatever they were calling it now—to see who his life insurance and pension beneficiaries were.

"Come on, HH. I can't divulge that information to you. Anyway, I already gave that info to Rikelman."

"Oh, I was trying to help him out, sir. Sorry to have bothered you. Hey, on another matter, when will you be appointed captain?"

"A lot will happen when Tustin gets back from the academy. I'm just in a holding pattern. It depends on who the chief is going to be. If he's from inside, I'd be next up, but I wouldn't be surprised if the city manager holds it up until that decision is firm. But I have a great job here. I can come and go as I please; the work is exciting, and I'm still learning a lot. Now, can I ask you a question? When will you get off your ass and study for sergeant?"

"I'm like you. I have a great job. I come and go as I please, and I am still learning. But I am thinking about it."

"Think harder, HH. We need guys like you to challenge themselves to go after positions of increased responsibility. You owe it to the department and your family."

"We'll see, sir. We'll see."

His cell phone rang. "Gotta go, Lieutenant. Bigger name on the other line." He had no idea who it was, but it was an excellent way to close the conversation.

*   *   *

"I got your message regarding a letter from my GM explaining our level of cooperation. What's the matter? Don't you trust me?" It was Getty, and there was no doubt she was pissed.

Howard tried to recover and put her on the defense. "That's not the point, Nicole. We need to cover our asses on this. My boss wanted it in writing that you have the OK to move forward with this. Is that so unreasonable?"

"I don't like it" was her immediate response.

"There's a lot of things we don't like that we have to do, Nicole. Just get it done, and we can continue the investigation." He had wrested control of the situation and waited for her reply.

"I'll call you when I get it. If I get it."

Now he was sensing some trepidation on her part. "What do you mean by that? He's on board, is he not?"

She paused just enough to make Howard react.

"Nicole, he *is* on board with this, right?"

"He will be." She hung up.

53

He brought Rikelman up to date on Bowers's car being sold and advised him about his conversation with Getty.

"Once we get the letter from the GM, we can start moving forward. Until then, do not do anything more about it. As a matter of fact, I think Barber and I will visit him once we get the letter."

Hamilton agreed with the strategy. "Should I go by and pick it up? Would that be OK?"

"As soon as you hear it's ready, let me know. Then I'll decide." Rikelman had a way of ending a conversation.

"Got it. My plate's full right now anyway."

Hamilton returned to his office to ensure he finished entering everything Getty had given him in a spreadsheet designed just for the case. *Better to be organized at the beginning of this one.*

As he was about to close his door, Phil showed up. "HH, did you see the *LA Times* over the weekend?"

"Don't get the *Times*, Phil. There's not a lot of good stuff in there other than the sports page."

"Here you go." Phil tossed him the front section. "Take a look at page three. Our buddy Sparks is in some deep shit. Couldn't happen to a nicer guy."

Oh shit.

Howard took the paper to his office, closed the door, and sat down to read. The headline and article in the right column jumped out at him:

Los Angeles County Board of Education Investigating
Staff Members and Students Involved in a Possible Sex
Ring Conducted at Washington High School

Some school board members received an anonymous tip, including photographs, of a staff member and students participating in sex acts. The board of education has not named specific staff members or students. The investigators have determined that based on the photos' backgrounds, the events took place on school property.

I hope they do not try to trace the anonymous tip, but I think I covered my tracks. We'll see. Otherwise, I could be in some serious shit. Time will tell. But I had to nail that asshole one way or the other.

There was a door knock. Phil stepped in with a grin on his face. "What do you think, HH? Pretty good, huh? The restroom burned down, and one of our suspects is in deep trouble. I would say we closed this case out with a bang."

Howard tried not to make eye contact. "It sure looks like it, but I have to ask you a question."

"Shoot."

He had to try to pass the ball into their court, not his. "Did you or Don make the anonymous tip?"

"Is that an accusation?" Phil said with a smile.

"Just an inquiry," Howard said modestly.

"Well, knowing you are the supersleuth on the computer, it wouldn't surprise me if you were the culprit."

"Hell, it's not my case. I think you did it to close it out with a flair."

"No, and I didn't torch the restroom either, smart-ass."

The best defense is always a good offense.

54
CHAPTER

Howard thought about the repercussions of his move but was confident it could not be traced back to him. Sparks could try to accuse him, but anyone looking for the evidence could not determine it had come from his computer. In anticipation of an inquiry, he went into his system and erased the software he'd used and any possible tracking mechanism for someone with more knowledge than he had.

Now he could see that not making an arrest could sometimes solve a problem.

Another knock sounded on the door. It was Detective Anita Hernandez, a.k.a. Chili.

"Anita, good to see you. Come into my den." It was time to get back to some real police work.

"Howard, I need some of your time to help me with an investigation." In exasperation, she dropped a large case file folder onto his desk. "I don't know what I have, but I know something is going on with this case. I need a sounding board. This thing has me a bit flustered."

"Give me some background."

She talked about her investigation into a human-trafficking ring with prostitution and drug dealing.

Howard sat back and did a brief assessment. "Does this have anything to do with the recent uptick in the streetwalking prostitution on our border with LA?"

"It does. I understand you guys are working on it from your end, but I'm not concentrating on the streetwalking as much as on who is organizing it and what it all leads to."

"You might want to talk with the Everlys because it's their case. I don't think we've done much on it yet. We've all been on vacation."

Maybe I can pass this investigation on to the Everlys. That would be good.

"I know. I guess vice takes off during the holidays, but the hookers and traffickers know that, and it's why the activity has picked up. But that's not why I'm here." She paused for a moment. "I have found some bank records and accounts related to this organization. I think the cartels run it. I have an informant inside, one of the girls, and she's feeding me some information, but I can't make heads or tails of it."

"You do know a county-wide task force is working on this, don't you?" *Maybe they would pick this case up.*

"I just found out about it. I have a meeting tomorrow with a Detective Carvin to discuss it. She's coming here, and she says she knows you."

"We worked on a case a few years back. And she called me just before I went on vacation. I just got the information she sent and am going over it right now."

"I went to her when you guys weren't available. Can I give you some information and have you meet with us tomorrow?"

Turf wars inside and outside the department were constant: "Don't bother me with your case, or I'll take the whole thing off your hands. Don't try to dump anything on me, but maybe I can dump something on you." It never stopped.

Hernandez reached into her folder and pulled out copies. "Here are your copies. I have names, cars, and accounts but am unsure what to do with them."

Howard realized the ball was back in his court. "Give them to me, and I'll try to review them before tomorrow's meeting."

They agreed to meet with Bonnie Carvin in the big conference room tomorrow at one.

Damn. Looks like more spreadsheet work.

55
CHAPTER

Data entering was mind-numbing, so he was not paying any attention to numbers, names, and car descriptions as he entered the information Hernandez had provided.

Another knock sounded on the door.

"HH, we're going to code seven. Interested?" It was one of the Everlys. He was not sure which one.

"Let me hit Save, and I'll be right there." He wasn't going to pass up a break from data entry. And he wasn't going to ask Joanie—no sirree.

He jumped into the backseat of one of the UC vehicles, and when they arrived at the restaurant, he was glad to see Garcia and Morgan waiting for them. Wolford was on a day off.

Was the Barrio Queen the new hangout for the unit, or was it his imagination? Regardless, he felt he could use some male bonding time.

Everyone caught up on vacation activities and lamented the passing of BB Bowers. Questions arose about whom Rikelman would bring in to replace him, but everyone agreed that the conversation was for after the services. Garcia seemed to always work around any discussion of his deceased partner. That gave Howard some additional concern, but he would not be the one to confront him.

They returned to the station and went their separate ways. Howard felt refreshed and ready to go back to work. His voicemail chimed as he closed the door to get back to his spreadsheet. It was Marcia.

"Hey, Dad, I wanted to let you know I won't be home for dinner tonight. You're on your own."

He set that thought aside and returned to his spreadsheet. He was getting pretty good at designing various matrices to enter data he could manipulate. Two hours later, he was done.

He decided to go online to the *LA Times* to see if there were story updates on the school board investigation. A more recent article rehashed the old information and added that the board would not release anything further until the investigation ended. It was close to EOW.

His phone buzzed again—an unknown caller.

"This is Howard Hamilton. May I help you?"

"I certainly hope so," said the sultry female voice on the other end.

"I'm sorry, but I don't recognize your voice or number. Who is this?"

"I hope you will know the next time, but this is Lori. Lori Reynolds."

He remembered she had given him her number. He hadn't called. "I'm sorry, Lori; you caught me in a bit of a fog in front of my computer. I wasn't expecting—"

"Mel gave me your number. I hope you're not mad. When I didn't hear from you, I figured you may have lost or thrown mine away. I decided to follow up anyway."

"No, I still have it. I've only been back to work a few days and—"

"You don't have to apologize, Howard. I understand. Any chance I could get you to come to dinner tonight?"

He thought for perhaps too long for the circumstances.

"I understand if you already have plans with your kids. I just thought—"

"No, as a matter of fact, I'm free. Geoff returned to school in Arizona, and Marcia …" He thought some more in silence. "What time, and what's the dress code?"

56

Howard knew he must work on his social life. But he still wasn't sure he was ready for a Lori Reynolds type: bold, forthright, beautiful, and rich.

You might as well start at the top.

He did his afternoon workout in the gym at the station and decided to go home, shower, and change clothes.

He had to use his GPS to find her street in the hills along the coast. He had not paid much attention when Mel took him to the party at Lori's just before the holidays. The winding road led him to a cul-de-sac, where he passed her gated entrance and had to turn around.

He eventually pulled to her gate and entered the gate code she'd given him earlier. The mansion was unlike anything he had seen. Manicured Marathon grass on both sides of the entry, tall hopsacks trimmed to perfection, petunias, and vincas with a touch of arborvitae were a landscaper's dream. He hadn't appreciated it on his first visit because it had been dark, but it was certainly magnificent in the daylight.

I couldn't live like this—or could I?

He wore his newest Tommy Bahama dress shirt, casual slacks, and dark blue Sketchers. He put his off-duty weapon in his gun safe under the seat. He didn't think he would need it tonight and smiled at no one.

She said to dress casual, so here I am.

He walked to the entrance, taking in the lush landscape and stonework.

Eat your heart out, Guy Coyle.

Lori was dressed casually but still looked like she had stepped out of a magazine. A soft white dress jacket covering a powder-blue silk blouse, matching slacks, and dangling gold earring loops added to her attractiveness. However, her overall demeanor and graciousness made Lori Reynolds the complete package. For someone.

She wasted no time in hugging and thanking him for responding to her last-minute invitation. Her hair was pulled back, with either blonde streaks or brunette lines. He couldn't tell. She had an olive skin tone, as if she had been on the beach, with a fragrance to match. There was nothing that reminded him of Clare. Was that good or bad? Should he have brought her flowers?

She escorted him to an outside patio, where a chilled bottle of Patz and Hall chardonnay waited for him to pour. A tray of hors d'oeuvres tastefully on display—stuffed olives, shrimp, and bruschetta—made for easy relaxation. There was soft piano music coming from hidden speakers.

"Where is everyone else? Are you having others over?"

"Just you" was the quiet reply.

He poured them each a glass of wine. "I really like your garden. There's a touch of the English garden look I've tried to do in my backyard. But you nailed it. Can you give me a tour of what you have?"

They walked casually through the backyard's stone pathways, which led to a gazebo built midway into the hill. There were koi ponds on each side of the cobblestone path, with water casually trickling down perfectly placed rock formations.

She pointed out some of her favorite plants, knowing the Latin and the standard names nurseries gave them. The vines were almost overgrown. It seemed a manicure had taken place just before his arrival.

"Howard, if you don't mind, could I get you to bring the tray of munchies up here?"

He retraced his steps and returned with the tray and the wine. "Time for a top-off." He smiled.

The enjoyment of living in a dream with someone like Lori was not something he'd expected. He was getting into this lifestyle much too quickly.

Was this all a hallucination?

After considerable discussion regarding her garden, Howard opened her up with a question. "Lori, can I ask you something?"

She nodded for him to continue.

"What do you know about Mel's friend? The guy she's dating?"

"Everything." There was something emphatic about her answer.

He had to ask a follow-up question. "Do you mind sharing what you know?"

"I'm not sure Mel would approve. At least not right now. Maybe you could ask her. She's been like a sister to me, and sisters love to keep secrets."

"You're right, of course. I've been a bit hesitant. I think the world of her, and I don't want her to get hurt."

"She's a big girl, Howard. I have confidence she'll be OK."

One more question wouldn't hurt. "Have you met him?"

"Yes."

"Do you approve?" Howard was trying not to be so straightforward in his questions but was adamant he would find out more.

"He's handsome and has a great job, and from what I have seen, he adores her."

"Yeah, but ..." He hoped his hesitation would be filled with more information.

"I know."

They both knew what the *but* was without expressing it.

"Can we leave it there for now?" Lori was intent on changing the subject.

"Yes, I guess we should."

They talked about his trip to Big Bear, Marcia, and Geoff but nothing about his work. She was easy to talk with.

Too easy, Howard thought as he gazed at the landscape with almost a jealous tug.

From out of the blue, a question he was not expecting came: "Have you dated since you lost your wife?"

"Once or twice but not much, really." He sensed she had the same complacency he had about the dating scene.

"Same here. I just haven't found anyone to get comfortable with. At least not until now."

They both enjoyed the silence the two admissions brought.

There was a ring of a bell in the background.

"Was that the doorbell?" Howard seemed almost startled. The sound had awakened him from a trancelike state of staring at Lori, the garden, and the lush vegetation.

Her voice became softer than ever. "No, the oven tells us that dinner is just about ready." She paused too long before adding, "Are *you* ready, Howard?" She made direct eye contact with him.

He was unsure what she meant by the last comment. He knew he was experiencing a moment or series of moments he had not felt in a long time. The setting, company, and wine were doing precisely what was planned. But by whom?

"I'm ready," he said in as commanding a voice as he could muster for the moment.

57

The large dining table used at her holiday party had been replaced with a tastefully designed smaller table for four. Tonight there would be just two. Small votive candles floated in water inside an immense cauldron. Silver-and-beige linen napkins were placed on the table, right out of a page from Emily Post.

"I hope you don't mind, but I selected a red wine for dinner. It's a Wilson 2019 old-vine zinfandel. It pairs better with our main course. Will that work for you?"

"Of course, but if I may ask, what is the main course?" After saying it that way, he regretted his intonation.

She got it right away and gave it right back. "Us, of course," she said softly as she turned toward the oven. She was not going to let him see her smile.

He blushed, and he knew she saw his reaction.

"Well, I made a Caesar salad from scratch and homemade lasagna for the main course. Do you like Italian?"

"I love Italian, but it looks like a lot of work. And dessert?"

"It's never work when it's prepared for someone special. And dessert is a surprise. Will you open the wine while I care for some things in the kitchen?"

He gracefully used the bottle opener, removed the foil from atop the rim, gently removed the cork, and poured wine into each glass.

There was still piano music coming over the many speakers, but the songs were instrumental selections he recognized as coming from the '60s and perhaps the '70s.

Lori brought in the salads.

"The songs played on your sound system are familiar, but who is the artist?" he asked, hoping she would know.

"It's Richard Clayderman. Have you heard of him?"

"No, but I love it. I used to know the words to most of these songs, but I've never heard them as instrumentals."

"Something else we have in common, Howard. By the way, when do I get to call you HH like Mel?" She smiled as she placed the salads on the place mats.

"It's just my nickname at work. Not for—anyway, how you say *Howard* is so much better." He didn't know where he was going with that response.

"Please, let's sit." Lori took a chair across from him, reached out a hand, and said, "Will you say grace for us?"

Howard was surprised by her gesture and took her hand. The electricity from her touch went all the way to his shoulder.

When he ended grace with the standard "Amen," she held his hand and didn't let go. They locked eyes, and he knew it was over for him right then. The bell ringing in the kitchen broke the mood.

They toasted to a new friendship.

"Do you like the wine, Howard?" she said, emphasizing his name.

"I do."

The conversation continued as she cleared the salad plates and brought the lasagna. His portion was perfect. He sprinkled a touch of parmesan cheese over the noodles. It was still sizzling and smelled out of this world.

The conversation continued about Geoff, Marcia, and Lori's business.

"Can I help clear and do the dishes?" he asked after they had consumed another glass of the best red wine he had ever tasted.

"You do dishes too, Howard?"

"Of course. I come trained." He didn't mean for it to come out that way, but she laughed anyway.

"Come on into the kitchen then. It's an easy cleanup. We have to rinse and put them in the dishwasher."

"I can do that."

"While you do that, I'm going to freshen up and move our wine glasses into the living room."

Richard Clayderman was still playing but now in the living room. He seemed to move from room to room regardless of where they were, inside or outside.

Howard cleaned up the kitchen and walked slowly to the living room. He saw Lori sitting comfortably on a white couch with overstuffed pillows. She held her wine and his.

She patted the couch cushion, all the while keeping eye contact. "Come sit. It's a two-CD set."

58
CHAPTER

The next day, as he showered to get ready for work, he replayed the evening in his mind like a DVR on rewind.

*   *   *

They sat on the stark white couch with Clayderman in the background. Every move by Lori or Howard needed affirmation. Neither wanted to initiate anything they would be sorry for or have to apologize for abruptly. Both wanted some level of intimacy but were unsure if the other would accept or reject their actions.

Howard sat back and looked at Lori for signs that they were in the same place. Then it became an admission. Each wanted some level of intimacy and accepted whatever the other offered. They kissed softly, but the wine and ambiance took over, and they became more passionate. Heavy breathing and tongues intertwining overtook their senses—but only to a point.

Each held the other's face and, without a word, stared into eyes that communicated a loneliness that was no more. With his arm around Lori, they sat back and let the quiet envelop them. They listened to Clayderman's soft piano music, "(Everything I Do) I Do It for You," which continued to stir their desire for each other. His right hand held her left, and they heeded each other's breathing rhythm and began again.

She stroked the inside of his thigh but stopped there. He touched her breast area but only on the outside of the jacket. Then they both decided to stop, knowing there was time for more in the future.

They sat back to take into account what had happened. Perhaps both had known from the moment they met that this night was inevitable.

Howard spoke first. "Thank you for an incredible dinner, the wine, the music, and you. I think this is all something we each have to think about more, but I truly want this all to happen again. Do you?"

"I do, Howard. More than you can imagine."

"I think we should leave it here before we do something we may regret later."

"We have the time, Howard. We have the time." She reached out again for the comfort of the hug and the closeness they needed.

* * *

As Howard took the short drive to the station, he recalled the last moments of their time before he'd left her beautiful home. He knew the onus was now on him to make the next move.

But what would that be? Where was this all going to lead?

Should I invite her over to my home? Would she be disappointed in the average track home after what she has been accustomed to? Is she out of my league and merely looking for brief male companionship? Or is there more to be thinking about? Am I overthinking the obvious?

59

He walked into the station, and the buzz was unmistakable. He headed directly to the N&V office.

"HH," Barber said as he opened the door. "Lieutenant wants a quick unit meeting with everybody at nine. Grab some coffee, get caught up on whatever you're working on, and be there."

He put a pod in the Keurig and went to the watch commander's office while it was brewing. No Kip, just Lieutenant Harmon, who didn't even look up to see who was in the office. He was buried in his computer and never even turned around.

Upon returning to his office after picking up his brew, Howard checked his emails—nothing unusual. There was an online article Phil had sent him regarding the LA County Board of Education's exposé on Sparks, but it still gave no names or further information. Hernandez reminded him of his meeting with Bonnie Carvin. There was also a note from Mel, asking how he'd liked dinner last night.

What a joke. She probably knew all about it before my head hit the pillow. My pillow.

He cleared up a few other messages and saw that Donny had asked if they could meet after work at Home Plate. He responded with an immediate "C u there."

Everyone gathered as they took turns getting coffee. Rikelman appeared in rare form. Norman Bates had not appeared in a long time. Maybe that personality had run its course. Vivian might have had something to do with it. Who knew?

There was no written agenda, so they got right down to business.

"Before we get to the roundtable, a reminder: Bowers's funeral service is Friday. Everyone should be there. Al Garcia and a few others are pallbearers, but you should be in uniform unless you look like a dirtbag. The flyer is posted on the bulletin board. Do not be late."

"Lieutenant, sir." Graham raised a hand to be recognized. "Any idea who you're going to be bringing to team with Disney here?"

Garcia spoke up. "Jeez, Louie, his body's not cold yet."

"Just asking. Sorry. I may be out of line, but some guys have approached me, and—"

"Not right now, Graham." Rikelman put an end to that line of questioning. "Roundtable. Tell us what you're working on."

They went around the room, and everyone was brought up to date on one another's investigations. After saving Hamilton until last, Rikelman turned to him.

"I've been working on a few things to do with some cartels and information I've been given from an informant of Hernandez in detectives. I'm meeting with her and Bonnie Carvin from the HURT task force at one o'clock. Some of you remember Carvin from the Bresani case. She—"

"Whoa, Hamilton," Rikelman said quietly but firmly. "You might want to tell them what the hell *HURT* means."

"Oh, sorry. It's the county-wide task force on human trafficking. I think it stands for 'human undercover response team' or something like that. Sir, would it be all right to invite the Everlys? It may involve their *b* complaint," he said, referring to the streetwalking prostitution case they were working on.

"Don, Phil, are you guys available?" Rikelman asked the duo.

"Sir, if you want us there, we will be there. We're just closing out the park restroom caper and were going to work on a narco case we've been building, but that can wait." Don took some notes as he added his two cents.

Rikelman nodded. "Moving on. Now for some scoop. As you know, the POA has been lobbying the city manager to select Rod Tustin, newly appointed Captain Rod Tustin, as our next chief."

"That's great," Morgan and Wolford said at about the same time.

"Well, you also know that the Chief from Gardenia, Melendrez, has been lobbying for the job."

"That asshole." Al Garcia chimed in.

"Wait a minute, Disney. He's Hispanic. Don't you want an amigo up there?" Morgan said, pointing to the third floor. "We certainly ain't going to get a brother here. At least not yet."

"Yeah, I'd like an amigo but not an asshole amigo. They're the worst."

Howard had to jump into the conversation. "Shotgun," he said, referring to Morgan, "we may get a brother before we get an amigo. Have you met John Tenery?"

"Who the fuck is John Tenery?" Morgan said in a demanding tone.

"You've been in here too long. Check him out. He's on the night shift right now but will pass us all up."

"Can I get to the main topic before you guys chop each other's heads off?" Rikelman smiled when he said it, but everyone knew he had something else to share. "A bomb was dropped on all of us this morning. Captain Tustin called our acting chief to give him some interesting news: Tustin is not coming back from Quantico. It seems he will retire and stay there." Rikelman stopped to let that last message sink in.

Silence engulfed the room. Howard could tell it was a feeling of *WTF?*

60

CHAPTER

"Wait a minute, sir." Wolford finally spoke up. "Didn't you tell us he was married to Rose Tustin, Chief of Redondo? And don't they have a daughter?"

"Yes, he is. Or was. And yes, they do have a daughter. I think she's a teenager by now. It seems they've been split for a while, and while he was back there, he fell for some FBI person. He let his wife know, and, well, you know the rest."

More silence.

"What's he going to do back there? Quantico is all feds." Guitar Man Scotty Moore finally spoke up. "And yes, Graceland was outstanding, thank you very much, but I may have to remortgage my house. It was god-awful expensive."

"Thanks for sharing that tidbit, Scotty," Rikelman said. " Nobody knows what he'll do back there. Too soon to know or care. Does anybody want to join him?"

"Too fuckin' cold, man." Morgan added to the frivolity.

"Any other questions? Because that's all I know right now." Rikelman closed his notebook.

Garcia raised his hand once again. "Does that mean we could be stuck with the asshole from Gardenia, Lieutenant?"

"Could be, Disney. Could be."

"Not if I can help it," Garcia said sternly.

"What do you mean by that?" Graham finally spoke up. "We can get us an amigo and work on training this asshole to our liking."

"I don't think so, Louis. Not this one. Let's leave it for now, shall we?"

Rikelman stood up, signaling the end of the meeting. "Code seven,

149

and make sure you two," he said, referring to the Everlys, "get to that one o'clock meeting. Oh, HH, I need to see you for a moment."

Rikelman walked directly to his office, ushered Hamilton in, and closed the door.

"Two things. Barber and I have an appointment with the GM of Orchard Hill Mercedes this afternoon. It should happen while you are in your one o'clock meeting. Whatever you do, if Getty calls, do not answer your phone. I want her to stew a little bit. We're going around her, and she may be pissed. Too fuckin' bad. Got it?"

"Yes, sir. There is no problem at this end. And yeah, she is pissed. What's the second item?"

"Detectives and IA have a case they're working on and need you to do some research for them. I told Hospian he had to go through me and not directly to you."

"That's fine with me, Lieutenant. I'm not too fond of the guy."

Mainly because he's a lieutenant and an asshole who would love to catch me doing something wrong, and he was responsible for getting the Chief fired.

"Someone from inside here"—he flailed his arms to refer to the entire building—"is making lewd calls on a line that comes back to the department. They can't locate the line anywhere in the building. The phone company couldn't find it, and they scoured every office. Is that something you think you could do?"

"I don't know, sir. But why me? Can't someone else do this kind of work?"

"Maybe, but let me make this very clear. You're a confidential employee with incredible computer skills not many have here. The powers upstairs believe you can do anything; they trust you, as I do. Maybe you're more important than you realize."

The Norman Bates stare was unmistakable.

"Give me the number, and I'll see. How soon do they need it?"

"Yesterday, of course."

61
CHAPTER

The phone number returned to the telephone and computer-aided dispatch (CAD) room at the far end of the dispatch center. He pinpointed the location using a combination of privacystar.com/reverse-lookup, whocalld. com, and the phone company archives. It took him all of five minutes. Somebody hadn't looked hard enough.

He casually walked up one flight of stairs to the dispatch center and passed the 911 operators to the far end of the state-of-the-art CAD center. He looked around the room but could not see a landline phone other than the one on the supervisor's desk. There was a hum of dispatchers talking to 911 callers, while others were dispatching radio calls to patrol.

"Detective Hamilton, it has been a long time. You never come up here to visit anymore. What can I do for you?"

Donna Remington had been the dispatch supervisor for as long as Hamilton remembered. When she had come to the department, she had been on the p.m. shift, but when the previous supervisor had retired, she had taken over the day shift and never relinquished it. Eating all day at her desk—or, more accurately, grazing—had given her an extra thirty pounds. Her nasty smoking habit had given her a deep voice. He guessed she was approaching retirement herself, but he would not ask at this juncture.

"Hey, Donna, good to see you again. Is your phone here"—he pointed to the one on her desk—"the only landline instrument up here other than what the dispatchers have on their consoles?"

"As far as I know."

"Well, I'm on a hunting expedition as part of a project my lieutenant gave me. We're trying to clean up some old systems in the building. Where would I find the room that houses the phone systems? It's not in the basement, because I've checked," he lied.

"No, it's back here." She motioned to a solid metal door with no windows over her right shoulder. "Need to take a peek?"

"Can I?"

"If it's official business, I don't see why not. Here's the key."

Donna reached out to a small bulletin board leaning against the fabric wall of her cubicle. A large pin was stuck on it. Attached to the hook was a swirling piece of plastic wire with a 998 specialty key dangling in midair. She handed it to him.

"Is this key always here?"

"Always" was her terse reply.

"I promise I'll bring it back," he responded with a smile.

"That's OK. I have you on camera. That door is always monitored. All I have to do is bring it up on my screen here. Watch."

She opened her screen to show a full-color shot of the door. "It's on a motion detector, so I can see you enter and exit when you go in. Go do what you have to do in there and come out, and I'll show you when you're done."

"I have to ask: Has anyone other than me asked you to see the camera footage?"

"No, but I'm not sure anyone knows it even exists." She seemed proud of her little secret to conceal the camera.

Hamilton took the key and strolled to the door, looking for a camera. He couldn't find one. He opened the door and was hit with a warmth generated by the mainframe telephone computer system. He walked to the rear of the twelve-by-twelve room and found what he was looking for. Secreted in a corner was old telephony equipment. The city had not updated everything in the department.

He saw an eight-foot table with papers strewn about, an old-fashioned Rolodex with outdated numbers, and an in-and-out tray filled with old telephone records. An old box of Kleenex sat on the table, and used tissues were strewn about the desk and on the floor. On the table was a vintage landline phone instrument with push buttons for dialing purposes. There were four lines, but none were labeled at the base of the buttons.

They lit up, but there was no connection to an outside line on the first three. He tested each one. The fourth line was the jackpot. A dial tone told him it was a live line. He punched in his cell phone number to verify it, and it immediately rang. He looked at his screen, and there was the number he had been searching for.

He returned to Donna's desk with the needed information and handed her the key.

"Get what you came for?" she said with a smile.

"I think so, but where's the camera that monitors the door?"

"We can't tell you, Detective Hamilton." She laughed, trying to keep it lighthearted, and pointed to the top of a file cabinet. "Want to see you in action?"

She pulled up her screen, and he saw himself open the door and walk into the room.

"Is there a camera inside?" he asked as innocently as he could.

"No, at least I don't think so. But nobody ever goes in there except when the phone system goes haywire and needs repair."

"And do you know if the watch commander can monitor this camera, or is it just your desktop?"

"Just my desktop. To my knowledge, it's not tied to any other security cameras in the building."

Well, it should be.

"How long does the camera stay in the system when activated?" He tried to make it a simple follow-up question that belied his real intent.

"I think just for twenty-four hours" was the reply.

"Donna, thanks so much. You've been very accommodating." He gave her his best smile, at least under the circumstances.

"We aim to please, Howard."

"Well, I'm glad we can now be on a first-name basis. I won't be a stranger."

CHAPTER

He returned to his office and tried to think through his findings. *There comes a time when one does not need to know everything about investigations. This may be one of those times.*

"Lieutenant, do you have time for an update on that little assignment you gave me about an hour ago?"

"What part did you not understand?"

"I understood it all, and I finished. Want to know what I found?"

"Sure."

Hamilton filled him in about the phone room in dispatch, where the undiscovered landline was, and the type of security.

"Here's the weakness, sir. The key to this room is mounted on the dispatch supervisor's desk and pinned to a bulletin board—anyone who knew what that key fit could easily access the room. And there's a motion-detector camera with a twenty-four-hour loop. But you must know it's there, because it's not visible to anyone in the room. Only Donna knows where it is, and she can monitor it from her computer. At least when she's working."

"Thanks, Howard. That will be all."

"That's good because I'm not sure I want to know anything more. Particularly when IA's involved, but can I make a recommendation, sir?"

"Sure."

"Tell them to bring CSI and their black light." He tried to make his comment appear lighthearted. "And another thing. You might see if you can have that camera monitored by the watch commander. Right now, no one but Donna sees it."

Rikelman had a puzzled look on his face. "I think I got it." He was not going to pursue that line of questioning any longer. Then, almost as an afterthought, he added, "Oh, and, Howard, I asked Sam to join you in the meeting at one o'clock. Are you OK with that? I rescheduled with the Mercedes dealer."

"No problem, sir. You're the boss."

* * *

It was time for his one o'clock meeting. His stomach was growling, telling him he'd missed lunch again. It was not like a good cop to do that.

He muttered that he should do better time management with his code-seven routine as he walked to the detective's conference room. He entered to see a spread of sandwiches on a table, with the familiar Jersey Mike wrappings, chips, and bottled water—what a surprise.

"Anita, is this for me?"

"Not quite, HH; we'll have a roomful, but help yourself."

He sat in the corner with Barber after obtaining a tuna sandwich, potato chips, and water. "Detectives know how to live," he told Hernandez.

"We try to put our best foot forward when we deal with other agencies. Our last chief was big on that."

"He was good for a lot of things. I think we're going to miss him. More than we know."

She nodded her agreement.

"Why? Do you know something about the next one?" Hamilton had aroused her interest.

"What do you hear?" Anita was now doing the prodding. "Hey, we're in detectives. We don't hear much at all."

"Well, some people in detectives seem to know a lot." He brought her up to date on Rod Tustin and George Melendrez.

"I don't know about Melendrez. I'll have to do some checking. As far as Tustin, that's too bad. I'm kind of friends with his soon-to-be ex, Rose."

"Well, the POA has investigated George, and it's not that good."

Before they could continue the conversation, Bonnie Carvin and two people he did not know walked into the room. Then came Detective Sergeant Carmen "the Car" Anderson and someone he vaguely remembered. *Laidlaw?*

Introductions were made. Carvin introduced her team. Sergio Columbo was from Montebello PD, and Bobby Tucson was from Bell

Gardens. Laidlaw introduced himself to all as Pete Laidlaw, newly assigned to detectives and shadowing Sergeant Anderson as the officer in charge of the OIC of the crimes against persons, or CAP, table. Hamilton and Laidlaw acknowledged each other silently.

Hamilton recalled that Laidlaw had been Morrison's partner a few years back and had transported a homicide suspect back to the station from Kensington Road in the Ginny Karsdon case. Laidlaw or Morrison had missed a wooden flute in the suspect's boot while searching him for transport. Laidlaw's nod told him he remembered.

"Sorry about Morrison," Howard whispered as Sergeant Anderson started the meeting.

Laidlaw nodded again, trying not to disrupt the start of what would prove to be an interesting meeting.

63

CHAPTER

Hamilton had his marching orders. Anita would coordinate with Bonnie and team up with Laidlaw. When Howard had the requested information, he would meet with the OHPD detectives to review it. He told them he would have something by tomorrow, Thursday. Barber took copious notes but said little. Sergeant Anderson wrapped up the meeting at about three thirty.

Hamilton returned to his office, got Barber's approval to work overtime, and closed the door. Then he remembered Donny talking about a meet-up at Home Plate. He texted that he would not be there until six and went to work on a spreadsheet he was preparing for Anderson and the task force. Carvin and Anita had given him bank account numbers, cars, and names to collate as much information as possible.

He could use all three screens to work on the data for the first time. But he saw it all quickly. He brought up Carvin's information; while not precisely duplicated, several accounts correlated with Getty and Anita's information. Cross-referencing the bank accounts from Anita's investigation, he saw that a few names coincided with what Nicole Getty had given him, and he started to create a picture. Some of the names were the same—and the cars.

He sat back and decided to make another spreadsheet, this time labeling where the information had come from, including all the cars, accounts, and people. Everybody had different styles of Mercedes. Carvin's information was tied into Getty's and Hernandez's. There were bank accounts, cars, and names he could cross-reference and tie into one another. He continued to code by source and then by account and vehicles. A picture emerged of one big organization.

This fuckin' thing is big. Enormous!

He looked at the clock, and it was five minutes to six. He texted Donny to say he was running late and closed out his computer.

As he walked out of his office and passed Barber, who was still working, he said, "Hey, Sarge, how did the meeting go at the Mercedes dealership?"

"Good, HH. I'll fill you in tomorrow. Don't forget Bowers's funeral on Friday."

"I won't, and I need to talk with you about the information I found after the meeting with the HURT task force and our detectives."

"A lot of shit going on, HH. We all have to stay focused."

"No shit, Sarge. See you tomorrow." He couldn't believe he still had the energy to get with his good buddy after everything that had happened that day.

He jumped into his car, headed for Home Plate, and hit Lori's newly added speed-dial number. He got her voicemail. *Good.*

"Lori, Howard here. I really enjoyed Monday night. Thanks. I meant to call yesterday and earlier today. I just got tied up at work. How about dinner tomorrow night at Bourbon and Bones? They have great steaks." He left it at that.

He pulled into a full parking lot at Home Plate and finally found a space in the fourth row, near the exit. A light fog was moving into the seaport at that time of night. It added to the mysteries that surrounded him.

I need a drink!

64

CHAPTER

Donny sat at the usual booth, wearing a floral Untuckit shirt, with Alcazar, Walker, and Tenery.

"Can you squeeze one more in there?" Howard said with a smile.

The four had drinks in front of them and were munching on the chips provided.

"Sure," they said as they scooted to tighten up the seating arrangement.

"What took you so long, HH?" Several asked the same question simultaneously.

"Just work. And I can't tell you about it, so don't ask."

"We know by now, or you'd have to kill us," Donny joked.

Howard ordered an 805 IPA and sat down, taking a heavy breath. "What a day, week, month. Jeez, our shop is going wild right now." Howard decided to get the conversation started.

"We know," Tenery responded. "Some days, I feel we're still in a war zone. What the fuck is going on?"

Alcazar spoke up. "It could be our new normal. It's been going on for the two years I've been here. While I was at the Academy, it was A. J. Johnson and Gabby Hayes, and now Morrison and that guy in your unit, HH."

"Yeah," Donny said, "but even the streets are getting weirder. Big-time car thefts and carjackings like crazy. I have cases I would not have had just a year ago."

They talked about the streets for a while.

Donny tried to change the subject. "Hey, HH, somebody is trying to get your attention."

Howard had not picked up on the soft guitar playing in the corner. He looked over his shoulder to see Samantha, or Sam, staring bullets through him.

"Where's Laurenti tonight? I don't see him behind the bar."

"Must have gone out for a while. He was here when I got here," Donny said.

Someone else was tending the bar, but Sam continued to sing in her soft '60s and '70s tone: nothing harsh, just background to all the cop shop discussions.

Howard turned to let her know he saw and heard her. "Be right back," he said to the booth.

He walked over as she finished her version of "I Really Don't Know Love at All."

"Where's Gary?" He fumbled to start a conversation as he dropped a twenty into the tip jar now visible to the crowd.

"Running some errands, but he'll be back. Are you looking for him?"

"No, I was looking for you." He tried to maintain eye contact.

"You lie." She laughed shyly.

"Hey, the only reason I came here tonight was to hear you play and to see you." He thought that might set her back on her heels, but she countered.

"I've been here the last five nights," she said, emphasizing *five*, "waiting for you to come back." She looked him directly in the eye with a strong sense of certainty.

"There's plenty of guys here. I mean ..." He wasn't ready for the comeback.

"I hear there's only one Howard Hamilton. And anyway, most of these guys are married and waiting for traffic to die down. And I'm not interested in longshoremen types."

"What? How did you know my last name?"

"I do my due diligence. You're a pretty good detective, but you obviously didn't do your homework on me. You have two kids, lost your wife a few years ago, and have not been seen with anyone since." She said it all with pride that she had one-upped him.

Just then, Laurenti came back through the office door. "Hey, Sam, good crowd tonight." He stuck out a hand. "I'm Gary Laurenti, and you're HH, right? We here at Home Plate try to get to know all the good guys. Hey, people still talk about you even when you're not here." Laurenti was making it a point that he had also been investigating and that his investigation included Howard Hamilton.

"Hmm. I guess I had better do my homework. Well"—Howard paused for just enough time to make his point—"I did do a little. Len Patterson said to say hi."

That statement put Laurenti on his heels. He stared at Hamilton for what seemed to be a frozen moment, grabbed an apron, and returned to the bar.

"I'm not so sure you should have said that," Sam whispered. "I don't know what that was about, but Gary didn't like it. I thought you were a nice guy, but you royally pissed him off. And I don't like people who upset my brother. I've got to get back to my music." There was a sternness in her voice that set him on his heels.

"Your brother?"

6.5
CHAPTER

Howard returned to the booth.

"What was that all about?" Donny spoke up for everyone. They all had watched the interchange but had not heard the conversation.

"Just a misunderstanding. Boy, I haven't pissed off somebody like that for a long time. And Sam was pissed too." Howard took another draw of beer and looked away from everyone. "I'll tell you more after I calm down. Can we change the subject for a while?"

"How about them Dodgers?" Tenery said, laughing.

"Hey, it's not even spring training yet, idiot." Alcazar realized what he had said and whom he had directed it to. "Sorry, sir."

Everybody had another good laugh.

After two beers and some nachos, Howard thought about what to do. He approached the bar. "Gary, can we talk? In your office?"

Laurenti took off his apron and walked without a word to the office, which was behind where Sam was playing.

She didn't look up as Howard was ushered into a room stacked with boxes of hard liquor, wine, and soft drinks. Laurenti sat in his desk chair and offered Hamilton a box of red wine to sit on.

"Listen, Gary. I don't want to get off on the wrong foot. Sam told me she had done homework on me, and I was a bit embarrassed." He went on to tell about how he had come to know Patterson and said that the subject of him and what had happened at Rampart had come up. "I felt like I had to counter with something, but I was wrong to do it that way. Sorry. I didn't mean for it to come out like that."

"Have you told anyone else? Like your buddies?" Laurenti looked him in the eye again, trying to see a sense of sincerity.

"Not a soul. I don't do that. My job is to keep secrets from these guys. I don't work IA, but I'm privy to a lot of proprietary information. I considered my conversation with Patterson to be just that. You can be assured it won't come from me. Others may snoop, but not me." He made sure to look him right back to ensure his point was made.

"Sam really took a liking to you last time you were here. She doesn't do that with everybody. She's been hurt too many times. I did some homework on you and told her you're a squared-away guy. What happened kept her back, but I'll talk to her." He reached out for the universal gentlemanly handshake that communicated a mutual understanding. "Full disclosure: she owns half of Home Plate. I couldn't have done it without her help. Get my drift?"

"I think I do, Gary, and I promise you I will treat her like she is your sister."

They both walked out with smiles, but Samantha was nowhere to be found.

Howard returned to the booth and found that Alcazar had left.

Donny jumped right in. "HH, what the fuck is—"

Howard waved him off.

"That singer packed up her guitar and left. Is there something we should know here?"

"Nope." Howard took the last swig of his beer, grabbed a nacho, and walked out.

66

Howard walked into the N&V office, ready to start his day. Standing before his door was the Wolf with her hands on her hips.

"Can we talk?"

"Sure, Pat, what's up?"

"When can I start shadowing you? Barber said the lieutenant approved it, and then it faded away."

"I've been tied up, but let's sit down. Can I get you a coffee?" He walked over to the Keurig.

"Sure."

He held both cups, so she closed the door, ensuring their privacy. The minute the door closed, she had her hands on her hips and looked at him with the evilest eye he had ever seen.

"What the fuck happened last night? Donny came home all upset. Muttered something about you, the bar owner, and a guitar player. What the fuck is going on?" Her voice rose as she chose her words.

"Good morning to you too, Pat. I had some personal things going on that I caused, and I needed to clear things up with the bar's owner and his sister. Nothing more."

"Are you sure?" She worked her way into a sitting position, facing him.

"Of course I'm sure. Why are you so upset?" He had not seen her so emotional.

"Donny has never seen you like that. You walked out and didn't say shit."

"What was there to say?" He threw up his hands in frustration. "I screwed up, took my lumps, and went home. I guess I was a little humiliated."

"Howard, we love you and want to know what the fuck is going on in your life that's causing you to withdraw from us."

"Hey, Pat, I'm OK. And I'm not withdrawing; I'm just adjusting to a new personal life. That's all." He turned to open his computer. "Let's talk about work."

She shuffled around but let it go for the time being. With tacit approval, she changed the subject. "Barber has me signed up for a cybersecurity school, but first, I must attend the intel school. Have you gone?"

"The intel school is great. I asked if I could attend the cyber school, but he said he would rather send you. I think you'll like it. Dennis Packer and some other guys I don't know are teaching it. But I think the idea is good. I can teach you much of what I learned in intel school, but cyber is another world."

"Can I ask—are you seeing anyone?" She would not give up on pushing his buttons regarding his private life.

"You sure know how to change the subject again, don't you? Yes, I'm kind of seeing someone."

Wolford was quick to counter. "Can we invite you guys over for dinner soon? If you're ready, we'd like to meet whoever it is."

"Give me some time, Pat. This thing just started, and I'm unsure I'm ready to share it with the world." His right leg was bouncing with a nervous beat that had no rhythm.

"We want nothing but the best for you, Howard; you know that. You, Donny, and I have something special. We would love to socialize as a foursome. As friends." She was trying to be cautious and not overdo her inquiry.

"I know. I just need some time. Let me get through this case I'm working on, and we'll sit down for some high-power training."

"You got it." She walked out, knowing she would not get any more information, at least not right now.

It was time to get down with some serious work. He hadn't checked his voicemail since noon yesterday. His phone rang. He glanced at the screen and said, "Oh shit."

67
CHAPTER

"Are we still on for tonight, Howard? I haven't heard from you." Lori tried not to show her impatience.

"I'm sorry, Lori. Work just seems to get in the way." He tried his most apologetic approach.

"As long as it's work, I'm fine with that. What time are you picking me up?" It was a sincere request, she thought.

"I have reservations for seven, if that's OK."

"That's great. Come a little early for cocktails, Howard. Maybe very early?"

The way she said his name created movement in his pants.

"I will, Lori. Looking forward to it." He tried to be heartfelt in his response after being caught off guard by her phone call.

He texted Marcia to tell her he would not be home for dinner and returned to work.

He saw more patterns in Nicole's, Anita's, and Bonnie Carvin's information. There was a knock on the door—Barber.

"Hamilton, be ready for a meeting with the lieutenant and me at ten. And bring all your shit from the Mercedes dealer and anything else you have."

"Yes, sir."

Hamilton spent the next hour and a half going through the data. Some things did not line up the way his past spreadsheets did. There were accounts with only six or twelve digits, and several of those showed up on all three separate pieces of information provided by Getty, Hernandez, and Carvin.

Four checking accounts showed up on separate ledgers; two had been used to purchase various Mercedes cars and Sprinters more than a year ago. He needed updated sales to ensure he was on the right track. Perhaps the lieutenant and Barber had gotten that information by meeting with the general manager.

*   *   *

"OK." Rikelman plopped the papers onto the conference table. "Here's what we got from the Mercedes dealer. By the way, HH, your informant had not told the GM about the details of her sales when she was involved with Bresani, but she did come clean with the latest transactions. There were a lot more of them this time around. She's a good source, and you handled her well."

"Thank you, sir."

"Mr. Jeff Dryer is a character right out of central casting for a car dealer. He's successful for a reason, and if we ever need any UC vehicles, he indicated he would provide them at no cost. We need insurance waivers to cover anything that may go wrong."

"If you don't mind me asking, what information did you get?" He didn't know too much, and it was bothering him. Howard wanted to get down to business.

Barber pulled the papers together. "Here's your copy. It's not as daunting as it looks, but what he did provide will be critical to our investigation. He gave us video footage of the suspects signing the paperwork. That will be invaluable, even though these are legit purchases but with dope money. It's all on this." He handed Hamilton a thumb drive. "We got more checking, bank records, and all the information on the sold cars. You'll see it all there," he said, pointing to the papers he moved in front of Hamilton. "He'll send us the plate information once they register the cars with the DMV."

"Lieutenant, I have some information that does not make sense right now. I need some time to analyze it. Can I get Wolford to assist me? I can coach her and see if she can pick this stuff up, but I'll need some help."

"You got it, HH. We'll make that happen. I can team Morgan up with Garcia for a while."

"One more thing." Hamilton sat back in his chair to prepare for a statement he had to put on the table. "This thing could get big. And quick. It reminds me of the Bresani case, when we had to call in LADUECE.

Let's start thinking about doing something like that. Maybe turn it over to HURT?"

Rikelman stared at Hamilton with a severe look of concern and appreciation. "Let me give this some thought with the higher-ups. Today's our last workday this week, but we have Bowers's funeral tomorrow. You go through the data we showed you, and let me know what you find. We'll probably need a few days to review all of this. We're looking at some serious asset forfeiture here."

"Got it, sir. See you tomorrow, but if I could get Wolford for the rest of the day and next week, that would help."

"You got it."

68

CHAPTER

The Bowers funeral was exceptionally somber—and strange. Hamilton saw that the Presbyterian church was not that different from Saint Elizabeth's. It was not as elaborate, with marble and gold fixtures, but the church was tastefully appointed. It looked like a wedding setting, with the bride's family on one side and the groom's on the other. There were two families, one on each side of the aisle. One wife, Betty, and her child sat on one side, and on the other side were Barbara and her two children, along with Bowers's assumed brother and sister.

As Hamilton and Flowers entered the church, they were handed programs with Bowers's picture in uniform and a rundown on the service and burial site. Interestingly, there was a list of the family under his name:

Barbara Bowers
Bonnie Bowers
Robert "Bobby" Bowers Jr.
Betty Bowers
Bycho Bowers

Did anyone else notice that everyone has the same initials: BB?

Smartly, the rest of the command staff divided up, with Pierson behind Barbara with one captain and the other two captains on Betty's side. The lieutenants were evenly divided, as were the sergeants and officers. Interestingly, Hamilton noted that Kip Bennett, only a sergeant but one who was always in command, was sitting next to Pierson, whispering in his ear periodically. There was little doubt Kip was coaching his every move. Behind the uniforms and detectives were family and friends from who knew where. City staff, including the city manager, were nowhere to be seen.

The service went smoothly, honoring God and his disciples but not saying much about Bowers. Father Mike shared the altar with a minister no one knew. No doubt Father Mike was in charge, but he surrendered to the minister as much as possible. The minister looked as confused as his congregation for the day. There was a table set where a casket typically would have been placed, with two gold-plated urns and a photograph of Bowers in uniform with an American flag proudly displayed. Everyone assumed the urns held Bowers's ashes.

Hamilton wondered how the procession and burial service would be carried out. Bowers was given the full benefits a fallen officer would have received, just as Charlie "Gabby" Hayes had been when he succumbed to a heart attack while waiting to testify in court. Heart-related issues were deemed job-related in the world of public safety.

There were two separate limousines outside the church, one for each family. Barbara had a large support group who processed out of the church first, followed by Betty and her child. Without a casket, the chief decided to have two officers—Al Garcia, his partner, and Tony Morgan—carry two urns out of the church, holding them with white gloves. Neither officer could be in uniform, as they looked like dirtbag undercover cops, but they were pleasantly attired in their best suits and ties.

Everyone gathered outside the church as Garcia and Morgan handed the ashes to two other officers for a moment to escort each widow to her respective limousine. Garcia took Betty's arm, and Barbara took Morgan's. They made their way to the limos, which were mysteriously not in front of the church but off to the side parking lot.

Al Garcia looked like shit. His hair was disheveled. He was unkempt for an event such as this. He had bags under his eyes, either from not sleeping or from crying—or both. And Hamilton knew why. Garcia held on to too much information about Bowers and his personal life. Howard had found out about the two families and confronted Garcia a few days before he asked Rikelman to talk with him. Garcia had admitted to him the entire story about Bowers keeping two families. But it was not Hamilton's story to tell. It was Garcia's, and they both knew it. Howard was hopeful that Garcia had the intestinal fortitude to clear the air as much as possible, at least with his boss.

OHPD motorcycle officers were stationed behind the limousines. An official from the church advised everyone to follow the procession to Redemption Cemetery, which was a few miles away. The black-and-whites were behind the motorcade, detective cars lined up, and the rest of the attendees were advised to follow.

Everyone arrived after the limos had parked next to a burial ground plot prepared to accept Bowers's remains. The families lined up in the chairs specifically for them, while others stood around the grounds—interestingly, on the graves of others who had long passed.

After everyone was seated, Father Mike and the minister said a few words and talked briefly with the widows, whispering words no one would hear.

After the brief prayers, Lieutenant La Bonge assembled all uniformed officers to one side and called everyone to attention. There was no doubt about what would happen next, at least for the police personnel there. But the friends and family were startled. In the distance, a seven-member US Army detail with rifles at port arms stood ready to accept the inevitable command.

The twenty-one-gun salute startled everyone. Birds flew from trees, and women flinched at each volley, while others looked around to find out where the sounds had come from.

After the final volley of shots, a lone bugler started the inevitable Taps from the other side of the burial site.

Hamilton thought this was how a burial for a fallen officer should've been. And they all had been during his time on the job. The tributes, from A. J. Johnson to Charlie Hayes and Bud Morrison, were as they should have been.

The contingent worked with Chief Pierson to prepare for the presentation of the folded flags to the widows. Typically, there would've been one flag and one widow, but that day was different.

Chief Pierson took the meticulously folded American flag, wearing white gloves. The chief, smartly dressed in his uniform with four stars on the collar, walked deliberately to the army representative and saluted methodically as befitting a military and police funeral. The question was, which widow would receive a flag first?

Barbara was the lucky recipient. Pierson had some quiet words with her and the two teenagers, and everyone let the silence fill the air as birds returned to the trees, chirping, glad the gunfire had subsided.

Chief Pierson took the second flag from Lieutenant Rydell in the same fashion and walked to Betty and her child, who were sitting alone in the front row on the opposite side of Barbara and her family. Again, he had a short but quiet conversation with a hand salute of the flag after he stood from his kneeling position.

Immediately after the two flag ceremonies were completed, the crowd seemed to shuffle and become restless, ready to leave and get on with the day. But there was one more event that all would remember. Al Garcia approached Barbara and presented her with the urn he had carried from the church. No one could hear the conversation, but she rose from her chair and walked with him to the plot of land set for the burial.

Almost simultaneously, Morgan walked over to Betty, whispered, and escorted her near the same spot Barbara occupied. Each widow put half of Bowers's ashes on the small stand created just for such an event. Hamilton watched the events unfold, with Mel Flowers, Donny, and Wolford standing near him. The next event startled many of the onlookers. The widows turned to each other, hugged briefly, conversed, and returned to their seats.

Lieutenant La Bonge called the uniformed detail back to attention. Father Mike announced that the services were complete. There was no mention of a reception or gathering to be held in celebration of Bowers's life. That was probably a good thing.

La Bonge dismissed the uniformed detail, and the event of the year was finally over. Everyone quietly walked to his or her car, not daring to say a word.

Hamilton knew he did not have the entire picture of the Bowers saga, nor did he want to. OHPD had its intrigues, but most would never see the light of day or a headline, thank goodness. Sometimes being a confidential employee sucked.

69

CHAPTER

Howard had difficulty focusing on what was said. He was there in body only. He could not get his mind off last night. *Wow!*

* * *

He arrived at Lori's at five thirty after making a reservation at Bourbon and Bones for seven. They enjoyed a glass of wine and light snacks before leaving for dinner. Hamilton filled Lori in on the events of the past few days.

After arriving at the appointed hour, they were escorted to a table in the corner, somewhat secluded from the main dining room. Howard followed her and the maître d' and could tell she attracted a lot of attention as she passed several tables of onlookers. She was a dazzling lady.

Howard started to order a red wine for the table, but she asked if they could start with a dry martini. The wine would come later. He agreed, and they discussed his children, her unfortunate lack of offspring, and generalized comments about her week. She told him she had recently started growing her company specializing in ladies' cosmetics and was doing well. He was impressed.

He kept looking at her. She was stunning. There was no doubt her dress had not come from Marshalls. Her makeup was light and tasteful. Earrings dripped from her lobes like raindrops. She did not have hair out of place except where she wanted it to be. Her sparkling eyes glistened from her jewelry.

He saw it when he picked her up but held off any compliment until they were in a more intimate setting. He wasn't used to thinking about compliments, even though he'd frequently told Clare she looked good in a particular outfit or dress.

Lori was different. She glowed. Whether from a tanning booth, makeup, or whatever, she took good care of herself. It was all working, and it all looked natural. She had an aura, and when he was talking to her, he knew she was talking directly to him. She was captivating.

They talked of their career plans for the future, as vague as he was, and hers for the company. There was a question burning inside him that he finally decided to ask but only after he had consumed the martini and selected a glass of wine to go with the dinner.

"Lori, why me? Why do you seem interested in a simple guy like me, when you were married to the corporate world? Plenty of guys in corporate would love to have your companionship." He finally spit it out. What would be her response?

"Pretty simple, really, Howard." She reached for her wineglass and offered a toast. "Here's to simplicity." She set her glass down and reached for his hand. "I have had a complicated corporate life. It's not as glamorous as it looks. It's hectic, stressful, and full of phoniness."

"Are you saying I'm simple and therefore—"

"No, no, my dear. You are real—the real deal. I feel like I've known you for a very long time. Mel talks about you with such reverence. She brags to her dad about you, and that's why the date situation for my party worked out so well. She told me she looks up to you like a brother, not someone she would be interested in. That was when I knew I would like you right away. We both joked that you have three qualities many guys out there do not." She wasn't going to let go of his hand.

"I know; she told me. I bathe, don't do drugs, and have a legitimate job with benefits."

"I have to ask: Are you seeing anyone else?" She said it as their salads arrived.

Ground pepper was casually tossed atop the butterleaf lettuce, and the waiter disappeared, attentive to the intimate conversation.

"Not really," he stuttered. "Are you?" He'd thought of Samantha for a moment. But he only talked to her; he wasn't seeing her.

"Not really."

They laughed at each other's response.

Lori said, "Since we met in person, you're even more than I expected. It's our third time together, and I can't get you out of my mind. You have swept me off my feet, Howard Hamilton, and I mean it." The martini and wine were also getting to her.

"Oh boy" was all Howard could say. "You come right out and say it, don't you?" Now she had him laughing.

"We're not kids, Howard. When do I get to call you HH?" She laughed to break the tension.

By then, the main course was needed to calm the emotions and clear the head.

"I have to say I have been kind of feeling the same." *Damn.* He regretted it right after he said it.

"Kind of?" She looked him directly in the eye. "What do you mean *kind of*?" She wasn't going to let him off the hook that easily.

"I guess I'm just not as good at expressing my feelings as you are. For the last few years, I haven't had to. Can I take that back and rephrase it?"

She nodded.

"Let me put it this way." He paused to take a bite and sip some courage. "I've had trouble trying not to think about you. It's complicated. I'm deep in a big case right now, and we've had some other things going on, but it all pales compared to thinking about you. I try to compartmentalize, but all I think about is the next time I'll see you. And here we are." He waved one arm to emphasize the ambiance that prevailed all around them.

Each of them knew what was coming next. They hurried through dinner and finished the wine. It was all perfect, but the evening wasn't over.

There was casual banter as they drove to her home high in the Sparrow Hill section of Orchard Hill, which he had never dreamed he would see, let alone be privy to entering.

Rather than parking in the cutout for passenger drop-off near the front walkway entrance, she asked him to pull all the way up in the driveway, closer to the garage. She escorted him through the rear door that led directly to the kitchen. Discussing the events that would follow was unnecessary because both knew they were headed for completion—but it was the start of a relationship that would grow.

She reached into the cupboard, pulled out two drinking glasses, went to the ice maker, and filled the glasses. She set a half-and-half carton on the counter and reached into the liquor cabinet for a bottle of Baileys.

"You mix the drinks, and I'm going to get comfortable. Bring them up when you're ready," she said. There was a slight emphasis on the *you're*.

He found a serving tray and slowly walked up the stairs, carrying the two drinks. Which bedroom was hers? He heard sounds from behind the most oversized door, pushed it open with his foot, and was met with Lori in all her splendor, barefoot, in a short slip and not much more.

Every part of her was breathtaking. Her breasts sat up as if at attention as she walked toward him, took the tray, and led him to her bed. He tried to undress quickly but still did not show his nervousness. But it had been way too long.

Soon they were between the sheets, examining each other and staring into each other's eyes. The kissing led to the petting and touching of each sensual part. She removed his underwear and took off her slip over her head while on her knees, looking at him with a longing he had never seen. They lay side by side and held each other for a long moment. They would cast away their pasts and focus on what would come next.

Each seemed to know when it was time for the next move. They kissed again, and then she went down to his throat and licked his neck as her hands moved slowly around his chest, feeling each hair and touching his nipples. The sensation had him concentrating and trying not to get too excited, not just yet. She knew where she was headed next; she slowly moved her tongue down his belly to his groin and, finally, used her hand to place his erection in her mouth.

She spent some time moisturizing his cock with her saliva, moving it in and almost out teasingly. She finally moved back up to him and purposely kissed him to bond their body fluids. Then he was prompted to do the same. He had difficulty leaving her neck and breast area but eventually knew where he needed to be. But it was the journey he enjoyed the most.

Her breasts were full, supple, and sensitive to the touch. He found every crevice with his tongue and thought he might have even brought her to climax a few times with his efforts. He gently pushed her onto her back, found the top of her pubic hair, and continued to move to her sweet spot. His tongue found it and lingered there so long that he had to be prompted to come up for air. He moved up to her, and she reached for his cheek, kissing and licking her fluids from his face.

He entered slowly. He could tell she wanted him on top, at least for now. But he was surprised when she said quietly, "I don't want this to last too long. You are right there, and I need to come, and you need to come. Please. Please. Now."

At that moment, they both found what they had been yearning for.

70

While looking forward to next week and the case he and Wolford were putting together, Howard also looked for his time with Marcia and Bentley. Working in the English garden, doing manual labor, and thinking about Lori were all uppermost in his mind. He now realized he had strong feelings for her, but things looked full of twists and turns. Returning to the soil would sort that out.

Howard returned home from some errands and found Marcia vacuuming the living room.

"Wow, the dutiful daughter acts like a little Miss Homemaker." He laughed and hugged her in a way that only fathers could do. It had been too long between hugs, and he held her tighter than usual. "Thanks."

"We haven't seen each other since Thursday morning. I had to leave for school early this morning. I know you had the funeral today, but I didn't hear you come in last night."

"I know. I haven't seen you much all week. I got in late."

He would not add anything more and hoped she did not pursue it. The truth was, he'd left Lori's house at about seven thirty and returned home, hoping Marcia had already left. He'd gotten lucky. Again.

"I have a surprise for you, and I hope you're OK with it." She was smiling as if she held a big secret. "I've invited my new best friend over for dinner Saturday night. Do you have any plans?" She set the vacuum handle down to give full attention to the conversation.

"Just hanging with you. Who's this friend? Have I met her before?" He wasn't ready for the response.

"Yes, you have. It's Mel."

"Flowers?" Howard asked incredulously. *What is going on here?*

"Yes, we've been talking on the phone. We had lunch, and I thought having her over for a sit-down dinner would be nice. Here." She pointed to the dining room table to make her point.

He thought about it for a little too long. "Marcia, I—"

"I know, Dad, but I like her. A lot. She's like an older sister, and I think I need that right now."

"Do you think she feels the same way?" Howard knew Mel liked Marcia but was unsure how this scenario would play out.

"I think so. I mean, we haven't discussed it, but—"

"OK, I get it. That's fine. But I can't think of anyone better if you must have a new friend. What's the menu?" He knew his back was against the wall and caved into his persistent daughter.

"I thought we'd barbecue if it doesn't rain."

"You mean I'd barbecue, don't you?" He laughed to break the tension that had built. "OK, I'll run to the store in the morning. Let me check on what we need." He walked toward the kitchen and shouted, "What time did you tell her to be here?"

They were now a room away from each other.

"I told her to come early, like four thirty. And thanks. Oh, by the way, she asked if she could bring a friend."

"A guy?"

"No, her girlfriend. She said you know her. Lori?" She turned the vacuum cleaner on in case he tried to respond.

71

CHAPTER

Hamilton heard the vacuum start up again and smiled. He knew exactly why she did that—so he couldn't protest her plans and make a fuss. But he wasn't going to protest. The more he thought about it, the more he liked it.

He spent the afternoon working in the garden, pinching the blossoms on the hydrangeas, pruning his Arabian lilac trees, and ensuring the weeds were minimal. It was his way of putting everything at the forefront of his mind behind him, at least for a few hours. And Bentley was the best. He would lie down next to where Howard was working, and every time Howard changed to a new bush, Bentley would move with him. He figured that even the dog missed having him around more.

He made his grocery list for the Saturday night dinner, got In-N-Out for himself and Marcia, and settled in for a movie in the evening. His first Friday night date in a long time would be with his daughter.

Hamilton, do you know how long it's been since you did this?

As he left the garage to get lunch, his phone rang—it was the Wolf.

"Pat, what's going on?"

"Hey, HH, I just wanted to update you on something I've been working on."

"Shoot," he responded as he climbed into the SUV on his way to his errands. The phone switched to the car speaker.

"After the services this morning, I asked Barber if I could go in for a few hours to work on our project. He approved it. And I think I may have discovered something. Got a minute?"

He wasn't about to burst her bubble of enthusiasm about this case. "Sure." She'd piqued his interest.

"I came in and bumped into Hernandez. You know, Anita?"

"Yeah," he said as he backed out and headed to the market.

"We chatted about her case and the info she gave us. She told me about her CI and gave me other information to research. The story about her CI is horrendous. Wait till I tell you about that."

"Whoa there, Pat. Slow down. How much of this can wait until Monday? I'm tied up today and the weekend with family things." He had to rein her in.

He didn't want to go into more detail than that.

"Well, most of it. Except for one thing I need to know right now."

"And that is?" He was not expecting what came next.

"Did you ever hear of Red Dot when you were working on this case on the computer sources you have?"

"No, what is it?" Now she had him. *Damn.*

"It's a debit card the cartel is using and abusing. I have some card numbers that don't match what you gave me. Sorry to bother you, but I'll be working here for a while. I'll show you on Monday. OK?"

72

Marcia set the table and prepared the salad, and Howard took to the barbecue for his patented chicken and sweet sausages menu. So far, the weather had cooperated. When he heard the doorbell, he was outside, ensuring the grill was clean. He froze for a moment to collect his thoughts.

He let Marcia greet the guests while he finished ensuring the barbecue was ready. He kept his fancy apron on as he entered the house to welcome Mel and Lori.

Mel was wearing casual jeans, a light-colored blouse, and a jacket, just like the fashion model she was. On the other hand, Lori wore beige dress slacks and a satin blouse with a necklace that made her eyes sparkle. She carried a light sweater.

"Whoa, I didn't know there was a dress code," he joked as he undid his apron to show his stylish slacks, shoes without socks, and an open-collared light cardinal sweater. "You ladies look fantastic." He hugged Mel, grabbed Lori's hand, and kissed her gently. "Marcia, this is Lori. We've been seeing each other. I mean dating."

"Gosh, Dad, I know. Mel has kept me up to date on your activities, even if you haven't. I just haven't had a chance to meet her in person." Marcia turned her attention to Lori. "Hi, Lori. I'm Marcia." She reached out a hand, and Lori pulled her in for a comforting hug.

Mel and Howard stood in awkward silence for a moment. At least it was uncomfortable for Howard.

"Well, come into the living room. I have munchies and some wine."

Howard was going to make this as easy for everyone as he could. He poured the exact wine they'd had on Thursday night. She noticed. He excused himself to get the barbecue going.

"Can I join you, Howard?" The way Lori said his name sent chills up and down his spine.

"Sure, come on out."

Bentley followed without being asked. They walked to the backyard, and Lori stopped to admire the garden.

"I forgot you mentioned you had an English garden too, Howard. Or can it be HH yet?"

"Yes, we have a garden, but it is not quite up to your standards. It's still a work in progress. And yes, HH is fine. Anyway, Clare and I started this a few years ago. Some simple plants, pots, and, you know, some personal touches."

This was the first mention of Clare. But as he started to explain, he put one arm around her waist to comfort her. Or was it to comfort himself? Lori made everything easy.

"Wait here while I get the meat and veggies."

He quickly returned, as he had prepared everything before their arrival. He put the plates on the side table and returned to her side. She was kneeling to pet Bentley and solidify a friendship.

"Thank you for coming. I've been very excited since Marcia told me and—"

She reached up and kissed him with a full, open-mouthed kiss that melted him. They held each other and then took a moment to step back.

"This is beautiful, HH." Smiling, she looked again at the foliage, pots, and vines.

He put the chicken and sausages on the grill, sprayed the tinfoil, put the veggies on, and closed the hood. He retook her hand as they walked along the cobblestones he and Clare had placed in the gravel.

"And so was Thursday night," she added.

Howard nodded. *It will be OK. It will be OK.*

After he led them in grace, it became one laugh after another. Bentley took his position, sitting between Lori and Howard. He held hands with Lori and Marcia during the prayer, gently squeezing gratitude for everyone's presence. Mel was in rare form, as was Marcia. Lori was poised but bantered back and forth in a more reserved manner.

After all, she was in Clare's home and didn't want to overstep her boundaries.

She looked for family photos but didn't see any. At least not on the first visit. At least not in the rooms she had been in.

Howard didn't catch it, but Marcia looked at her watch. It was seven. Just then, the phone rang.

Right on time.

She walked to the landline, trying not to look excited. "Hi, Geoff from Arizona." She announced it for everyone's benefit. She listened attentively and then said, "Hold that thought. Can I put you on speaker?"

Greetings were exchanged.

Marcia paused briefly and said, "Geoff, meet Mel and Lori. They're here for dinner."

Howard was trying to figure out what was going on.

"We should've done FaceTime, Marsh. I'd like to see who I am talking to."

"Next time, Geoff. What's going on in Zona?"

Geoff jumped right in. "Hey, Dad, remember I said I might have some Super Bowl tickets for you and Marcia?"

"Yes" was the somewhat tentative reply.

"They came through. The people who put the game on hired a bunch of us Sun Devils to help with security all week and during the game. In exchange, we got two tickets. The players and coaches get eighteen each, but we only get two. My buddy will give me two more. We get in big trouble if we try to sell them. I have to turn in the names of those using them by the first of the month. Two for Marcia and what's-his-name and two for you. They're not quite in the nosebleed section but in the stadium."

"His name is Brandon, Geoff. Brandon," Marcia said, getting frustrated with her brother.

"OK, Marsh, Braaandooon." He dragged out the name to further her frustration. "Dad, you can bring whomever you want. But get me the names by the first for sure. It's the Bengals and Kansas City Chiefs. I'm rooting for the Bengals."

Everyone else said in unison, "I'm rooting for the Chiefs."

Howard attempted to seize some control of the conversation. "Geoff, I'll call you later to discuss, but save those tickets. They're gold."

"Don't we know it. But family comes first. Talk to you. Nice meeting you, Lori."

Everyone said goodbye to Geoff.

73

"Wow, Dad, the Super Bowl. What do you think?" Marcia kept the rhythm of the evening going. "What's for dessert, Dad?"

Howard took the hint and moved into the kitchen.

"Can we help?" was the faint appeal as he walked with a smile.

"I have this."

He returned with four slices of cheesecake fresh from the Cheesecake Factory. He refreshed wines and sat to enjoy.

"I hope it doesn't conflict with this big investigation I'm on, Marcia."

Mel jumped in. "Hey, HH, don't damper Marcia's plan here. This is a once-in-a-lifetime experience for her. And with her dad? I think you're not as indispensable as you may think over there," she said, referring to the department.

Lori looked on, not wanting to get in the middle of this conversation.

Howard took a long gulp of wine. "I know, Mel, but—"

"No *buts*. I don't think they'll do much on Super Bowl Sunday. It could wait."

Howard sat back. "I won't work that day if I have anything to say. Is that what you want to hear?" He reached for his glass and sipped this time.

The statement got rousing approval from the table.

"So, Dad, who are you going to take?"

Howard stood up to walk toward the kitchen. "Anyone else want another slice of cheesecake?" No one answered. "All the rest for me, I guess."

Going to the kitchen gave him time to think. He came back, sat down, and looked around the table. "Have I been set up here?"

"What do you mean?" was the universal response.

"My investigative skills tell me that something is going on here. Mel

185

invites me to Lori's house for a holiday party as her *date*." He used air quotes for emphasis. "Marcia and Mel become friends and go to lunch, and then Marcia invites Mel for dinner. She brings a friend, Lori, who I've been seeing. We have a very nice dinner, and Geoff magically calls at seven with his Super Bowl announcement. Did I miss anything?"

"Well"—Lori finally chimed in—"perhaps I can fill in some of the missing pieces." She looked at Mel for approval, got a nod, and moved on. "You have some of the pieces—the important ones. Except for ..." She paused for effect. "Mel has someone she sees who could not make the party I threw during the holidays. But Mel has been talking about you for months, HH, and I told her I was interested and wanted to meet you. Very interested, as a matter of fact." Lori looked to Marcia for assurance.

The room got quiet for a short moment, and then Lori continued. "I told you the guy I had to accompany me was a friend, and he is—a family friend. But I wanted to go on a blind date with you, so I arranged it. Our second date was dinner at my house. Then our third was dinner at Bourbon and Bones. And here we are." Lori beamed with pride at how she presented the circumstances and saw, with relief, that Marcia approved.

"I didn't stand a chance, did I?" Howard said.

All three, in unison, responded, "Nope."

Mel broke the atmosphere with "How about those Chiefs?"

74

CHAPTER

Everyone contributed to cleaning up—even Bentley. There was nothing more said about the Super Bowl. It seemed to be the elephant in the room, and no one, not even Marcia, wanted to touch it.

Mel wrapped up the evening with "Hey, I've got an early roll call in the morning, so Lori and I will head out. Thanks so much for the dinner, wine, and, most notably, the companionship. What a great evening!"

Howard looked at Lori and decided to take a chance. "Mel, if it's OK with you, I'll take Lori home. I'd like her to stay for a while—if that's OK with you, Lori?"

Mel looked at Lori and then at Howard. "Sounds good. I'm outa here. See you at the shop, HH." She said it with a smile and a hug. "And, Marcia, we will chat this week, OK?"

The rest of the evening was spent making sure Marcia and Lori got to know each other. Lori took time to delve into Marcia's plans for the future and shared with her the business she had created, which got Marcia's attention. She even asked about her relationship with her boyfriend and where it was possibly headed. Howard became the fly on the wall, content with listening and adding a few comments.

Marcia was the one to bring the conversation to a close. "Dad, we have to get up early for church. We didn't go tonight, so early for me is better."

Howard got the drift quickly.

He took Lori home and walked her to her door, and they kissed good night for a long time. Each longed for the other but knew it was not the time. She complimented Howard on raising wonderful kids, thanked him again for dinner, stared directly into his eyes, and asked if he would call her soon.

He drove home with a lot on his mind: the evening set up by Mel, her relationship with Marcia, his feelings for Lori, and how to handle the Super Bowl issue. There was one other thing he had been wrestling with since all of this had happened.

Should I be going to communion after what Lori and I did in the intimacy of her bedroom? Should I discuss this with Father Art in confession?

How would he talk to Lori about this? And what had Pat discovered that had made her call over the weekend?

Howard and Marcia went to Mass and the Cheesecake Factory for brunch. The rest of the day was spent with their chores. Of course, all the conversations were about Mel, Lori, and the Super Bowl.

They saw Disney Garcia and his family at church but only from afar. He waved across the aisle but decided not to talk with him after the service. He explained to Marcia who Garcia was and that he worked in the same unit—nothing more.

Al Garcia still looked like shit.

75

Like magic, it was almost time for the meeting.

Hamilton wanted a jump start on Monday, so he arrived early and got an early workout in the station weight room. A note on the conference room whiteboard reminded everyone of the meeting. He saw Pat sitting at a computer in the conference room but did not acknowledge her. He walked directly to his office and opened his screens, checking emails and his landline for messages.

He looked at his calendar and saw he was slated for his three-day asset forfeiture school that week. *Damn, a lot going on right now.*

He glanced at the spreadsheets he had been working on all last week but could not convince himself to delve into the minutia that was there without a few cups of coffee. That was his priority.

He entered the conference room to a relatively sparse group. No Disney Garcia, and Barber had not arrived yet. Rikelman was in his usual seat. He handed out a limited agenda with only a few obscurely titled items and seemed to be in a pleasant mood.

Vivian must be doing some good for him.

"Sorry I'm late," Barber said, bursting into the room with a stack of papers.

Rikelman didn't acknowledge him but casually conversed while everyone got coffee and enjoyed the doughnuts the Wolf had brought to brighten everyone's morning. Joanie would not be in for a few days, as she was taking time off for family; Rikelman said so in a conversation with Lou Graham, but everyone heard.

"OK, let's get started, shall we?"

There was no Norman Bates stare, and what was that smile on his face? *Must be getting some pretty regularly.*

"We're going to be part of a big operation going down, but I won't talk about it right now. Don't anybody start anything without my OK. Oh, and I want to thank everyone who attended BB's services on Friday. I know the families appreciated it."

Silence in the staff meetings meant agreement and the OK to move on.

He referred to the agenda item entitled "Personnel." "As you can see, Al Garcia is not here. I have assigned him to administrative leave until an investigation is completed. He will be home and must check in every two hours during the day."

Howard looked around for reactions and didn't see any. Was he the only one who knew what was going on? What were the dolphins saying? He would have to find out later.

Rikelman continued. "We obviously have a vacancy in the unit and need to fill it. I have three applications from patrol guys, but feel free to do some recruiting yourself."

Barber walked to the whiteboard and put three names up. One of the names was Tenery.

Morgan immediately spoke up. "Thumbs down on Tenery. I checked him out. He doesn't have enough street time, he is too rigid with his military shit, and I'm the black in this unit. Don't need another one. No disrespect, but …" He stopped there.

"I think we have the idea, Shotgun. Find somebody you think will fit in, but Sam and I make the final decision. Got it?"

There was silence.

Graham spoke up. "Can I ask what's going on with Garcia?"

"No, you may not" was Rikelman's quick retort.

They all went back into their cocoons. Nothing more needed to be said.

Howard looked straight ahead.

"The next topic I have been thinking about is grooming standards. We may be a narcotics and vice unit, but we don't have to look like street urchins. While you don't have to adhere to patrol's hair requirements, I don't want to see any more long, shaggy, and unkempt looks. Got it, Scotty? You're starting to look like that quarterback from the Jacksonville Jaguars. Don't know his name, but—"

"Trevor Lawrence," someone said.

There was more silence. It was clear no one was going to cross the line today.

Rikelman was on a roll. "While I'm on the subject, you know there's a lot of talk about language used in the workplace, much of it directed at offensive words and name-calling, but I want to talk about something somewhat related. I'm talking about using street language, the language you use when operating out there, and bringing it into the station. To the workplace. I don't like it, and I don't think it's necessary."

Morgan was the first to respond. "You mean like the street talk the brothers use? I know I sometimes bring it in here, but so do the other guys."

"And that's my point. I know I'm getting picky. And let me add another one. We don't know what they say when Graham and Garcia talk in Spanish. But some could take offense to that."

"Just you white guys," Graham said with a smile, trying not to offend.

"I'm just saying let's elevate some things here. We have Wolford in the unit, I may add another female, and I think we have to prepare to be …" He was now rambling and stammering to make his point.

Hamilton stepped in. "I think we all understand what you're trying to say, sir. And we get it. We do. What's next?"

Rikelman looked around the room and obtained consensus. "Next item. Admin has announced the date for the sergeant's test. Don't anyone laugh, but it's April Fools' Day."

They laughed anyway.

"It's always on a Saturday around the first week of April, but this year, that happens to be April Fools' Day."

Hamilton was going to take a chance. "At least they didn't schedule the lieutenant's exam that day too."

His comment brought down the house, with everyone, including Rikelman, enjoying the barb.

76

As the meeting broke up, Howard looked to Wolford to discuss their project and let her know about his upcoming school. Then his phone rang.

"Hello, Nicole," Howard said, trying to get a smile over the phone as he walked to his office.

"Hello my ass, Detective Hamilton. You hung me out to dry with my boss. Your bosses came to see Mr. Dryer here, my GM, and he went through the fuckin' roof."

He could sense the anger. "Hold on, Nicole. I didn't know they would talk with him, but because this case is so important, they felt they needed to meet with your boss. They told me after the meeting, or I would have given you a heads-up." He was unsure he would have told her but wanted to appease her somewhat. He decided to put her on the defense. "Had you told Dryer everything?"

"Well, no, but then I had to. My job may be on the line here. I'm scared of him and some of these customers I'm dealing with, and I use the term *customer* lightly. Thanks to you guys."

"Let me see if I can get the OK to talk with Dryer about your situation. I can take some blame and take the heat off you."

"Would you?" She was now again in a defensive posture. "I would appreciate it." She was calming down, at least on the phone. "By the way, these guys called me today and said they needed two more Sprinters by tomorrow and didn't care what color or equipment. They said they'd get them customized. I know it takes ten days, and they need to start the ball rolling now. What do you think that means?"

"I don't know what it means, but I have an idea." He was going to change the subject. "By the way, do you know who does the customizing?"

"There's only one company that has that kind of turnaround. I referred

192

them to Continental Chariots in Anaheim. They're in an industrial complex right off the 57 freeway and Anaheim Stadium. I can get you the address."

"Let me see if I can talk to Dryer. I'll get back to you."

Hamilton immediately looked for Barber and filled him in.

"I'd prefer that the lieutenant OK that, HH. Let me see." Barber knew his decision-making boundaries.

Five minutes later, Barber had the answer. "OK, this is how it's going to work. Take Wolford, and record the meeting. Do not—I repeat, do not—let Getty attend the meeting. Just you guys. Then let me know how it went."

"Got it."

Hamilton checked out a pocket pen recorder from the 007 room and called Dryer's office. The meeting was on. He told Wolford they could grab a sandwich on the way.

"Sounds good, HH. Want to give me some more details as we go?"

"Of course. Would I lead you down a blind alley?"

77

Hamilton decided not to park in front, where the customers parked. He opted to enter at the service entrance and park in an obscure spot, hoping not to be noticed. He saw that the Sprinter headquarters and Nicole's office were on the right of the customer parking, while the main showroom was on the left. Used cars were spread between the two buildings, creating pathways. Somehow, a Dodge Charger did not fit the motif.

They walked to the rear service door, asked for the manager, and were directed upstairs. The waiting room oversaw the Mercedes showroom, which featured cars of every style and color. All, he surmised, cost more than $100,000. A somewhat matronly woman in her midfifties led them into a well-appointed office, introduced them to Mr. Jeff Dryer, and asked them to be seated.

Hamilton sized Dryer up right away. He was a smooth businessman, dressed well and living the good life. He was bald, with a white goatee and glasses; in his midsixties; and getting ready for retirement after selling a hell of a lot of cars, including to the cartels. Wolford just thought he was a dirty old man. Maybe they were both correct.

They got to the business at hand. Introductions and business cards were exchanged. Hamilton made it a point to compliment Dryer on his business, the layout, and the cleanliness that screamed wealth. He thanked him for the information and the company's level of cooperation with the department. He acknowledged Dryer's meeting with Rikelman and Barber and purposely overstated his appreciation of Nicole Getty's efforts. He would not mention how he and John Bresani's girlfriend, Nicole, had met. That had been another book and previous life.

Dryer got direct. "I think we've given you quite a bit of information that should help your investigation, have we not? So why this visit?"

Wolford stepped in. "Sir, we appreciate what you've done for the community and us. While we could access DMV records for the plates to be issued to all of these vehicles, we would appreciate it if you could provide that information. And we have a few more requests."

Dryer nodded for her to continue.

"We would like you to place GPS tracking devices on the two Sprinters the suspects are picking up tomorrow. Putting them in places where they would not be detected, even with electronic search locators, would be very helpful. Your people can do it better than we can, I'm sure. We can deliver them to you early in the day."

Wolford sat back as the signal for Hamilton to bring the meeting to a close.

"Sir, we would be remiss in not thanking you and Nicole for your work. We know you may not see these clients again after tomorrow's sales." He paused to make sure he was getting his message across. "I'm also concerned that Nicole may have felt she overstepped her boundaries. Believe me, with what you have given us, the outcome will significantly benefit the greater Los Angeles County and maybe even the Southern California region. I hope you find a way to recognize her efforts in all of this." He wanted to stress her contributions without appearing to go overboard.

"Let me be clear, detectives," Dryer said as he pushed his chair away from his expansive desk. "I think I know the message you're trying to send. I have put a little fear in her regarding this matter. And for a good reason. She did overstep a bit, but she's served us well, and her job is not in jeopardy. Once this is completed, she will be quietly recognized for her work with you." He nodded that the meeting was over and approached the desk to shake hands.

But Dryer had something else on his mind. "I am the incoming president of the Orchard Hill Chamber of Commerce. I will get installed on Thursday before the Super Bowl weekend. I would like you both to be at that luncheon as my guests."

Hamilton smiled warmly. "If this investigation is completed by then, you can be assured. Right, Pat?"

78

CHAPTER

"We have a lot of work to do," Wolford said as they left the OHMB parking lot.

"No shit, Sherlock" was his retort. "Where did you come up with that GPS thing?"

"I've used it before, and those damn things never stay on the car, even with the magnets. I think they can do a much better job," she said, referring to the dealership.

"Agreed. It looks like Nicole is safe."

"Hey, HH, you don't have the hots for her, do you?"

"Hell no. I have something going now that I don't want to screw up, and adding somebody like her would do just that. Anyway, she's just an informant."

"And when will you tell Donny and me about this *something*?"

"Soon. I'm trying to take this slow and—well, later. We've got work to do."

"When we get back to the station, I want to show you my workup on everything. You'll be surprised."

"Hey, I've got a surprise for you too. I'm in a three-day school until Friday. I'll check in, but it'll give you some time on your project."

"Great. I need to put some stuff together, but come on in, and I'll show you what I have."

* * *

Wolford rushed to the office. Hamilton was not far behind. She went to the 007 closet and brought out some sizeable white Post-it sheets with names and figures written all over them.

"See if you can get Hernandez to step in while I set up, would you, HH?"

Howard did her bidding. Hernandez and her partner, Jake DeLeon, followed him into the N&V conference room, where Wolford had set up her charts. She had taken it upon herself to ask Barber and Rikelman to sit in.

She grabbed a ruler like a schoolmarm and walked everyone through her analysis. She was a little nervous. "This is what I've worked up. Thanks to Howard's spreadsheets with information from the first group of sales at OHMB and the second one we just received, I could compare it with the info Anita and Bonnie Carvin of the HURT task force provided."

She pointed to the list of suspects. "First, out of the twenty suspects we've identified with all three separate pieces of intelligence, five were in on the Bresani case you guys did a few years back. We see the same names on Anita's list here. See?" She pointed to make sure everyone saw the same names. "That means we're dealing with the Zeta cartel again. Only they've come back even stronger. Two names showed up on Bonnie's list. The other fifteen still must be identified through our Backoffice and maybe even DEA."

She set the first Post-it aside and went to the next one. "Howard identified ten cars purchased at OHMB by the cartels, all with either cashier's checks or from a Mexican bank just south of the border. Six are Sprinters, Mercedes's big vans, and four have powerful engines. All four-doors have massive trunk storage space. I think they're called the S550 and AMG models. Tomorrow they're delivering two more Sprinters to the dealership. We should be there. I'll talk about that a bit later."

"I have a spreadsheet on PowerPoint with license numbers, VINs, color, and even photos. That's the next phase," Hamilton added. He then waved to Wolford to continue.

Even Rikelman was not going to interrupt her.

She took a breath. "This is all rough stuff, but I want to get through it before diving in. We have much more work to do, but once you see what Howard and I have come up with, we need your input and where we go from here."

Hernandez shyly raised a hand. "We should probably have a rep from the task force in on this."

"I'm a step ahead, Detective," Rikelman said, "but wait until we get this rough stuff out to all of you."

Hmm. Hamilton thought about that statement. Rikelman acted as if he knew what Wolford had been working on.

The next sheet listed bank accounts that showed one of the suspects as the depositor, including the dates and sources of funds.

Howard felt compelled to add, "I have copies of all bills of sale, credit reports, bank transactions, and the owners of record. I'll be doing deep searches to ensure we tie each one of these suspects to each car."

"Like I said, guys, this is preliminary stuff. I wanted you all to see what we had going." Wolford was excited. "Here's the best one."

She reached for her next Post-it. At the top of the page were boxes filled with twelve numbers each, with at least ten boxes filled in. On the left side were locations, such as Walmart, Fry's, and other smaller retail outlets.

"These are accounts with a bank out of Pakistan via the company RIE: Shabadmetro Bank. They issue debit cards like candy to anyone who wants them. The numbers you see here are just examples of the accounts."

Silence filled the room.

"The cartels use these to transfer the money to their relatives worldwide. Howard and I will track this funding area, but be assured they are in high numbers."

Howard raised a hand as if he were in school. "Teacher, can I add something here?"

Everyone laughed.

"I believe they need the Sprinters to transport people, not just drugs. Anita, we hoped you could meet with your CI ASAP to get some intel on this. We believe this is going to happen sometime after the first of February. They wanted the new Sprinters for a reason. We found out where they get them customized and will need some help with surveillance. This thing could be enormous." He looked to Rikelman. "We need to talk offline, sir."

79

CHAPTER

Hamilton spent the next few hours discussing the findings with Rikelman, Barber, and Wolford. Hamilton pointed out specific cars he had seen when the unit took down the cartels and when Bresani was killed. Howard made his plea.

"Lieutenant, I believe this case is above the capabilities of OHPD. The HURT task force needs to be involved, perhaps with some gang expertise and additional technology assistance. They need to take the lead here, not us."

Rikelman responded quickly, "Once again, you are right. This thing is out of hand. We need more resources than OHPD. We have major officer safety issues. We could easily be outgunned and outnumbered. I'll make it happen."

Rikelman started briefing the command staff and making calls to the HURT OIC, Captain Peggy Dial of the Los Angeles Sheriff's Department. The wheels were in motion for a ten o'clock meeting Friday at HURT headquarters in an industrial building next to LADUECE and the Backoffice. Both were located in the City of Industry, a unique municipality gerrymandered around unused land in Los Angeles County, primarily for commercial purposes. If most law enforcement didn't know about it, they were safe from the cartels or other local gangbangers discovering their whereabouts.

Barber assigned Wolford to work with Hernandez and her CI. He coordinated the assignment with the detective supervisor to ensure no jurisdictional issues between detectives and the narcotics unit. Rikelman and Captain Markham would meet with the HURT teams, and Hamilton and Barber would work on all the information collected thus far. Barber assigned Graham and the Everlys to visit Continental Classics to see what they could find regarding van conversions and their nefarious customers.

Hamilton worked on cleaning up what the Wolf had started with her Post-its. First, he needed to dive into the debit card company RIE to find out more. And he did. As the industry labeled it, RIE was a GO2bank that only used debit cards with no fees, just transaction rates based upon amount. The underground had discovered this banking method and its use for the international transfer of money—all tax-free.

Mobile wallets, Apple Pay, Google Pay, JPay, or MoneyPak could use chip-enabled encryption and lock protection from cybercriminals. Money could move from a bank or a checking account or transfer to another card without a trace. Kiosks were in Walmart, Fry's, Kroger, and other stores, permitting funds transfer to more than one hundred countries. They even paid almost 5 percent interest on $500 or more without tracing anything with a tax identification number.

Hamilton could not believe what he was finding. The movement of money without a trace or audit was designed explicitly so that cartels would not have to transport large amounts of cash once their ill-begotten gains were made in the dope trade or human trafficking. They had found ways to move money electronically or with debit cards, transferring small amounts under the $10,000 threshold banks sought.

He knew he had one more area to discover but couldn't think of what it was. It was bothering him. He needed to think.

He got one last cup of coffee and returned to his desk. He called Lori and arranged a late date for drinks and a night snack at Bourbon and Bones. He needed the distraction because this case was consuming him. He knew he would not be EOW by six or even seven. He called Marcia to tell her he would not be home again for dinner.

"Dad, Geoff called again. Have you decided who you'll take to the Super Bowl?"

"I think so, but I'll let you know when I get home."

"Lori?"

"I'll let you know." He clicked off.

Then he remembered his wild-ass idea. He called the Everlys and discussed it with them as they headed to Anaheim to visit Continental Classics. Then he jumped into his car, went to a local Ace Hardware, and found what he wanted. He would be ready when he and Wolford went to OHMB tomorrow to meet with Dryer and get him the GPS devices to install on the Sprinters being prepped for the cartels.

Such fun.

80
CHAPTER

Howard had the evening planned. He was looking forward to dinner with Lori. Hopefully, it would be a pivotal moment in the relationship. While his mind was on the big case at work, he decided to do whatever he could to compartmentalize everything. He wanted this evening and this relationship to work.

As hokey as it sounded, he stopped by the local Bristol Farms and picked a bouquet of roses: yellow and red mixed with a splash of greens and baby's breath. He still marveled at the driveway and approach to the most beautiful home he had ever seen.

What was he doing in such a setting? With this level of a woman? He never would have dreamed he would know, let alone sleep with, someone like her. She had looks and money and was an intelligent businesswoman.

Look at this home! Roman pillars opened to an entrance out of *Gone with the Wind*. The landscaping would take years to mature.

Howard set all those doubts aside as he reached out to ring the bell. He didn't have to ring, because she opened the door as his finger reached for the button. With as much bravado as possible, he placed the flowers in front of her face with a "To the most beautiful woman I know."

"Well, hello to you too." She laughed. "I wasn't expecting this. You are just full of surprises, aren't you?" They hugged and had a kiss that lingered longer than planned. "Let me put these in water and get a wrap. I'm starving."

They drove to the restaurant in constant conversation. Lori was excited to talk about a new line of cosmetics she had discovered. She would have to take a brief trip to Austin, Texas, to seal the deal. She went on about her new find and her excitement about seeing him that night.

"Too many good things are happening in my life right now, Howard, and the most important one is you."

"I'm glad to hear that. I mean about your business. And me. Can we talk more about it over another great dinner here?"

They arrived at Bourbon and Bones and were escorted to another perfect spot in a dark corner of the dining area.

"So, Howard, tell me about your week."

He told her just enough to satisfy her interest but tried not to get bogged down in the details.

"There's a lot of work to be done, but it looks like it'll all come together. But that's not what I want to discuss." He became serious as he waved away the waiter.

"Is this bad news? Is it about your family? You look so stern. Is it us?"

"It is about us." He used a moment of silence to reach out and hold her hand. "I've been alone for more than two years now. I found you—well, you found me, really. We've both been trying to find—you know what I mean. I guess I'm trying to say I think I'm falling—I am falling for you in a big way, Lori. There. I needed to get that off my chest." He wasn't going to use the L-word, not yet.

"Well, Howard Hamilton, I have news for you too. I fell for you long ago. At my holiday party, I knew it was you I wanted, needed, and needed to want, if that makes sense."

Neither knew why, but their hands tightly squeezed the other almost to the point of pain. Then the tension was released.

"I think I'll order a bottle of the Grenache."

They sat back, breathed, and stared intently into each other's eyes.

"Maybe we should just get a room."

They laughed so loudly that others at surrounding tables smiled at them in quiet support.

It was another perfect dinner. They decided not to have dessert but ordered cappuccinos instead.

"I do cook, you know, Howard. We don't have to eat out all of the time. And by the way, I made a nice dessert for us at home. Do you like carrot cake?"

"Do I like carrot cake? It happens to be my favorite. You really know how to get to a guy, don't you?"

"Everything with us seems to work, Howard. Everything." She looked at him with a longing that melted his heart.

"I have one more question. Will you go to the Super Bowl with me?"

"I wondered who you would take after Marcia and Geoff staged that call. I thought you would be asking someone else, because you hadn't brought it up since."

"Lori, there is no one else. It's you. It's all you."

"It's all you too, Howard. And since we've met, it's always been you." The silence meant so much right now.

She decided to add something a little more straightforward to the conversation. "And by the way, I hope you know it's a little late to get a place in the Phoenix area during that hectic time."

"I didn't even think of that." He sat back, perplexed. "Maybe I'll call Geoff to see—"

"No worries, my dear. I have a condo in Scottsdale. Got it covered." She smiled like the Cheshire cat.

"You never cease to amaze." He shook his head in disbelief.

"I always want to amaze you, my dear Howard. Always."

81

CHAPTER

Lori dropped another bombshell on him as they indulged in the carrot cake dessert. She had been talking to Marcia about working with her in her business. He was convinced it was all a conspiracy, but he loved every minute.

After spending another night with Lori, he knew the relationship was more than he ever had anticipated. But it was causing significant logistical problems, not to mention getting raised eyebrows from Marcia. He showered at Lori's but had to go home to change clothes.

He went directly to a nondescript office building in Segundo for his class on asset finance. He wasn't looking forward to it, because it would take him away from his investigations, but once he got into the subject matter, he became increasingly excited about its potential. He learned the laws relating to seizing property that were associated with and benefiting criminal investigations. It would be invaluable with the case he was working on and could be added to his résumé for future use. He was taught how to do a financial questionnaire and seize vehicles, boats, residences, and airplanes. Three days went by quickly.

* * *

It was quiet around the office that day. The Wolf reminded him of the meeting with the GM of the Mercedes dealership. He would be ready. Then he remembered the lieutenant and Barber meeting with the HURT task force at their headquarters. It looked like another operation similar to the Bresani drug-smuggling case a few years ago—perhaps even more extensive.

Wolford interrupted his catch-up on emails. "HH, got a minute?" It didn't matter, because she continued to talk. "I met Friday with Anita;

her partner, Jake; and her informant." She was referring to Detective Hernandez and Jake DeLeon. "What a story. I have to tell you about it."

"OK." He sat back from his computer to give her his full attention.

"Gina, the CI, was taken from her parents at twelve and sex-trafficked from Mexico to the LA area. She's been working on the streets, acting as a mule to carry drugs and delivering money from the cartels to various businesses, for almost ten years. She knows about the cars and vans transporting people illegally crossing the border. She is giving us everything they are doing now. I'll fill you in later on that." Wolford had to curb her enthusiasm and take a breath and a sip of coffee.

"Hold that thought while I get a cup going," Howard joked.

"Anyway, here is the big item. Well, that was one of many things she told us about. Do you know those numbered accounts? The ones we couldn't figure out what they were? You'll never guess what they are."

"OK, I give up," Howard said as he raised his hands.

"They're accounts from prisoners—Eme cartel members serving time. Those RIE debit cards are used to deposit big money into prison accounts. She told us they could also transfer these cards from one prisoner account to another, which is how they pay contract hits and drug smuggling from inside. And some of the prison guards are in on it as well."

She took another breath and referred to her notes. "We figured they were going to at least four different state prisons without any trace. At least a hundred various cartels or local gang members are involved. Jake has identified Ironwood and Chuckawalla Valley prisons in Blythe and Northern California. We can't figure out the account numbering system."

Howard sat back in amazement. "Does the lieutenant know about this?"

"I called him over the weekend. He has the information but not the details. They're attending the big meeting at HURT this morning while we go to the Mercedes dealer."

"You said there was more?"

"Yup. You know the Sprinters they've been getting from your CI, Nicole?"

He nodded.

"Well, at least five have been customized with seats to hold at least twenty passengers."

"This Gina will have a bounty on her if they find out where we got all this information." Howard could tell Wolf was emotionally involved with Anita's CI and the case.

"They have long-standing pickup spots along the coast of Orange County. Every Thursday, they go down there and pick up at least one hundred illegals along the beaches. They bring them up from Mexico on small pangas, land early in the morning, and use local gangs to escort them from the beaches to the waiting vans. They use walkie-talkies to communicate within a short window to escape detection. And there's more," she said as she looked at the clock. "We'd better head to our meeting."

Howard grabbed a to-go cup and his backpack as they left the station.

82

The Wolf could not stop talking. "These people must pay the cartel up to eight to ten thousand dollars to bring them to the United States. We are really concerned for this CI's safety. We may have to relocate her after this is over. I can't wait for the lieutenant and Barber to get back from their meeting. What's in the backpack, HH?"

Howard could see she was getting worked up over every aspect of the case. "Slow down, Pat. You're going to have a heart attack. You'll see when I get there."

He parked the Charger in the rear service area to ensure Nicole didn't see them enter the dealership. They went directly to Dryer's office and were escorted in by his matronly assistant.

"Good morning, detectives. Can I get you some coffee? You look like you could both use it."

They both nodded.

"Two with just cream—no sugar," Howard said.

Dryer greeted them, wearing casual slacks, a starched white shirt, and no tie. "The customers are taking delivery of the Sprinters this afternoon. I understand you have some requests for us?"

"We do." Howard reached down into his backpack. "As we discussed, we have two GPS devices for your technicians to install where they can't be discovered. You said you could do that on our last visit. We're covered with a search warrant."

Dryer nodded.

"But we have one more request." Howard reached into his bag again, produced two cans of spray paint, and set them on the desk. Each can was labeled *Cardinal*, with detailed information in tiny print to provide all the legal knowledge required for the unique product. "This is a clear liquid paint that is luminescent when a particular light is used. It doesn't glow in the dark but can be detected with specific illumination. I'd like you to apply it on the roofs of the Sprinters, large enough to be seen from the sky. Can you do that?"

"No problem, Detective Hamilton. Let me call somebody right now to get on this before it's too late."

"You little devil, HH. Where did you come up with that?" the Wolf whispered as Dryer made the call.

Howard just smiled.

Dryer hung up his phone call. "OK, now it's my turn. I'm unsure how to do it, but I'd like to get some acknowledgment of our cooperation here. While I'm not too concerned with losing business from this type of clientele, there has to be a way for my dealership to be recognized for our efforts."

"I'll talk to my boss, but we've got to be careful. These people are not above retaliation if they find out the source of our ʾestigation. People who've crossed them have been found with their body parts strewn along the highway in black bags. That's not a pretty sight."

Dryer paused to take in that statement. "I'm sure you can find a way. When is all of this supposed to happen?"

"Let me put it to you this way, sir." Howard repositioned himself to ensure he sat up straight with his best command presence. "We have a lot more work to do on this. Your information is not the only piece of the puzzle. We have more intelligence we need to use before we decide on anything." He wasn't going to give him anything more than that.

"I don't suppose you could have anything available for my installation as president of the chamber of commerce, could you?"

"You mean by the week before the Super Bowl?"

"Yes."

"I don't think so, sir. Think longer term. But we'll keep you posted. Probably after everything happens, but not before."

"We'll accommodate your requests, detectives."

There was no doubt the meeting was over.

Wolford and Hamilton walked back to their car, constantly aware of ensuring Nicole Getty would not spot them.

"That was a nice trick on the spray paint, HH. Where did you get that?"

"Read about it" was his quick reply. "I also have the Everlys using it at the Continental Classics location. They should be doing that right about now. But without anybody there knowing. Not sure we can trust those people."

"Cool. Really cool, Howard," the Wolf said as they returned to their car.

"Right down my alley."

83
CHAPTER

The four-day work week turned into day five, with overtime on the horizon for just about everyone. Rikelman and Barber returned to the office in the late afternoon. Wolford and Hamilton gave them an update on the meeting with the Mercedes dealership and what the Wolf had discovered with the new accounts. Hamilton decided to bring up the issue of Dryer wanting to get some recognition for the dealership's efforts with Rikelman.

Rikelman smiled. "We'll figure something out for Dryer. I'll talk to the acting chief. Detective Hernandez met with us at HURT and brought up the new accounts. Bonnie Carvin from the task force has some other information, and I asked if she could give it to you two. I think that will be our biggest contribution to this case, along with some bodies for surveillance. Right now, Captain Dial and HURT will run the operation."

Everyone agreed with the strategy.

Rikelman added, "I'll tell her to bring the California Department of Corrections and Rehabilitation, CDCR, to work with us and INS. I want you two," he said, referring to Wolford and Hamilton, "to do a PowerPoint workup for our next meeting with all that shit you have." He waved his arms to point out Hamilton's office. "I want to wow them as much as possible."

The Everlys walked in and gave Howard subtle thumbs-ups.

Phil spoke up. "We got an excellent look at the Continental Classics operation. Quite an impressive business. They trick out almost every kind of van and RV you can imagine. We think they know who they're dealing with, but as usual, it's all about the Benjamins." He took out his phone and downloaded photos to his computer so everyone could see them. "We took some pics of the vans we're looking at."

The photos showed the start of the installation of bench seats much like those found on a school bus. There was a small bathroom and sink in each van.

Don pointed to a photo of the overlay of the lot where all vans were stored. "At least three of them will be completed within ten days. The other two vans are equipped with storage bins that look like they're lined with heavy fabric. I think it's for storing drugs and ensuring our K9s don't detect them." He moved to exterior shots of the vans with front and back plates depicted.

Don continued to stare at the collage of photos on his screen. "The manager told me the last part of the remodels would be a wrap around the exterior to depict a business of some kind. You know how they put a picture of a dog for mobile grooming or a carpet-cleaning machine? That kind of thing. He indicated the customers would bring that in later in the week, as they were getting those done off-site. He is going to send us photos when the work is completed." Don leaned back to admire his handiwork.

"Oh, by the way, we didn't have enough GPS devices to mount on all of them, but I think we took care of three. I couldn't find any more in the 007 room."

"I took two early this morning. Sorry. Didn't sign them out," Howard said sheepishly.

"Uh-oh." Phil laughed. "You are in deep shit. That's a felony around here, HH. Barber will have your ass."

"I know." He cringed. "Beat me. Did you take care of that other business I asked for?"

"We did." The Everlys chimed in with a duo response.

Howard and the Wolf exchanged smiles.

Rikelman indicated there would be a quick unit meeting at four o'clock to bring everything together. That gave everyone an hour to prepare his or her little piece of the gigantic puzzle.

84

CHAPTER

The Wolf knocked on Hamilton's door with a strong sense of urgency. "HH, I just had a quick meeting with Anita Hernandez. She got a call from her CI, and you won't believe this."

"Come on in, Pat. Sit down, and take a breath. You can't get excited about everything that goes on around here. We take things in stride. You'll have a coronary if you keep this up." He offered her a chair.

"I know, but I've never been involved in anything like this. Hell, I just trained bomb dogs in Iraq and handled radio calls here. This stuff is complicated."

"I know it is. That's why we take it slow and methodical. What do you have?"

Wolf jumped right in. "The CI says they've set up an operation like a war room, not just for the drugs like meth, fentanyl, and coke but also for business scams. They have over thirty corporate LLCs and use them to submit phony requests to the federal government for loss of business because of the COVID crisis. They even have a phony call center. And they're getting checks in left and fuckin' right."

Howard responded, "This is getting crazy." He rubbed his face, moved his hands through his hair, and breathed. "That scam has been widespread throughout the country because there are no damn checks and balances to audit who's legit and who's not. Jeez, isn't anybody paying attention other than us?" He pursed his lips and shook his head. He wouldn't get into the politics of it all, but it bothered him.

Wolf sat back and sipped on her third cup of coffee. "Do the math. If they have thirty companies and phony up at least ten or more employees with counterfeit Social Security cards, they could bring in over a million bucks a month of your and my money. Fuck this. We've got to do something here."

"We will, Pat. But let's be a bit more deliberate here. Can we get any information regarding the names of these companies? If so, I can get a lot of details and send them to the feds. I heard they had a task force of their own working on things like this."

"Anita said her CI would work on it, but it may take some time. These guys are raking in millions with the charges for smuggling, drug sales, and these other scams."

"And it's all right under our noses, Pat, but we're the ones who have to go by the rules. Be a little sneaky, but go by the rules. We have to fuck with them in ways that drive them crazy. And we will." He was getting control of his emotions, but he could feel his blood pressure rising.

"How do we do that, HH?"

"Think about it, Pat. They use all these vehicles. Maybe they get some flat tires. They use walkie-talkies. Maybe their frequencies get jammed. We'll have GPS on them to track where they go and see where they conduct their legitimate business, and we'll talk with those people to try to sway them from doing business or use them to our advantage. That's all I can think of right now, but you think about ways we can screw with them. Talk to Donny, Anita, or Jake to get some ideas. Make it a game."

"You've given me some good ideas, Howard. I'll get back to you."

"In the meantime, Pat, get me as much as possible from the CI so I can go to work. A lot of the information on LLCs is public record. I have sources to drill down on those kinds of things. I'll teach you all about it, but you'll learn more in the intel school with Packer."

"Can't wait for that school, HH. Do you have time to meet us at Home Plate after EOW tonight? Maybe then I can relax a little."

"Maybe. Have to check with Marcia first."

"Anybody else you have to check with, Howard?"

"Maybe."

His phone rang, and a familiar name appeared on the screen: Guy Coyle.

85

"HH, got a minute?" Guy Coyle was a retired LAPD lieutenant who lived in Orchard Hill and had become Hamilton's outside mentor. He had great insights and always wanted to know the inside scoop on what was happening in the city. Coyle rarely said hello.

"Always for you, Guy."

"Any chance we could have a beer tonight? I have something to talk to you about."

"Jeez, Guy, I can't. I'm tied up at work and have plans with Marcia." He left out Wolford's invitation to have a beer at Home Plate.

"Early morning coffee at Peet's at seven hundred hours? I promise it'll be worth it. And I'm buying."

"Does a scone or blueberry muffin come with that offer?"

"Of course. See you then." He hung up.

God, it's great to have another friend who's a guy. Too many women in my life.

He called Marcia to plan a late dinner, perhaps seven or so. They wrapped up what could not wait until Monday, and everyone promised to have just one.

Home Plate was not as busy as expected for a Friday night. They headed for their favorite booth, and Howard looked around for the guitar music and Sam. The only sounds were the TV, which showed commentators talking about the Super Bowl and the weekend playoff games, as well as the usual crowd noises. There were no new paintings or other artwork, but Laurenti was behind the bar. They caught each other's eye.

Hamilton excused himself from the booth and went to the corner where Sam usually set up to play. "Hey, Gary, where's Sam? Not around tonight?"

"Not around, period. She's gone." Laurenti continued his bar duties.

"What do you mean *gone?*"

Laurenti threw a towel over his shoulder and put both hands on the bar. "She went back to Sausalito. She didn't like the vibes here in So Cal and Pedro. The only person she warmed up to was you, and that didn't go as far as she wanted it to. And when you weren't in for a while, she packed up and headed back to a place where she was more comfortable."

"Well, I've been busy. Really busy with work and a few other things." Howard wouldn't go further than that explanation, at least not with Gary.

"She said you never asked for her phone number or made it a point to come in more frequently after your little talks. Anyway, she couldn't warm up to anyone here. You know how women are. The guys here are either married, drunks, or Grizzly Adams longshoremen she didn't care for."

"Would you give me her number so I could at least call her? I owe her that much."

Laurenti grabbed a napkin, wrote down her number, and handed it to Hamilton. "Hey, Hamilton, one more thing. I got a call from Len Patterson." He paused for a moment to let it sink in.

"And?" Howard said.

I wonder how much he told him about our little talk. I don't want him to think I was prying into his past. That wouldn't be good.

"Well, he apologized for not giving me a heads-up on his conversation with you. He also said you were a good guy—a straight shooter." Gary wiped down the bar as he talked. "I told him I'd already figured that out."

"Good to hear, Gary. About him and you sizing me up. I am a straight shooter. I don't shoot from the hip; I take my job and, I guess, life seriously."

"Give her a call. She'd like that."

Howard went back to the booth, thinking about his conversation with Laurenti.

"What was that all about, HH?" Donny said as he shoved an IPA in front of Howard.

"Oh, nothin'." He let some silence fill the air. "Hey, I have an idea. Would you and Pat like to come to the house tomorrow night for dinner? There's someone I'd like you to meet."

"Sure," Donny quickly responded, "but we already know you're dating Flowers."

"Flowers! Fuckin' Flowers? I'm not dating her," he said in too loud a voice.

"You've been awfully quiet of late, and everyone sees you huddling with her at the station. So the dolphins went to work."

"Well, you can tell the dolphins they're wrong. You'll meet someone I've been seeing tomorrow night, and it's not Efin Flowers."

The IPA went down quickly.

86

Howard kept the promise of one beer and headed home. The conversation at HP was always more important than the beer. On the way, he called Lori, got caught up on her daily activities, and asked if she would come to dinner on Saturday night.

"Well, that's a pleasant surprise, Howard. Dinner at your place? Will Marcia be there?"

"Yes, and I've invited my best friend on the job, Donny, and his wife, Pat. I think it's time you meet them."

"I'm always interested in meeting your friends, my dear. I think your friends are more down to earth than mine. And I guess it is about time."

"You may find them more interesting, but I must warn you: they are different."

"Different is good, my love. What time?"

They agreed she would come early, perhaps three, to help prepare for the feast.

* * *

Hamilton walked into Peet's at precisely seven o'clock to see Guy Coyle with coffee in hand and talking to Sophia, the barista.

"Here he comes now, Sophia. Give him whatever he wants."

They both laughed at Howard. There was apparently some joke he'd missed.

"Your regular, HH? Anything to eat? Guy says he is paying, so I'd take him up on it."

"Blueberry muffin warmed. And maybe I'll take one to go if he's picking up the bill."

They laughed as Guy coaxed him to a booth in the back of the coffee shop. It was still too early in the morning to sit out on the patio.

"How's it been going, HH? We haven't talked in forever."

"It's been crazy, Guy, but it was your dime, so what's going on? Bring me up to date on your activities, and maybe we'll have time for my stuff."

"That's fair. Well, you remember I mentioned I was seeing someone?"

HH nodded, trying not to interrupt.

"Well, it's getting a little serious, and there are a few impediments, let's say."

"OK."

Interrogation technique number one was to say little.

"Well, she's still married. I mean, she's going through a nasty divorce. And to top it off, she will get a new job."

"That does sound a bit complicated. I mean, I'm also seeing someone, and it's kind of getting serious. When do I get to meet her?"

"You're going to meet her in a few weeks. I told her all about you. I hope you don't mind."

"No, I don't mind. I haven't told my girl about you yet, but—"

Coyle held up a hand as each took a drink.

Howard broke his muffin in two. "Want some?"

"Maybe later, Howard, but there is something you need to know."

"OK."

"She's going to be your new chief."

"What?" Hamilton sat there with his mouth open. He took a moment to digest that comment.

"Your new chief."

"I heard you, but—"

"I'm seeing Rose Tustin. She's Captain Rod Tustin's soon-to-be ex. She's the chief at Redondo, and when she heard you lost your chief and my friend, I encouraged her to apply."

"I thought Melendrez from Gardenia was coming over."

"I heard your POA put the kibosh on that. With Rose, they get a twofer."

"What do you mean?"

"Rosa Delgado Tustin. Need I say more? But she's solid, HH. I promise. Great lady, a great cop, and a great administrator. Ask around."

Hamilton's head was swimming. "I will, but how did you guys hook up?"

"She was an LA Sheriff's lieutenant before she became the Redondo Chief. When I was with LAPD, we went to a management school together. We stayed in touch and became professional friends. We thought alike and hit it off, just as friends. We stayed in touch, and I was there when she needed a shoulder."

"I don't know what to say, Guy. Has this hit the press or anything?"

"Not that we know. It was only confirmed yesterday afternoon. We think it'll be announced tonight. You know how politicians are. Make hard decisions on Friday afternoon, and see how it sizzles over the weekend."

"Well, this is a big wow. I'm not sure how to respond, but congrats to you both."

"She's going to do this alone for a while, HH. I won't be in the picture right now. I hope you keep that under your hat." Coyle was always thinking ahead.

"Got it, Guy. I think I'm going for a refill. Then I'll tell you about Lori and, if we have time, the case I'm working on."

"I'm yours, HH. That was a big load to get off my chest. I wanted to tell you about her, but she swore me to secrecy, and it drove me crazy every time we got together, you know." He stumbled on his last few words.

Howard told how he'd met Lori but briefed it down.

"Sounds like you got set up by the best. I know Melanie, and she would not take no for an answer. Lori sounds like an incredible person. I know you can't replace or replicate Clare, but she sounds like a match made in heaven by Clare."

"You know, Guy, I never would have looked at it that way. Thanks for that little bit of insight." Howard contemplated Guy's words for a moment.

"But, Howard"—Guy sat back with his last cup of coffee—"what's wrong with Mel? She's a great lady. I hear she's a top cop, and I know she's a nine or ten to boot. Why not her?"

"Truth be told, she's more like a sister to me than somebody I may be interested in romantically. We tend to see each other as family, not as part of a personal relationship. And anyway, she's involved with someone right now." He would not describe Mel's relationship with a married man.

Howard checked his watch. "Hey, look at the time. I gotta run. I'll update you on our big case sometime next week. Count on it. You've dumped enough information on me to make my head spin."

As Howard started walking out the door, he returned to Coyle. "I almost forgot the most important thing, Guy. I've decided to take the sergeant's exam. Thought you should know."

"That's great, HH, and I'll help you get there with some good study material. You still have to take tests in your department, right?"

87
CHAPTER

Lori showed up right on time. She dressed in her usual casual elegance of tan slacks, a soft blue blouse showing modest cleavage, and a necklace that Howard thought he had only seen on Princess Diana. She surprised him with a bottle of their favorite Grenache.

"Now we have two bottles to work on," he said as they laughed and hugged.

He gave her some backstory on Donny and Pat to ensure she knew whom they were dining with.

"Donny has been one of my best friends on the job for years. We've gone through a lot and saved each other's butt more than once. Pat—well, she's a bit different. She's not a girlie girl, but she has a good heart and is as intelligent as anyone I know. And she was in the army, trained bomb dogs in Iraq and Afghanistan, and transitioned to OHPD."

"I can't wait to meet Wonder Woman and her boy toy," Lori said, laughing at her comment.

Howard walked into the dining room as Marcia set the table for six. "Why six, Marsh? Who else is coming that you didn't tell me about?"

"Just Mel. She's working but will try to get approval from the watch commander for her code seven here, if that's all right. She only has less than forty minutes, but I thought I'd be—"

"That's fine, Marsh. I would have liked to know, but it may work out OK. Did you tell her what time?"

"I told her around six, if that's OK." Marcia was now looking for approval for her oversight.

"Perfect. Donny and Pat will be here about five thirty, so it should all work out."

Howard thought of Wolf's comment that everyone was convinced he and Mel were an item.

The Simpkins showed up at the appointed time. After meeting Lori, Pat was somewhat subdued. She pulled Howard aside.

"Jeez, if I had known about this, I would have dressed up more, HH. Give me a heads-up next time."

Howard hugged her and whispered, "No worries. You look great."

Introductions were made, and Donny gave Howard a thumbs-up after meeting Lori for the first time.

Drinks were served, and Howard joked about wearing jeans while Donny wore nice dress slacks. The laughs about the wardrobe made Pat a bit more comfortable with the circumstances.

They were just about ready to sit down, when the doorbell rang. It was Flowers. She walked into the entryway in full uniform, with her radio still blaring police calls.

"Hi, everybody. I'm starved." Her warmth and beauty filled the air as she turned down her radio.

Everyone sat in his or her seat, and Howard said, "May we all say grace?"

Bentley came to his side as he made the sign of the cross and led all in the blessing.

Donny spoke up first as the food was passed around. "Howard, aren't you going to introduce Mel to Lori?"

Mel, Lori, Howard, and Marcia broke out in laughter.

Mel took the floor. "Let me tell you and Pat the real story here." And she did. "And you guys thought HH and I were dating?" She had another laugh at Donny and Pat's expense.

"Well then, Mel, who are you seeing?" Donny decided to be direct about it.

"Nobody at the moment," she said, looking at Howard and Lori with a slight tear. "I'll be right back. Have to use the head." She excused herself, and Lori followed.

Lori led her to the far bathroom and closed the door. Mel couldn't hold back the tears.

Lori hugged her until the sobbing stopped. "I've never hugged anyone in uniform, Mel. But for you, I'll make an exception. What's going on?"

Mel broke down. "It's finally happened. We broke up. He's staying with his wife. His Chief is coming to our department and will be taking her place. He didn't think it would be the right time to do anything but break up with me. His fuckin' image is more important than me."

There was disappointment and hurt all wrapped up in one set of emotions.

88

CHAPTER

Lori held Mel for one more moment of consolation. "OK, Mel, get yourself together, wipe your eyes, and finish your shift as best as possible."

Mel regained her composure, straightened her uniform, and splashed her face to freshen up.

Lori knew she needed some additional consolation. "Come by the house about ten tomorrow, and we'll hash this out, OK?"

Mel returned to the living room with Lori and thanked Howard and Marcia for dinner before excusing herself to return to duty. Donny and Pat had no idea what emotional turmoil Mel was going through. They said their goodbyes as well.

Everyone pitched in to clean the table and place the dishes in the dishwasher. Donny and Pat thanked Howard for dinner, promised to reciprocate, and went a little overboard in their excitement for Lori and Howard's newfound relationship.

"Well, that was quite an evening!" Lori exclaimed after all the company had left. "Do you have any Baileys to top this off?" She laughed. "Howard, by the way, do you mind if I spend the night? I don't think I should be driving home. I still have some business with Marcia, so I can sleep in her room, if that's OK?"

"Business? What kind of business? What am I missing here?"

Marcia jumped in. "Dad, I told you a little about it, but Lori wants me to help her with a new line of products. I thought it was a good idea for her to bring her stuff here so she could go over it with me and spend the night. I have twin beds in my room, you know, just for girlfriends to sleep over."

He realized he had lost control of the situation. "Who am I to argue with you two? But only on two conditions. Lori agrees to go to Mass with us and the Cheesecake Factory for brunch afterward."

"Gosh, I don't think we've discussed this, Howard. But I would love to go to church with you. I grew up Catholic and used to go to Mass all the time. I just fell away from it over the years. And I've never been to the Cheesecake Factory."

Howard stared at her momentarily, collected his thoughts, and responded, "Well, you won't be able to say that after tomorrow. But you need to fill me in on Mel. What's going on?"

"Let me get my little suitcase and overnight bag from the car, and I will do just that."

"You mean this was already planned?"

Both Marcia and Lori laughed and shook their heads.

"Everything but church and the Cheesecake Factory," Marcia said with a hug.

It was all coming back to him now. Had he lost control of the family while Clare was still alive? Of course, he had given it up. He had control at work but needed to look at family differently. The academy taught the strength of command presence and how to handle any situation. One could step in and fix something, but Howard had learned one must always leave the command presence at work.

The family was different. Everyday life didn't fit neatly into command and control. The tools on his duty belt were useless at home. Hamilton saw his relationships blossom as his life changed and his children became young adults. He saw that the foundation of his command presence was failing him. He was ready to accept many things that happened at home, whether happy or tragic, and he had done so. He couldn't always be influenced by his need to take charge.

With what was happening with Lori and Marcia lately, his only control now was his response to whatever came next.

89

Howard knew it was going to be a crazy day. He would spend the entire week preparing for perhaps the most significant case he or anybody at OHPD had ever worked on. But he still could not get Sunday out of his mind.

*   *   *

Lori and Marcia sequestered themselves in Marcia's bedroom and only came out for a glass of wine to acknowledge that things were going fine. He woke up to coffee and avocado toast to get everyone an early morning start before Mass. They attended with Father Art and Deacon Rex Holcomb presiding.

Hamilton gave Lori a quick rundown on Holcomb. Besides being a deacon at Saint Elizabeth's, he was a retired LAPD officer who was an expert in satanic cults. Rex had assisted Howard in a case a few years back, and they remained friends. After services, he briefly introduced Lori to Father Art and Rex before they headed to the Cheesecake Factory.

Walking into the restaurant was eerie for Howard, but he said nothing. The hostess recognized him and asked if he wanted their usual booth.

"Of course," Marcia responded.

It was the same booth the family had used for years. Clare, Geoff, Marcia, and Howard had been staple figures on Sundays. Sitting with Lori and Marcia was different.

Marcia caught her father's eye and smiled with an "Everything will be fine, Dad" look. And it was.

*   *   *

But now a workday like no other was waiting for him and the entire N&V Unit.

He was early for a change and slipped into the workout room to push some iron. The unit members started dribbling in as the clock approached seven thirty. Written on the whiteboard was the message "Staff meeting at nine. Do not be late!"

Rikelman entered the office at seven thirty and immediately went to his office with a summons for Hamilton to follow. "Sit down, Hamilton. How was your weekend?"

"It was good, sir. Perfect."

What is going on here?

"Did anything happen, or did you talk to anyone about what is happening here?"

Howard figured it out. "I heard we're going to have a new chief. And before you ask, I know it's the current chief at Redondo, Rose Tustin. Captain Rod Tustin's ex. Or soon-to-be ex."

"You have great intel, Howard. Mind telling me how you knew?"

"Well, I had two different sources; each confirmed the other, but I would rather not reveal them now, if you know what I mean."

"That's good, Howard. You shouldn't reveal your sources. But be careful with what you hear, and verify your info before you act on anything."

"I will, sir, but no action is needed."

"I'll announce it at the staff meeting—oh, and another piece of information. Actually, it was really why I wanted to talk to you. Remember I had you track down a number a few weeks back? The one you traced to a back room upstairs by dispatch?"

"Yeah, I was wondering what that was all about."

"Do you know Tony Platt? He's a longtime patrol officer, working nights mostly."

Hamilton thought for a moment. "I do. I worked around him a few times. Seems like a good guy. Isn't his wife a dispatcher here?"

"Yes, she is. Thanks to you, IA put a phone trap on it to see who was using it. That number was used for a series of lewd phone calls to women all over the county. It turns out that Platt was the culprit."

Howard looked at Rikelman and mouthed, "What?"

"Yup. Platt knew where the key was kept, because his wife worked right next to the desk where it was hanging. He would casually visit when he was in the station, walk over, pocket the key, and disappear into the room. IA followed him on Saturday night and took him into custody after he made two phone calls they were monitoring. They also got him on camera entering the room."

"What an idiot," Howard said, shaking his head in disgust.

They both sat back to take in the moment.

"Did they use the blue light I recommended?" Howard asked.

"Yes, and again, you were right. It's pretty messy in there. By the way, they probably won't file charges on him, but we did get his resignation." Rikelman wiped his hands as if he were washing them.

"Anything else, sir? It's not even nine o'clock on a Monday." Howard got up to leave. "One last question, sir. Was his wife working at the time?"

"Yup."

"Like I said, sir, an idiot. And we don't need idiots here."

90

T he most surprising thing about the staff meeting was not about the new chief, Platt, or the extensive investigation everyone was working on. Al Garcia was back and in complete Disney form. He looked rested, energized, and glad to see everyone. He'd gotten a haircut, and his wardrobe was upgraded. No one, not even Howard, knew why he had been off for over a week, but everyone suspected he had been suspended for something to do with Bobby Bowers. The standard response was "It's a personnel matter."

Some of the guys were surprised by the announcement of who the new chief was, but as Scotty Moore eloquently said, "It doesn't matter who's up there." He pointed to the ceiling. "I still do the job here. Not going to affect me."

He was right, but everyone enjoyed letting the dolphins talk about Rod Tustin not returning and hooking up with some fed on the East Coast.

No one in the unit really knew Tony Platt, so other than the fact that his behavior tarnished the badge for everyone, it didn't seem to matter. The sympathy was all directed at Kathy Platt, the sexy dispatcher voice everyone drooled over. Platt would go on the list with Bresani and others who had tarnished the badge.

Rikelman and Barber spent time discussing the cartel and human-trafficking case. There was to be a big meeting on Thursday at the Backoffice, the intelligence think tank for LA County and the entire Southern California area. Only Barber, Hamilton, and Wolford would be attending with Rikelman. Of course, the barbs resounded with lip-smacking and oohs and aahs.

Rikelman announced that Disney would be loaned to detectives to work with Anita Hernandez and Jake DeLeon until the investigation was completed. He had developed a rapport with Hernandez's informant during an interview, and they did not want to inhibit that communication.

Hamilton and Wolford had their work cut out. They both spent the next few hours going over everything. It was impressive, but some holes needed to be filled.

"As stupid as this sounds, we don't know what these seven-digit numbers Anita's CI gave us mean. We think we know but have some more digging to do." Howard was talking to himself, but Wolford heard his muttering.

The meeting adjourned, and Pat and HH went directly to their office.

"Saturday night was great, HH, and I like Lori. She is a real girlie girl, and I'm not. I guess I have to warm up to her a bit."

"Well, get used to her, Pat. She's going to be around for a while. A long while, I hope."

"I'm happy for you, HH. Donny and I both. And she gets along well with Marcia. I couldn't believe that. Hey, not to change the subject, but I had this great idea yesterday, HH."

"And?"

"I have this old Army buddy, George DeLap. Good guy, but we were just buds, you know."

Howard's silence gave her permission to continue.

"I remembered he's now a prison guard at the Ironwood State Prison. That's one of our target prisons. Maybe he can help us."

"Wouldn't hurt, Pat. Get him on the line."

It took Wolford more than thirty minutes to finally locate him at the prison, only to find he was coming in on the night shift. They were not going to give out his number, so she left a message for him to call and said it was important.

"He'll be in at three, so let's keep working until then."

91
CHAPTER

T hree o'clock came and went with no call from DeLap. At four o'clock, Pat's cell phone rang.

"George here, Pat. Your message said it was urgent. Hey, good to hear from you."

Howard overheard the conversation, as Pat put him on speaker. They had not spoken in more than five years, so there was much to catch up on. She told him about working at OHPD and said she had an investigation on which she could use his help. After more than ten minutes of small talk regarding their careers and personal lives, Wolford finally got down to business and introduced Howard, saying it would be a three-way conversation.

"Sorry I couldn't call earlier. It takes me about an hour to check in, do a briefing, and get to my assigned pod. I oversee twenty-five inmates. So how can we help?"

Howard held a hand out to advise Wolford he wanted to take the lead. "George, thanks for making yourself available. Pat and I are working on a case where we discovered a series of debit cards with easy transfer capability that somehow ended up in your prison, Chuckawalla, and two other state prisons in Northern California."

"Is it the Red Dot cards?"

"Yes," Pat said excitedly.

Howard continued. "We found that funds are deposited into some accounts in your facilities, but we can't figure out your numbering system."

"It's a seven-digit code to identify our facility and the account user. The first two digits are the number of the facility, and ours is twenty-five. The remaining five numbers are associated with the inmate who holds the card. Most of our inmates use them as trust and commissary accounts to buy things here or pay for phone calls. Each card has a PIN they use for the phone calls, and they get them swiped at our commissary. We've even found that they trade them for favors or privileges. They are like a currency here."

Now we are getting somewhere.

Both Howard and Wolford were taking notes.

Howard said, "We knew some of that, but you gave us more details we lacked. OK, can I ask a few more questions?"

"Sure, but I don't know much more than that."

"Do you conduct any investigations regarding their use in the prison system?"

"Well, we've had a few times when Eme, the Mexican Mafia, has used them to pay off a contract hit here. We house a lot of Eme characters—but not as many as Chuckawalla and the other locations you mentioned. They seem to use them like candy."

"Is there someone we could talk to at your shop to assist us with drilling down on some of the accounts?"

There was a long pause. Then DeLap came back to the phone. "Sorry, but I have to handle an incident here. Can I put you on hold?"

"Of course," Pat responded.

The pause gave Hamilton and Wolford time to formulate some additional questions.

"OK, I'm back. There was a minor scuffle, and we had to break it up. Happens every day." The lack of excitement in his voice told volumes.

Hamilton got right back on track. "Do you track the use of cards and the deposited amounts?"

"That I couldn't tell you. As I said, we did find them used for that contract hit, but nothing lately. They use it for phone calls, food from the commissary, toilet items, and just about anything in exchange with other inmates. Deposits are generally made from family, but I think they can only send nine hundred dollars on each transaction."

Pat chimed in. "Is there someone, like in accounting, we could talk to?"

"I can give you a name and number, but he may have to get permission to talk with you or answer questions. Maybe even a search warrant. You know, even these idiots have some privacy rights."

Hamilton could tell he was done with the conversation and needed to return to his duties.

DeLap provided the name and number. "Great to hear from you, Wolford. If you ever get tired of the street, come on up here. We have all the OT you can handle, and the work is usually pretty easy."

They said their goodbyes and developed a checklist for the next person to talk with.

92

They needed a different strategy for their next call. The Wolf had taken advantage of a personal relationship with DeLap to get this far. Talking with a perfect stranger would be more difficult. Now that they had figured out the inside phone line numbering system, they could call any unit using the online directory on the state prison website.

They dialed and were surprised the call was picked up on the first ring.

"Steven Pomeroy here" was the greeting—precisely the person they needed to talk to.

Hamilton decided to keep it formal. "Mr. Pomeroy, this is Detective Howard Hamilton, and I have Detective Pat Wolford on the line with us. Your name was given to us by George DeLap."

Hamilton took the silence on the other end as a cue to continue. He laid it on heavy. He talked about working on a task force for human trafficking, drug transportation, and dealing. He made no mention of OHPD. He went into detail to ensure Pomeroy knew they were serious.

"Our investigation has led us to four state prisons where these cards are used extensively. We can get a search warrant for specifics, but we need some general information if possible."

"I'll try to help as much as I can. You're the only one ever to ask for my help. I've been trying to get someone to pay attention to what I've been seeing, but no one here seems to give a damn. You've got to understand, sir and ma'am"—he lowered his voice to almost a whisper to avoid being heard on the other end—"the people who run this place are stupid. Everything is designed to keep the inmates in, but they don't want to pay attention to keeping the bad stuff out. No one looks at the money floating inside around here. No one. Except me."

HH and Pat looked at each other with grins.

"Well, Mr. Pomeroy, you can be assured we will listen. But first, can we ask you some questions?"

"Be my guest, detectives. But first, let me close my door."

Hamilton updated Pomeroy on what they knew of the Red Dot cards.

"You are correct on most of what you told me. The inmates can only get exactly nine hundred ninety-nine dollars per deposit. But it can be one right after the other, and that's what I'm seeing with certain inmates, if you know what I mean."

"You mean Mexican Mafia types?" Pat felt the need to jump in with that question.

"Yes, ma'am. It's used like an EBT card that welfare recipients get. They can keep adding money to it like a bank. It's easy to transfer funds from one card to another, and if they have over five hundred dollars in the account, they get over four percent interest. Everybody gets interest, because I have never seen a card with less than one thousand in it. And I see them all."

"Mr. Pomeroy, we won't ask you about specific accounts right now. We only need to know how the system works."

"I understand, Detective, and you can call me Steven."

This guy is too good to be true.

Hamilton had an image of Pomeroy as a guy locked in a room with shirt sleeves rolled up and maybe even an eyeshade on.

"Steven, can I ask what you see as the average in each account?" Hamilton emphasized his first name to bond the newfound friendship. He could not resist.

"Most are over twenty-five thousand, and many are up to a hundred thousand. I'm glad you're interested." He was almost hyperventilating now. "Most everyone here also gets a stimulus check from the government because of the COVID stuff. I don't think that's right. I tried to tell my bosses, but they didn't seem to care. Oh, and here's an interesting thing I found out. I'm not sure it would interest you, but I thought it was strange."

"Try us," Pat said with a smile she hoped transmitted over the phone.

"In the system, particularly JPay, you can place a fraud alert on your card. It's designed so that anytime someone tries to use the card or gets an update on the balance that is not the cardholder, it notifies the person. For instance, the cardholder would be notified if you guys got a search warrant to look at the cards. But maybe I read too many crime novels."

"I don't think you read too many crime novels, Steven. I think you may have come across something very significant."

Howard and Pat nodded in agreement.

"Anything else, detectives? I don't think I've told you anything that would violate any of these guys' rights, have I?"

93
CHAPTER

Hamilton sat back to look at their masterpiece. "I think we're almost there. The intel from this case is piling up. I can't wait until Thursday's presentation."

"I've got more, HH. Watch this." She brought up another spreadsheet with numbers and data. "I took all the phone numbers from the Mercedes dealers' invoices for each car purchased by our suspects. Then I got phone numbers from Anita's CI and plugged them in. Some are the same, and some are different. Some are burner phones, but they've kept all T-Mobile accounts. I'm working on phone records."

"Pat, we can turn this over to the task force and let them get the search warrants. If they decide to do some surveillance work, they can ping them for locations and develop a mapping plot to see if there are any patterns." Hamilton was getting a rush just thinking about the possibilities.

"Howard, with all of this intel we've developed, it's like we have our own army to turn loose on these guys. This is awesome shit. I feel we need to tell somebody right now."

"I agree. Let's see if we can get the lieutenant and Barber to look at this."

The update went as expected.

"We need to give this briefing to the task force on Thursday."

Formulating a plan didn't take long. Rikelman seemed to be as excited as HH and the Wolf. They both could see his wheels were turning.

After Rikelman and Barber left Hamilton's office, Pat closed the door. "One more thing, HH. I may have overstepped my bounds here, but I've been talking to Donny about all of this," she said, waving a hand at their paperwork and computer screens, "and he may have something to contribute here."

"Like what?" He was all ears with everything Wolford had brought so far to the investigation.

"Well, Donny has become the department's expert on Carfax. Do you know what that is?"

"Carfax? Like car repairs?"

"It's a lot more than just repairs, HH. Just about every crime, carjacking, and kidnapping involves a car. Carfax has developed an app for law enforcement called Carfax for Police. It gets us data you can't get anywhere. Donny is working on getting it for the entire department so we all have it on our phones. I'm not sure where we are on it, though. He was talking about March or April, but we need it now for this case."

"But how does this help us?"

"There are a couple of things. We can trace ownership, service records, and collision repairs. We'd have access to every vehicle's history, including the original VIN, if they switch VINs, change out cars, or switch plates. We can even see if they paint the car a different color than when it came off the assembly line."

"OK."

"He's been working on a couple of cases where suspects are involved in multiple car crashes with the same vehicle, with the idea of collecting from an insurance company. After the car gets beat up to the point where it can't be used for insurance claims, they report it stolen. They make sure they don't just do it in one city, so they don't bring attention to themselves by one agency. Carfax gets information from insurance companies and feeds into the app."

"That's pretty incredible, Pat. Not sure how it ties in here."

"Me neither, quite frankly. But if you don't mind, I'd like to enter all of our cars from the dealership and those from the CI into the database and see what we get from Carfax for Police. Hey, it's worth a shot. What do we have to lose?"

"To quote a famous song, nothin.' Absolutely nothin.'"

They both had a good laugh.

"What song is that, HH?"

"I have no idea."

They laughed again.

94

CHAPTER

Hamilton used Tuesday and Wednesday to polish Thursday's presentation for the Backoffice meeting. Rikelman and Barber spent two days with Captain Peggy Dial and her staff at the HURT offices. Dial's people were involved in putting together a strike force that included multiple agencies, including INS and the Sheriff's Aero Bureau helicopters.

As a result of the information gained from the state prison contacts by Hamilton and Wolford, it was decided to bring in the California Department of Corrections and Rehabilitation and the Department of Homeland Security. The entire HURT unit of forty investigators from various agencies in the LA County area would be activated for the operation now named Torment. Captain Dial came up with the name because the cartels had tormented and abused the victims, and it was time to turn the tables and torment the suspects.

*　　*　　*

Howard managed to squeeze in time with Lori on Tuesday night but knew that Wednesday night would be taken up with preparing for the meeting at the Backoffice. Lori offered to prepare dinner at her place but only if Howard agreed to spend the night. She hinted in her conversation that the dinner she had planned would be special, and they had much to discuss.

What could be so important?

She coaxed him to come over early. Howard planned on engineering his EOW the best he could and confided in Pat that she was on her own if there was anything left to do after 1630.

Everything was coming together quicker than he anticipated. He decided to get a quick workout toward the end of the day, go home and shower, collect a few clothes for the next day, and surprise her by being early.

Hamilton pulled into the massive driveway, marveling at the home's size, beauty, and impeccable landscaping. He took it all in, seeing that the grass was manicured and the trees were trimmed to perfection, with enough leaves left on the ground to add to the setting. Many thoughts were going through his head about this new relationship as he approached the door and was greeted with a glass of wine, a smile, and a kiss.

"Oh, good. You came early. You can be my sous-chef and help me with the prep work."

She was as perky as she always was, but he sensed something else as they hugged and moved to the kitchen. Lori always wore the latest fashions, and tonight was no exception. She was decked out in a powder-blue pantsuit, low-heeled white shoes, and her understated jewelry. She glanced at his workout bag and tossed him an apron.

"Did you bring something to wear tomorrow? You didn't forget I asked you to spend the night, did you, Howard?" She loved to drag out her use of his name.

"Oh, no. I left my outfit in the car but brought in my other stuff: deodorant, shampoo, and other things I use. I'll get the rest later." He moved into his workspace on the kitchen counter to prepare a salad.

"That's one of the many things I wanted to discuss, my dear. Don't you think it's time for you to have some clothes here, at the ready, so you don't have to schlep your things in every time you get the invitation?" She smiled, moved toward him, and put her arms around his neck.

The kiss made him forget everything associated with work.

They resumed the prep work and sipped some wine, and Howard moved to the pantry to look for crackers to go with the cheese he was cutting. Lori followed, turned on the light, and continued her affection as she unzipped his pants, reached in, pulled his erection out, knelt, and took him into her mouth with a soft, gentle caress as his pants fell to the floor. She only spent a few minutes and then rose to kiss him.

"More later, Howard. Much more."

He shook off the fog of love, found the crackers, and made a design pattern for the cheese and fig jelly. He completed the salad preparation, and she showed him the stuffed manicotti she had prepared as she placed it in the oven.

"This will take a while, so let's take the cheese and crackers to the patio."

They talked about Marcia, her involvement with Lori's business, and her recent decision to major in business and accounting.

"She's a brilliant young lady, Howard. You should be proud."

"Oh, I am. She is so much like her mother. She never ceases to amaze me. Oh." He sat back on the patio chair, facing the small table. "I didn't mean to bring that up. About Clare."

Lori tried to assure him he was on safe ground. "Howard, that's fine. You don't need to be careful. Marcia and I talk about her all the time. I can handle it. I know how much she meant to you."

"Well, you never talk about—"

"Thomas? He was very good to me. Our last five years were, well, more of a business relationship than a marriage. He helped me establish myself, but there was little intimacy. I longed for it and could have found it elsewhere but chose not to. I think that's why the minute I met you and had the proper mourning time, I went after it. I mean you." She took a long sip of wine to ease the moment.

He smiled. "And I'm glad you did. I guess I needed to hear that. I wondered why it was so easy for you to take me to your bed, when this is where you and Thomas lived. I'm sure you saw my difficulty at my home."

"There's so much I want to discuss with you, my dear, but my lust gets in the way."

They laughed together once again.

"Is the salad ready?" she asked.

The dinner conversation continued with essential topics for both Howard and Lori. She talked about wanting to continue attending church with him, sharing his workday, and the trip to the Super Bowl. She continued to stress wanting him to be comfortable bringing several changes of clothes to her home. She asked more questions about Clare now that Marcia had brought up the issue.

"You make all of this so easy, Lori. It seems like everywhere I turn, you've made sure there are no difficult decisions."

She reached over to hold both his hands. "I've saved something for last, and I hope you don't mind."

"Something more? We touched on just about everything I can

241

imagine." Howard squeezed her hands and stared into her eyes with a longing that made clear dessert would have to wait.

"I've decided to put the house on the market and downsize a little. I'm unsure where to go, but I'll have time to consider it. But this place is too big for one. We'll have time to think about it. Never mind. I shouldn't have said it like that."

The silence was deafening.

Howard sat back in his chair, took a long drink of the Grenache, and stared at his plate. "You're not wasting any time here, are you, Lori? I mean, we've only been seeing each other for a few months, and you've made some life-changing decisions that involve both of us." He paused because he didn't want to spoil a good evening.

"Does that bother you, Howard? My plans are pretty simple. Develop my business, make personal decisions like downsizing, welcome you into my life, and love you. Whoops, I didn't—yes, I did. Damn it."

There was another long silence.

"Believe me, Lori, I'm ready for this as much as you are, but I'm just not used to moving so fast on everything."

"We have a saying in the business world, my dear. You snooze, you lose." She laughed at her attempt to ease the moment. "I know you're a cautious person. I see and admire it. I guess one of us has to be. I don't want to rush you, but this will all happen, I assure you, unless this is not what you want. Is it what you want, my dear?"

She got up from the table, moved to his side, pulled him up, and put her arms around his neck once again, kissing him on the neck with her tongue and pushing her body into him.

"You make this all so easy. I think I've said that before, but you do."

She pulled him by the arm, and they walked slowly up the stairs to a waiting bedroom. The dishes and dessert would have to wait.

95

Wolford and Hamilton rode with Rikelman and Barber to the Backoffice, leaving the station at nine. They took an older Crown Victoria, so the four passengers were more comfortable. They missed the commuter traffic and arrived ready to go. Barber drove.

Hamilton walked into the Backoffice, amazed at the enormity of the main room. It was out of a Pentagon war room, with various computer screens and monitors on the walls and a central screen over ten feet tall.

"You could launch a man to the moon from here." Wolford was the first to comment.

Rikelman moved his entourage to a side conference room, where Captain Peggy Dial and her staff were assembled. Introductions were made, and technical issues were handled to set up for what was to be a performance as much as a presentation.

Captain Dial reached out to shake with everyone but saved Hamilton for last. "I guess you are the man of the hour, Detective Hamilton. We've heard about your work and ability to analyze all the data gathered. You should be proud. Congratulations. I'm looking forward to your presentation."

Hamilton was unsure what to expect but found the captain charming, although she did not have the beauty that Lori or Mel exuded. Her handshake was soft but firm, and eye contact communicated she was expecting a lot from him today. Her command presence ensured everyone knew who was in charge.

"Yes, ma'am. Thank you, but it's all for naught unless we can bring these people to justice. I hope we can put some bad guys in jail with your group and everybody else involved."

"That's what we are here to do, Detective. But I warn you: we will be moving slowly on this operation to ensure we get everyone involved and no one on our side gets hurt. Let's do this."

Everyone responded to her command and moved to the main room, where the first slide for Operation Torment had already been posted on the big screen.

There were at least forty people in the room, but Hamilton only recognized a few of them. He saw Anita Hernandez, Jake DeLeon, and Al Garcia. Raid jackets told him INS, Department of Homeland Security, State Department of Corrections, Orange County Sheriff's Department, and HURT task force members were in the room. He would have to meet with them later to answer any questions.

He looked at Wolford. "Ready to go?"

"Absolutely," she responded.

Dial introduced the subject matter, went around the room for the attendees to identify themselves and their agencies, and asked everyone to hold questions until the end of the presentation.

Hamilton knew the information and could have presented it in his sleep. He had given Wolford sections to explain that she had worked up, and even though it seemed like ten minutes, it was 11:30 when he looked up at the clock. Silence engulfed the room.

Captain Dial started fielding questions. He and Wolford handled every question except for the information provided by Detective Hernandez. Anita responded, and by that time, it was approaching noon.

"Let's break for lunch, but the only people we need at one thirty will be the group from Orchard Hill and my supervisors. I want an INS, CDCR, and DHS representative and Orange County Sheriff's Department to attend this afternoon." There was no doubt Dial had a plan.

She ushered Rikelman, Barber, Hernandez and her team, and Hamilton and Wolford into her conference room, where sandwiches and drinks were waiting. They sat at the conference table and ate as Dial, her supervisors, and Rikelman huddled in a side office.

After twenty minutes, they all emerged, looking satisfied with their strategy.

"Here is how this is going to work." Dial jumped right in. "We'll do a dry run on our suspects next Thursday. According to our CI, they'll pick up over one hundred illegals from pangas along the San Diego and Orange

County coasts. We've identified Black's Beach in La Jolla, San Clemente Beach, Monarch Beach, and a spot just north at Laguna Beach. Only Black's Beach is in San Diego County, and the rest are in Orange County."

Captain Dial pointed to a map she'd brought up on her screen and projected for everyone. "We'll have aerial surveillance in the form of Orange County and LA County airships to provide air support. I want you, Detective Hamilton, and Wolford to be on those ships. We think we know where they will take the bodies, but we want to be absolutely sure. Detective Hernandez has identified warehouses in the Anaheim area to which they will most likely be deposited."

She paused for a moment, but no one had any questions. "I almost forgot one of the most important things. OCSO has offered Anaheim Stadium as the staging area for everything. They can land helicopters, and we could set up a temporary field jail if necessary. The baseball team is headed for spring training, so there will be only minimal staff, and the place is ours."

Hamilton raised a hand. "Why the dry run, Captain?"

"Good question. Our team has been working on some of these suspects for a while, but your information has brought it all together. We want these guys to get confident using the tactics and routes without being intercepted. According to the CI, they have already done one run. We'll give them two bites of the apple and then swoop down on the third. As I said, we must be patient and ensure everything is ready to go."

Dial looked at a calendar. "We'll target next Thursday, February second, for the dry run and the ninth to hit them with all we have."

The conversations continued with INS and the OC Sheriff's Department.

The representative from the Corrections Department approached Hamilton off to the side. "I have to ask, Detective: How did you get the information on the Red Dot cards and the money being laundered through our prison system?"

Oh shit, this could get ugly.

96

When in doubt, a stall was Hamilton's first reaction.

"Let me get my lieutenant to help with that question, sir." As far as he was concerned, everyone in the room was a sir or ma'am. He knew he was a low man on the totem pole and didn't want to get burned for answering this question.

He signaled Rikelman that he needed to talk.

After some discussion, Rikelman took the lead and walked over to the corrections officer, who had sergeant stripes on. "Hey, Sarge, my detective said you asked about the source of our information regarding the prison accounts. Is that correct?"

"Yes, sir. This is the first we've heard of such a large-scale insert into our system."

"Well, Sergeant," Rikelman said, and Hamilton immediately saw Norman Bates take over, "let me tell you something, Mr. CDCR. We have sources that you fuckin' guys don't. And they come from inside your organization. I'm not going to tell you where we got the information. That's for you to find out."

Rikelman started to back off. "I'm sorry, Sarge. It's just that we have been knee-deep in this stuff for a long time. You came in late in the game, and I was a bit defensive. Let's start over."

Rikelman ushered him to a side office. "All I can say right now is to look inside your department. I think you'll find what we did. It seems that all you are doing is just warehousing these guys and not keeping track of what the fuck they're doing inside. Got it? And if you have any more questions, call me after this thing is over. We'll go over everything with you. Don't bother my people right now. We're buried."

The corrections officer backed off and left the conference room quickly.

"That went well," Wolford said to break the tension.

Rikelman let his Bates persona go once the corrections supervisor left the room. He glanced at Howard with a look that said, "That's how it's done."

Everyone else ignored the confrontation.

Additional discussions were held to gather the information needed. Howard relayed the information he needed from the ground units to the HURT supervisors. He still needed to know if the suspects had changed plates and which wraps they would use on the Sprinters to tell which phony business they were portraying. He would require the radio frequencies of the walkie-talkies the suspects used, but he thought the information could be obtained on his scanners during the dry run. He also needed to talk to the two sheriff's departments' Aero Bureaus. There was still a lot of prep work to be done.

The ride back to OHPD was filled with lively discussions of Operation Torment. All were impressed with the Backoffice, Captain Dial and her people, and the overall enthusiasm for the operation.

"I just want to remind everybody of a couple of things," Rikelman said, talking to the windshield, with Hamilton and Wolford in the backseat. "This is not our operation any longer. We nurtured it, but it is now in the hands of the task force. Any information we get from now on has to be relayed to Dial's staff. I'll ensure Hernandez and her team know when we return to the station. Hamilton, do you know what needs to be done here?"

"Yes, sir, I think so. I have my list and will work through it with Wolford and keep you and Sarge in the loop."

"Any tricks up your sleeve, HH?"

"A few, sir. A few."

97
CHAPTER

Head calls were in order upon arrival at the station, and to-do lists needed to be developed. As Hamilton and Wolford were preparing to hibernate in his office, Rikelman asked Hamilton for a moment. Barber followed into Rikelman's office.

"Close the door, HH."

Uh-oh, what did I do now?

"You haven't done anything wrong, Howard, if that's what you think. If anybody did, I did with that corrections asshole. Anyway, if you hear from him, let me know. I need to apologize. But probably not until this caper is over. Anyway, that's not why I called you in."

"OK."

"As you can see, this thing has ballooned out of proportion. But that's a good thing, in my estimation. You started this thing, and I want to see you finish it. I want you to flashback to that presentation you made in that room. You were a low man on the totem pole, yet you commanded much respect because you had the evidence, stats, and material needed. And information—I mean intelligence—is the key here."

"I see that now, sir, but—"

"Where I'm going with this is, you need to get your ass into the books and start studying for sergeant. You need to get high on the list, do your time in patrol, and let me bring you back here, where you belong. Sam has a one-year plan to retire, and I'd like you back here to fill his position when he leaves. The Wolf can take your spot with some training, but you need to be in a position of increased responsibility around here, not just sitting on your ass."

"Whew, that's a lot to unpack, sir. I've been thinking along the same lines, and that's my plan, so we're on the same page. It's just that this takes a lot of time, and I need to prioritize my off days to study."

Barber jumped in. "We'll help with all of that after this case. Just start accumulating the needed material, and you'll do well."

Rikelman nodded in agreement.

"One other thing, HH. I don't know what or how this new chief thinks, so anything can happen. I won't say you're bulletproof, but we don't know much about her other than she was Tustin's wife—now ex-wife."

"Hey, I'll take my best shot, sir, and if it's not enough, so be it."

"That is nothing more than we would expect," Barber responded.

"Oh, one other thing, sirs. I have Super Bowl tickets in Arizona. This operation takes place on the ninth. Will there be a problem with me taking off on the tenth?"

"How the fuck did you get Super Bowl tickets, HH?" Rikelman gave him a look that would have killed an ordinary person.

He explained that his son, Geoff, was at ASU and told the entire backstory that had led to his getting tickets.

"Do you have a place to stay? Hotels are not cheap for these things. At least that's what I've been reading in the papers." Barber sat back with renewed pride in Hamilton.

"Got that covered too, sirs."

"Hamilton, you never cease to amaze us. Who the fuck gets tickets to the biggest game of the year?"

"I only have one thing to say, sirs."

"And that is?" Rikelman bit on the statement.

"Go Chiefs."

98

Hamilton walked out of Rikelman's office with his head spinning.

Focus, focus, and more focus.

It wasn't just the topic of the sergeant's exam. It was the case with everything else in his life, from being a dad to ensuring God understood his intentions and actions with Lori.

He needed to make one quick call before settling in with Wolford and tightening loose ends.

"Guy, can I drop by at EOW around five?"

The call to Guy Coyle was long overdue.

Five o'clock could not come fast enough. He and Wolford wrapped up everything for the day with phone calls and data dumps. He texted Marcia to say he would bring dinner home by about six thirty.

Guy's Craftsman home never ceased to amaze Hamilton: a manicured lawn, neatly trimmed boxwood hedges, and flowers planted for the season and in the right places. The painted trim glistened with white enamel, and the shake siding was the typical washed stone gray. It was right out of a magazine.

"City police! I have a warrant" was his greeting after three knocks in rapid succession.

"Enter at your own risk" was the response behind the door.

The standard man hug followed the greeting as Guy handed Howard an ice-cold beer. "Let's go to the patio for a few minutes before the sun goes down."

On the patio, Guy asked, "So what's happening in our little city, Howard?"

Howard filled him in on his case involving human trafficking and narcotics smuggling and the enormity of its proportions.

"It's become huge, Guy. I never thought I would be involved in something this big. I'm just a peon doing grunt work, and now I find myself in an international case."

"I told you that you were a shit magnet, didn't I?"

They laughed at the term Guy has used since the Karsdon homicide case several years back.

"It's pretty exciting, but I'm a bit exhausted with all the brain work I've had to put into it. I miss the streets."

"Well, Howard, those days will return to you but only if you study your ass off to make sergeant. If your department is like the rest, they'll promote you and throw you back on the streets to supervise other gunslingers."

"I think I'm more than ready, Guy. The hours are killing me. Plenty of overtime but no days off, and I think I'm getting a hunchback from too much computer time. I'm feeling like a nerd, not a cop. I sit in a fuckin' cubbyhole of an office and stare at screens. I haven't put cuffs on anybody for a long time. I'm really a street cop at heart. This doesn't seem right. And with all this, I need to pay more attention to my personal life."

"Do you have one?"

Howard told him about Geoff at ASU, Lori, and the connection between Lori and Marcia. He omitted any reference to Sam at Home Plate or his association with Gary Laurenti.

"This calls for another beer. Are you ready?"

"No, I'll pass. I've got to pick up takeout for Marcia and me tonight."

Coyle left the patio and returned with one more beer for himself, mounted on top of a banker's box. "Here you go, Sarge."

"What's in the box?"

"Your future—that's all. In this box is the study material you can use to prepare for the test. Some of it's outdated, so you need to update the sources." He set the box down and took a swig from a new beer. "I have sample tests for the written and oral exam, case law, search and seizure, and other odds and ends. If OHPD is like every other department, they'll use a standardized state test, and all of this info is based upon those instruments. You'll have to add your department policies, but that shouldn't be difficult. Here you go."

Coyle set the beer down and handed the box to Hamilton with a big smile, finishing with "Sarge."

"Wow, I can't thank you enough, sir. I mean Guy." He still had trouble viewing Coyle as a peer and friend. "I have to ask you a big question now."

"What's that?"

"What's going on with you and Chief Rose?"

Coyle paused to look away for just a moment.

"You're still seeing her, aren't you?"

"Yeah, but it's still on the QT until the divorce is final. She starts in your department on Wednesday, the first day of March. That's the first city council meeting of the month, and she'll get sworn in with a big hullabaloo. I'll be there but somewhere in the back row."

"I don't plan on attending, Guy. I want to stay in the background. The sergeant's exam is on Saturday, April Fools' Day, if you can believe that."

"Of course. I understand. I'll help with the oral board prep later, but I'm confident you'll do well." He walked Hamilton to the door. "Get your ass inside the books, and don't come out until the test."

"Right now, that's one of us with confidence, Guy. Thanks for the beer."

99
CHAPTER

All the teams were working on their regular cases. Barber was still vetting applicants for Bowers's replacement, but everyone was notified partner changes could soon be made. The Everlys were the only ones unhappy with that announcement.

Hamilton wanted to take the time to make sure all the information he had compiled was sent over to the HURT task force for their search warrants. His information would be the key that locked up a lot of bad guys.

He also had one other task but dreaded making that call.

"Hello, Sam. This is Howard Hamilton. Please call me back." He left his number in her voicemail.

Maybe that'll be enough. She won't call back, will she?

He needed closure because he thought he may have led her on and then just walked away.

Within two minutes, his phone rang, and he saw the number.

"I'm sorry, HH. I was outside cleaning the deck and didn't hear the phone. How are you?" Sam sounded bright and perky, more so than when he had seen her at Home Plate.

"I'm good, Sam. I hope you don't mind I asked Gary for your number."

"Not at all. He told me."

"So you took off pretty quick. I didn't even get a chance to say goodbye."

"I know. Pedro was just not for me. To tell you the truth, Southern California was not for me. I'm much more comfortable up here. Did Gary tell you I came back to Sausalito?"

"Yes, he did."

"Well, I got my old houseboat back and am living the good life in the marina again." She sounded comfortable with her new surroundings.

Howard went for the line he had rehearsed for at least a week. "I just wanted to call to tell you I'm sorry we didn't get to spend more time together. I really enjoyed your music and you."

She laughed briefly. "Let's not kid ourselves, HH. You had no time for me, and I could see that. In another life, you and I could … Anyway, I saw that you either were not finished grieving for the loss of your wife or maybe had something else going."

"It was a little of both, but—"

She interrupted him. "No need to apologize, HH. I get it. We can still be friends. Hey, if you're ever in the Bay Area, call me. And if you get over where you are right now, who knows, huh?"

"Thanks for understanding, Sam. You're the best."

"Not best enough, I guess. Thanks for the call, Howard. I really do appreciate it." She hung up.

Howard would have to consider his call to Sam something he'd needed to get done.

He couldn't do much more on the most significant case of his career, so he let his mind drift to Lori's many comments of late. She was going to sell her home and downsize. He had to do some serious thinking. There was no way he would ever consider selling the house he and Clare had built, or would he? He had to decide if the relationship was heading where he thought it was going.

He didn't know what Geoff's plans would be. He knew Geoff might never return to Orchard Hill. It would be just him and Marcia. And Lori. Would there be a time when Lori would ask to spend the night at his place—and not to use the twin bed in Marcia's room, as she had recently? While it was faint, he still could feel Clare's continued presence every night as he slept.

Thanks to Lori's influence, Marcia was in a perfect place right now. She had a steady relationship with Brandon, but Howard didn't want to think about his only daughter in some stranger's arms.

His career was another thing, however. He was plateauing in the new position he had pioneered. It was time to mentor Wolford and move on. What if he didn't make sergeant? Would he go back to patrol? Would he apply for a detective slot with Donny?

He decided to spend that night organizing the material Coyle had given him to study for the sergeant's exam. He would get additional direction from Barber and Rikelman and plot out time each day to review the various exam components. But after the big case, he longed to return to the street.

With those issues to contend with, his guidance would come from various sources. He would seek the counsel of Donny, his best friend, but away from the Wolf. Then there was Guy Coyle. And Father Art. He knew what he wanted to do but was hesitant to pull the trigger without some reflection from those he trusted.

Maybe he would stop by the church on his way home.

100

Howard's priority for the week was Operation Torment DR, or dry run. Intelligence from Hernandez's CI said they would send the pangas from the northern tip of Mexico to the four designated landing sites of Black's Beach in La Jolla, San Clemente Beach, Monarch Beach, and Laguna Beach.

Local gangs had been recruited to escort all immigrants from the boats up through the beach to a predesignated location, from which the Sprinter buses would take them to another point in Orange County. This was all to be done before daybreak, under the cloak of darkness. By the time all passengers were loaded onto the Sprinters with blacked-out windows, the sun would rise, and it would look like just another dog grooming or plumbing contractor going to work. No one would be the wiser.

The staging area meetup was at four in the morning at the Anaheim Stadium parking lot.

Hamilton and Wolford were to be picked up by the Aero Bureau choppers at Anaheim Stadium. From the air, their job was to monitor the Sprinters as they went to their intended locations, follow them to the pickup point, and then follow them back to a safe harbor someplace in Orange County. The plan was to fly at an altitude high enough that cartel surveillance teams would not pick them up but low enough that they could spot their intended targets. With the tricks Hamilton had played weeks prior, it would be easy.

* * *

Hamilton met Donny for lunch on Wednesday at the Barrio Queen. He was looking forward to some authentic Mexican food again.

"Are you and Lori that serious, HH?"

"I think so, Donny."

"What do you mean you think so? You either are or aren't."

"We've never proclaimed the L-word if that's what you mean. We know we like each other, and I think she loves me, but we're both afraid to say it."

They each ordered the taco and enchilada combo with Arnold Palmers.

"Don't you think it's time to do that?"

"Well, I talked to Father Art about that."

"Father Art? What—"

"Yeah. How does a priest who has never been married have so much insight into relationships? He made so much sense. The guy was clairvoyant with his insights into marriage, even his views on priests' celibacy. He stressed living together to ensure compatibility. What priest would do that?"

"Hell if I know. Whoops." Donny laughed at his attempt at humor.

"I know you're not religious, Donny, but you should meet him. He expresses his thoughts from a practical and logical perspective. He stressed that the most important thing we could do at this point was to stay close to God and ensure I brought Lori back into the church's fold. If all those elements were addressed, it would work out for everybody, including Geoff and Marcia."

"I get back to my question. Are you guys serious? Are you in love?"

"Well ..." Howard stammered, trying to find the proper response. "It seems like we talk around it. She tells me how much I mean to her. I do the same, and we seem to spar around like kids waiting for the first person to drop the l-bomb."

Howard talked about the sale of Lori's house, what he should do with his home, Geoff and Marcia, and the issues yet to be addressed. By that time, their food had arrived. The waitress could see their weapons under their shirts and asked if they were detectives.

"Yes, ma'am, OHPD's finest," they said simultaneously, as if it had been rehearsed.

She commented on how much her customers talked about the department and their support, while other cities were being torn down and defunding the police.

"No one here I've talked to wants anything to do with those other crazy cities. More and more people are just staying here, supporting our local businesses, because you always seem to catch the bad guys."

"Great to hear, Geri," Hamilton said. He looked at her name badge to call her by name. "Is that your real name or your waitress name?"

"Real name. Why?"

"Sometimes people use a phony name when they're working. Just had to ask."

"That's me. Geri."

Donny and HH thanked her for her attention and vowed they would see her again. They made sure to leave a big tip.

"See how easy it is to have a conversation with the opposite sex, HH? Go try it at home."

Nobody likes a smart-ass, even if it is your best friend.

Howard mulled over his next comment. "Hey, can we talk shop here a little?"

"Sure, what's up?"

"I'm not so confident of my next steps. I've been studying for the sergeant's exam, but my habits suck. Barber told me he was retiring in a year and said the job was mine if and when I made sergeant and did my time in patrol. That's a lot of stress." Howard motioned to the waitress for another Arnold Palmer.

"Yeah, but you are up to it."

"I'm not so sure. With this new chief coming in, who knows what she'll do with the promotional process? We all may be working for fuckin' Flowers."

"You can't control that, buddy. Just knuckle down. The worst case is you come over to detectives. I'll find you a spot."

They parted ways, agreeing to catch up again soon.

* * *

Howard would be ready for that damn exam.

But then there was Lori. He knew he wanted to make it work, but how would he handle the L-word issue? He decided the best way was also the easiest.

"Dinner tonight at Bourbon and Bones?"

"What time will you pick me up?"

"Earlier the better," Hamilton responded, wanting to ensure he didn't get cold feet. "Five thirty at your place. See you then."

Reservations were made, the office was organized and cleaned up, and he was out the door. He stopped at home for a change of clothes, freshened up, and, finally, stood tall at her door.

"You sounded like you were in a hurry, Howard, so I'm ready. But first, we need a small glass of wine to celebrate."

As usual, she was dressed for success. A black top with light sequins and black slacks accentuated her shape and ensured all would take notice.

Uh-oh, what did I miss?

"Do you know what today is?" she asked.

"Uh ..."

She laughed and put a hand on his chest. "That's OK, my dear. You aren't expected to remember, but today is our six-week anniversary of meeting at my dinner party. Six weeks—can you believe it?"

This was the moment he had been waiting for. He took a deep breath. "You know, Lori, I think that's why I fell in love with you. You never forget the small things that make me realize how lucky I am. I do love you, you know."

Lori started to reach for her drink, stopped, and turned to face him. "Are you just saying that Howard, or—"

"I am saying it because I mean it. I've fallen hopelessly in love with you and want you to feel the same."

They moved in closer but still had enough space to maintain their conversation.

"I've been in love with you since day one, Howard. I think you know that. I never wanted to say anything, because I was afraid you wouldn't feel the same way."

Her gaze told him she was serious. Their eyes locked as they both set down their wine to kiss and embrace with the passion each of them now knew was more than lust, more than heat, and more than just a close relationship. It was what each of them had longed for, and now, finally, they had arrived at the same spot at the same time.

They never made it to Bourbon and Bones. They never made it to the bedroom.

101

Hamilton felt comfortable about the overall direction of the most extensive investigation he had undertaken since becoming a police officer. As much as he wanted to be part of the boots on the ground when D-day came, he knew he was needed up in the air, directing and tracking the bad guys. For the most part, his work was done, and it was a matter of execution by the task force.

Wednesday was Operation Torment dry run minus one. It would be a short day because all unit members were carpooling to Anaheim Stadium and the staging area to shadow the cartels at three o'clock the next morning. It would be their first time in a six-passenger LASD Aero Bureau helicopter for Hamilton and Wolford.

All unit members, including Rikelman and Barber, arrived Thursday morning. The Wolf and Hamilton had driven separately, not knowing when their part of the operation would end. They walked over to the two helicopters participating in the day's campaign. According to the pilot, Sergeant Dan Broderick, one was a Sikorsky H-3; that would be the lead scout ship.

"You two will be in our newest purchase, a Eurocopter Airbus AS350B2. It holds six passengers, but you two and a member of the HURT task force will be observing." Broderick ran a hand over the fuselage as if petting a dog. "This is my new baby. As you can see, it's a three-blade prop with new Garmin instrumentation. State of the art. It even has the built-in blue fluorescent light system you requested, Detective Hamilton."

"Looks like everything is built in and ready to go. How long can we stay up?"

Broderick smiled again. "We can stay up almost a complete shift, or four to six hours, based on our speed. She holds over one hundred forty gallons of fuel and has a range of over two hundred eighty miles. Capacity is thirty-five hundred pounds, so we should be light and ready for the big time."

The Wolf said, "I flew in the Sikorsky Black Hawk in Iraq. It seemed much heavier and bulky compared to this sleek baby."

Broderick stepped back in admiration. "Hey there, Detective Wolford, you went up in the mother ship. Yes, it is much more durable, but this isn't for combat, just aerial surveillance and transport. We'll be cruising at about one hundred twenty-five knots until we reach our destination. Circling will take up a bit of fuel, but we're OK."

Wolf continued her query. "I was an EOD K9 handler, so they dumped us behind the lines. Where do you keep these ships when they're not in use?"

Broderick smiled at her knowledge of helicopters. "We're staged out of Long Beach Airport, right up the road from here. We cover the entire county with a large fleet supporting patrol and detective units. The Euro is soft and quiet, so we can get low, and no one can hear us until it's too late."

"That's exactly what we need for this operation, Sarge. Let me tell you what we have in mind." Hamilton finally got a word in.

* * *

Captain Dial and her staff held the briefing inside the stadium and within walking distance of the helicopters. She was her usual efficient self, with a command presence that communicated she was in charge of Operation Torment.

"We'll do this again next week for real, so, everyone, enjoy the dry run. Ground units, stay out of sight of our targets. We have GPS on their cars, so the Backoffice will track them along with Hamilton's people."

She displayed on a PowerPoint presentation photos Hamilton had sent over depicting the various Sprinter vans, white, gray, silver, and black. All had commercial wraps showing a dog groomer, plumber, florist, or handyman.

"We'll meet back here after we put our targets away with what I hope is a lot of confidence they do not know we are watching. Any questions?"

Dial fielded a few questions and asked people from her team to answer them. There were more than forty in attendance: nine from the OHPD narcotics unit and others from various surveillance teams from the HURT task force, LASD, and OHPD detectives, including Hernandez, Jake DeLeon, and Al Garcia.

Hamilton only knew his responsibilities but assumed everyone had a critical assignment.

Operation Torment was big—very fucking big.

102

CHAPTER

Hamilton and Wolford were given flight instructions, helmets with built-in headsets, and plenty of room to spread out behind pilot Dan. Broderick warned them of the forty-two-inch span of the blades and told them to stay low when boarding. Howard and Wolford slowly crouched to the chopper, not wanting to even think of raising their heads near the whirling blades, which could cut heads off easily. They took off quietly and banked south, heading for La Jolla in San Diego County.

In her briefing, Captain Dial indicated that the San Diego County Sheriff's Department would be operational for D-day. However, because this was a dry run, at her request, SDSO would monitor the radio frequencies the task force personnel used on a just-in-case basis.

As they approached the San Diego coastline just before dawn, visibility was as clear as the eye could see.

Howard pointed to the caravan of pangas as they inched along the coast. "See how they almost move as if they're tied together? I hope we get this kind of visibility next week."

"Don't count on it," Broderick said through his headset.

The pangas moved north, breaking water swiftly across a relatively calm ocean, oblivious to the eyes in the sky watching their every move. The boats appeared to be overloaded from their capacity of fifteen. More than likely, the cartels would cram at least twenty or more on each, regardless of the safety issues. It was all about the money.

It was like precision clockwork. Five pangas were lined up about one mile from shore. As they serpentined through the waters, the first boat peeled off and headed for the beaches of La Jolla. Even in the dark, the magic eye from the Eurocopter could track their movements. A group of six or seven, assumed to be gang members, was seen huddled on the shore.

One Sprinter van was parked on the first street that parallels the ocean, waiting for pickup.

Hamilton directed the observer seated on the right side of the cockpit to shine the blue fluorescent light on the van. To his surprise, the letters *OHMB* glistened in the night, letting him know Jeff Dryer had a sense of humor. He had asked Dryer to mark the recently purchased vans with the fluorescent paint he had provided. Dryer wanted to get a commercial in for his business. Everyone in the airship had a good laugh.

Hamilton and Wolford watched from their position more than fifteen hundred feet above the ocean as the vessels, loaded with at least twenty people, landed quietly on the shore. The teams of gang members working with the cartel members were waiting and assisted the passengers in getting out of the boats. It looked as if some of the new arrivals were lined up and released to follow another gang member one by one as they quickly walked up a steep incline to the waiting bus.

"Sergeant Broderick, sir, can you turn on the blue light so we can better see those things left on the beach?"

"Your wish is my command, Detective. Watch this." Broderick circled the chopper and streamed the invisible beam toward the beach.

From what they could discern, some occupants could go from the shoreline to the waiting van, and others appeared to be detained. They saw a small, noticeable pile of illuminated objects on the beach. It seemed they had cut wristbands from some immigrants and released them, while others kept the wristbands on and were segregated from the remaining group members. Hamilton's intel indicated the wristbands would illuminate under the specialized light they were using.

Hamilton activated his mic and announced, "I remember from my conversations with Anita Hernandez that her CI said there were markings on the wristbands indicating if they had paid the cartel fees. Some had the money but only agreed to pay when they got here. Others had to make specific arrangements or face the cartel's wrath. If all fees had not been paid, they would be detained until arrangements could be made. That's why the markings on the wristbands were important. They had codes for who paid and who owed."

The fifth panga came close to shore but quickly unloaded two or three boxes and returned to the remaining boats continuing north along the shoreline. Hamilton and Wolford watched as suitcases or cartons were unloaded and handed off to other members of the cartel waiting on the beach. Was this clothing of the migrants or drugs? Next Thursday's operation would reveal much that they did not know about this operation.

Wolford jumped on the frequency. "Sergeant Dan, can you contact the San Diego County Sheriff's to go to the site and retrieve the discarded wristbands and anything else they may find down there?"

"Roger that, but it will take a few because they're not on the scene for today's dry run."

"Got it."

That information would prove invaluable in identifying the codes on the wristbands used by the cartel to keep track of their prey.

103

CHAPTER

Hamilton reached into his backpack, pulled out his laptop, and opened a software package provided by Packer in the intel class.

As he opened the database, he explained to the Wolf, "You'll learn this in Packer's class, but watch this. You won't find this in any typical hardware scanner. Look below. They're using handheld radios to communicate. They probably have them on the boats. The local gangs escort everybody, and the Sprinter driver has one."

He moved the laptop so she could see where he was going on the screen. "This software-defined radio system, or SDR for short, uses my laptop to receive the frequencies they're using. It can decode to find out which radio frequency is used."

"Don't we need a search warrant, HH?"

"I gave the information to Dial's people, so they'll put it in if they feel it's necessary. But this is open source, so anybody can monitor these frequencies. You'll learn all that in the school."

He moved his cursor around to two sites. "Watch this." He smiled deviously at Wolford as he called up the Family Radio Service (FRS). "This shows fourteen radio channels available, which operate on fourteen specific frequencies. The most common use of this is families on vacation or security companies who need to localize their communication."

Hamilton displayed a screen with channel 01 and a frequency of 462.5625. "You see, we have channels 01 to 14, and the frequencies go from 462.5625 to channel 14 and frequency 467.7125. I'll scan all fourteen channels to see if they use the FRS system." It took him two minutes.

"This is above my pay grade, HH."

"No worries, Pat. It won't be after the class."

He toggled the cursor around various databases. "Nothing there, so let's go to the more sophisticated General Mobile Radio Service, or GMRS. I think this is where we'll find them."

Hamilton opened a new page listing sixteen channels and sixteen frequencies different from the FRS. "This system is more robust at fifty watts, allowing the signal to transmit farther. It generally requires a license, but the FCC is so lax it's seldom enforced."

Wolford was all eyes. "I can't believe it. Are you shittin' me, HH? This is incredible James Bond type of stuff."

"There are a few other RFs we could search, but let's look." He ran the software program through all sixteen channels. "Bingo! There it is. They're using GMRS channel 7 frequency 462.700. Let's listen."

He turned up the volume and heard the Spanish language from one person to another. He could make out some of the words because it was more Spanglish than pure Hispanic language.

"These guys are pretty sophisticated if they know about this radio frequency system." Howard made a note of the frequency and channel and closed his laptop.

He turned to the Wolf. "You'll pick up on this fast. It's just the tip of the iceberg regarding radio frequencies. The old-time dope dealers used CB radios, and that was easy. These guys are a notch above all of that. But it's still analog, so it's not that difficult if you know what you're doing."

Wolford just shook her head in amazement.

"One more thing, and I'll shut up and let you learn more from the school. I can set it up like an email or conference call so the command post base station at Anaheim Stadium can listen in, as we will next week. I can also have the Backoffice people monitor and record it. Cool stuff. Don't you think?"

"Right now, I don't know what to think. You have so much crammed into that head of yours. I'm not sure I can grasp it all."

"Hey, it took me a year and a half to get this far, and I don't think I've scratched the surface."

CHAPTER

The following two hours were spent tracking the remaining drop-offs at San Clemente Beach, Monarch Beach, and Laguna Beach. All were choreographed like the La Jolla drop-off. The Backoffice techs tracked the Sprinters with GPS, which the Everlys and OHMB had mounted inside each van. The surveillance ground units had followed the first Sprinter to an industrial park in Garden Grove, just north of Anaheim Stadium.

Broderick turned the airship north and headed for the staging area at Anaheim Stadium. "Get what you needed, detectives?"

"I think so," Hamilton responded, "but it's very frustrating from up here to see what we saw and not do anything about it. I can't wait until next week."

The headsets used for communication were working perfectly.

"I see this all the time. We track homicide suspects, dope dealers, and others; bed them down; and wait two or three days before the ground units go in to take them into custody."

"I don't know how you see it from up here, but I need hands-on down there. Being in this ship is great, but you're too far removed from the street," Wolford said.

"I spent ten years on the street in patrol, worked detectives, made sergeant, and went back to patrol for two years before coming here and getting my wings. I've had my time in the street. It's a young man's job— well, young women's too. Being up here, I can participate in many cases and do what I love—fly—and go home safe every day."

Safe unless you crash.

Broderick advised everyone to prepare for landing as they saw the big *A* sign coming up off the 57 freeway.

"This is almost surreal," Hamilton said to Wolford as they approached the colossal sign announcing Anaheim Stadium. "I feel like we are at Disneyland or in a movie."

"I know, HH. I think I see the Matterhorn from here," the Wolf said.

They waited for Broderick to land the chopper, took care in exiting the airship, and gave a thumbs-up to Broderick.

Everyone reconvened in the conference room. Captain Dial conducted a debriefing, reviewed specific assignments, and advised them they would be in touch during the week for any modifications to Operation Torment.

Hamilton met with his counterpart in the HURT task force, gave him information regarding the radio frequencies used, and updated him on the fluorescent markings on the vans. It was great to have just one contact point with the task force. It made the transfer of information much more straightforward.

According to Hernandez, all vans eventually wound up at an industrial park, where additional processing, payment arrangements, and other issues were addressed, such as the migrants' final destination in the United States.

The CI told Hernandez and Garcia that those who had not paid were interviewed to determine their ability to pay, threatened, and, in a few cases, assassinated on the spot. The bodies were shoved into fifty-five-gallon barrels and loaded onto trucks for an unknown destination. Children were kept with their parents, but if there was a young teenage girl, she would be separated and moved to another location in Southern California to perform acts of prostitution with the oversight of a pimp or madam.

"I sure wish we could be on the ground next week to take these assholes into custody," Wolford said.

"Me too," Hamilton responded. "Being up in the air is fun, but there is nothing like taking those guys into custody, getting the cuffs on, and marching them to jail. Nothing like it."

Just then, he saw the Everlys as they returned to the command post from their surveillance responsibilities. "Hey, Don and Phil, you guys did a great job marking the tops of those vans with *OHPD*, but the Mercedes dealer did a one-up. They marked theirs *OHMB* as a commercial for the dealership."

Both Everlys got a good laugh.

"Well, HH, those assholes won't be laughing next week when we put the clamps on 'em and seize those Sprinters. I can't fuckin' wait," Phil said.

"I think this is a SWAT operation for the takedown next week. I'm concerned with the weaponry they may have and their numbers at that industrial park. Too much for us to go in and seize everything and wrap them up in cuffs," Howard said.

Captain Dial was walking past them and overheard their conversation. "We're a step ahead of you on this, Hamilton. Sheriff's Enforcement Bureau and SWAT are ready for next week. I think you're right. They'll have armament more than just handguns. This operation has too many moving parts, and I hope we've planned for all of them."

"Yes, ma'am. Roger that." Hamilton spoke for all who had joined the conversation. Then he approached Captain Dial off to the side. "I have a special request."

105
CHAPTER

Wolford and Hamilton drove back to OHPD at about noon after grabbing sandwiches at a local Chick-fil-A near Anaheim Stadium. Hamilton's phone rang when they were discussing the operation of D-day minus one. It was Geoff.

"Hey, Dad, I've not heard from you in a while."

"Well, Geoff, just been busy with work and stuff. How's it going at ASU?"

"Great, but I wanted to check in to see if all of your plans have been made for coming to the Super Bowl. Things are crazy over here, and hotels are booked solid. I don't want you to miss out. And you know it will be the Chiefs and the Bengals, right?"

"Yeah, go Chiefs, I think. I like both quarterbacks and coaches, so I'm a bit torn."

"Well, over here, it's about fifty-fifty too. I'll be working outside of the stadium, but I think you, Lori, Marcia, and Brandon will get to see a great game."

"Let me check on our accommodations, and I'll get back to you to tell you where we will stay. Will we have time to meet Marty?"

"Of course. That's one of the reasons I want you guys over here early. We'll have two days before the game if you come on Friday. I'll make the dinner plans. You just get here, Dad."

The conversation between Geoff and Howard was going rapid-fire. They seemed to be on the same page.

"Got it. I'll let you know."

They hung up with an agreement to reconnect.

"Wow, going to the Super Bowl, HH? That's right after this thing goes down. You timed it well." The Wolf was impressed.

Howard explained Geoff's connection for tickets and Lori's condo in Scottsdale. Howard pointed the Charger toward the interconnecting freeway that would take them back to Orchard Hill.

"Have to ask, HH: Are you going to be OK with Marcia and Brandon being, you know, together over there in the next bedroom?"

"Hmm. Honestly, Pat, I haven't thought about it. But now that you mention it, no, I'm not. Gotta think through this."

"How old is she?" Wolf asked innocently.

"Nineteen."

"Do you think they've slept together?"

"Brandon and Marcia?" He posed the question in a serious mode.

"Yeah, Brandon and Marcia," she responded with an "Are you serious?" look.

"I don't know, and quite frankly, I can't get that picture in my head."

"Well, you'd better think this through. She may plan to do it and not ask for your OK."

He turned onto the freeway that would take them home. "Let me call Lori. Do you mind?"

"No, but what has she got to do with it?"

"Well, it's her condo, and I want to find out if it's a three-bedroom or if she has a fold-out couch."

"What? You're kidding, right?"

"No, I'm not," he said as he hit speed dial for Lori.

"Yes, my dear?" was Lori's answer to his ring.

"Hi, Lori. We're returning from Orange County—Pat and me. Geoff called to make sure we were on track for the Super Bowl. We're staying in your condo, right?"

"Yes, it's all set. It's turnkey, and all we have to do is walk in."

"Well, is it a two-bedroom or three?"

"It's a three. Why?"

"Marcia and Brandon are coming too, so I want to ensure enough bedrooms."

"You mean so they can have separate rooms?"

There was a long pause as Howard tried to be as casual as he could. "Yes."

"Have you discussed this with Marcia?"

"No." There was a short pause, and then Howard meekly asked, "Would you?"

"I will, but you might not like the response."

106

CHAPTER

There was silence for the next ten minutes as they exited the freeway to the surface streets of Orchard Hill.

"HH, I know you're a religious guy, but today's young people are, well, you know, more modern in their thinking." Discretion had never been one of Wolford's strong points.

"I must think this through, Pat. I get it, but it'll take some thinking about it."

They arrived at the station and returned to the N&V office. Barber and Rikelman were already at their desks.

"I just got through briefing the acting chief about this morning. The new chief doesn't start until the first of March, but she and Pierson are talking. I told him that things went as planned," Rikelman said.

"They did," Howard responded. "But it was very frustrating to see all those crimes being committed, and we just did nothing."

"I get it, HH," Barber said, "but the greater good and all that bullshit, you know?"

"Hey, Sarge, OK if we go EOW? Pat and I are a bit tired, getting up at o-dark-thirty."

"We all are, HH. Everybody is done for the day. See you on Monday."

Howard remembered something he needed to confide to Rikelman. "Oh, Lieutenant, do you have a minute?"

"Sure, HH, what about?"

They walked into the lieutenant's office but did not close the door.

"Well, I've been studying for sergeant, you know."

"Uh-huh."

"Any possibility the new chief will change the process? Like no written exam and just an oral board and package review? I've heard other departments are doing that. But it sounds like it would be too political."

"I don't think she'll even get to deal with that issue. Finding the ladies' room will be her priority in this maze of a building. But I'll do some checking. You might call soon-to-be captain Rydell because he's over HR and will probably have some insight."

"Thanks, Lieutenant. As always, you have the answers."

"Not always, HH, but that was an easy one."

On the way to leave the station, Howard walked through the detective squad bay, looking for Donny.

"Hey, Donny, we just returned from South OC, but I wanted to chat with you for a minute." He motioned for them to enter an unoccupied interview room and closed the door. "I just wanted to thank you for the prompting about Lori and—"

"What happened?"

"Well, it went much better than expected after I stumbled through the L-word issue. With Clare, we never said it that much. It was just understood. When you have a new relationship and feel like you feel, I guess you have to express it. So I did. And boy, did it pay off in dividends."

"I don't need the particulars, but you have a find there, a quality lady, so don't mess it up. You're a lucky guy."

Hamilton stretched, yawned, and leaned on Donny's desk. "I know, Donny. Thanks to you, I got over the second-love jitters. I'm tired."

"That's what friends are for, HH."

"Isn't that a song?"

They both had a good chuckle.

107

CHAPTER

Howard planned to spend the weekend with Lori, looking around the South Bay with her and a friend who was a Realtor. Lori had an offer on her home but was still considering it. Moving was always challenging, even if you stayed in the same zip code.

He got up from his nap at about four in the afternoon, just as Marcia came home from a long day at school.

"Hey, Dad, have you talked to Geoff?"

"Yup." He yawned and stretched to get rid of the cloud in his head. "He was concerned about whether we had arranged to stay in Arizona for the Super Bowl. I've verified with Lori that we'll stay at her place in Scottsdale. I just have not gotten back to him. I had a long day—or night. I'm not sure which." He stretched again and decided to wash his face.

Marcia followed him into the bathroom. "Dad, can I say something?"

"Of course, Marcia. What's on your mind?"

"Well, I've been thinking about this trip to Arizona and staying in Lori's condo with you and Brandon." She talked to the mirror as Howard washed his face.

"And?" He looked up casually.

"I had a talk with Lori, and if it's OK, Brandon and I will stay with you guys, but I just want you to know we'll be sleeping in separate bedrooms."

"You're a big girl, Marcia. I understand the issues here. I'm just glad you told me in advance. I hadn't even thought of that," he lied.

"Lori told me it was more appropriate to do that, even though we have slept together. Just not overnight and with you around."

"I don't want to know the details of your private life. Well, maybe I do, but just be careful. I am still your dad, you know, and not your best friend to confide in."

"That's why I have Lori, Mel, and a few others, Dad. Thanks for understanding."

"Thanks for keeping me in the loop, Marcia. Love ya, but gotta do some gardening to make myself useful around here."

Sometimes things work out even if they have not been planned.

* * *

They spent Saturday and part of Sunday looking at single-family homes and town houses in the South Bay area. Living in a multimillion-dollar home and trying to downsize made the selection of homes for sale challenging. Lori opined that it had to be like her home, only smaller. She would know if it had a perfect canvas to work with, but thus far, nothing had appealed to her. Howard was just along for the ride.

His body may have been in the various homes visited, but his mind was on next Thursday and Operation Torment D-day. It was also on buckling down to study for the sergeant's test. Seeing what he contributed in that large room at the Backoffice had made him realize he had the skill set to accomplish more than he had been doing. He needed to be in a position of greater responsibility if he wanted to make an impact on crime fighting and take care of his community and even his extended community, as this operation had shown.

They attended Mass and finished house hunting in the late afternoon. Hamilton could tell Lori was flustered and tried to console her.

"Hey, the worst-case scenario is we don't find anything, and you have to move in with Marcia and me."

Did I say that?

Lori looked at him, perplexed. "You are kidding, right, my dear?"

"The offer is on the table, but I think you'll find something before escrow closes on your place."

He hoped he was right about that.

108

CHAPTER

D-day finally arrived in the shape and sound of an alarm clock at 2:30 on Thursday. Everyone met at the station and carpooled to Anaheim Stadium again. Howard asked Pat to drive so he could review some information he had compiled.

They arrived at the stadium just before four o'clock, as traffic was light for that part of the morning. There were more people than last time, by a large margin. LASD SWAT was gathered on one side of the parking lot, while everyone else walked briskly into the meeting room where Captain Dial would hold court.

From what Hamilton could pick up, SWAT would remain at this staging area until the signal to move toward the industrial complex, which would be the destination for the vans. Takedown would occur once all vans had arrived. When given the signal to move out, SWAT would find their staging area before the vans started showing up for their destination in Garden Grove.

Captain Dial had a spring in her step and a smile as she walked to the small podium to convene the briefing.

"Ladies and gentlemen, this is our Super Bowl, and we intend to win, no matter what. There will be only one winner, and that's us." She got a round of applause but tempered it to get through her agenda and talking points.

Dial announced one change in the ops plan. She had arranged for the San Diego County Sheriff's Department to pick up all gang members acting as escorts at the Black's Beach location and confiscate any radios or other items in their possession that would indicate a conspiracy to commit human trafficking. The Orange County Sheriff's Department would do the same at their locations. Everybody was going to jail today.

Hamilton raised a hand. "Captain, if possible, I would like them to go to the beach and pick up discarded wristbands again. I think we can use them in our investigation."

Dial immediately responded, "Does everybody get that? Make sure to relay to SDSO from our comm center. We will be picking up the gang members at each of the OC locations as well. Same drill. Let's roll."

It was time to rock and roll. Hamilton and Wolford walked over to Sergeant Broderick, advised him of a few changes, and jumped into the Eurocopter, just as they had last week.

There was a cloud cover coming off the ocean that would restrict visibility for flying along the coast. They had not planned for that.

"I'm going to go inland over Camp Pendleton and Oceanside from the east to La Jolla, the first drop-off point. This cloud cover, or fog or whatever you call it, may change our plans." Broderick sounded a bit distressed in his announcement.

He advised Hamilton they would be flying past the first point and coming in from the southeast. Hamilton was already monitoring the radio frequency used by cartel members and heard the chatter as the pangas made their way north from Mexico. He relayed the frequency connection information.

When they arrived at their first destination, the observer announced, "I can spot five boats about one hundred yards off the coast. Our cloud cover has lifted here, but no boats are moving toward shore. What do you make of that?"

Wolford said, "HH, do you think they spotted us up here and are getting spooked?"

Howard was intently listening to the radio chatter on the headset plugged into his laptop, trying to figure out why they had not landed the first boat. He held up a hand to say, "Hold off," because he needed to concentrate on what was being said on his frequency monitor.

"The mix of English and Spanish confuses me, but it sounds like they're not spooked. I think they were just late in getting to the location. Maybe the change in the weather affected them as well. The local gang members were not in place on the beach to escort the migrants from the shore to the van." He pointed to the beach area as the movement started.

Wolford acknowledged and continued to observe the activity below.

The first boat headed to shore. Hamilton could see they were moving too fast as they hit the breakwater. The panga tipped just then, and all the occupants fell into the water. They were only fifty yards from shore, and most could be seen swimming to the beach, where the waiting gang members would process them before they went up the hill to the waiting van.

Hamilton followed with his binoculars. "Hold on. I think I spotted something."

109

CHAPTER

Hamilton advised the command post about the incident as the migrants approached the shore.

"I spot at least two bodies, one small and one that appears to be an adult." From his vantage point, they bobbed in the ocean with little hope of rescue. "Sergeant Broderick, sir, I need to speak to the supervisor of the San Diego County sheriffs who are taking part in this operation. Can you make that happen?"

"Roger that." Broderick flipped some switches to bring up the SDSO supervisor.

Hamilton immediately identified himself and his location and advised what he was seeing from the air. "Hey, Sarge, once you pick up the migrants and take the gang members into custody there, can you get the wristbands dropped on the sand and anything else you find of evidentiary value?"

"Roger, sir. We're moving in right now."

Hamilton smiled that the sergeant called him *sir*, obviously thinking he was someone of importance. He and Wolford watched as the black-and-whites moved in with a combination of uniforms and plainclothes detectives in raid jackets. Hamilton breathed harder; his frustration was showing.

"I can see two bodies out there, Sarge—about thirty yards from shore. Is anybody with a wetsuit there with you? My info indicates the water temp is fifty-five degrees."

"Yes, sir, I have one in my SUV. Just for this occasion. We're on it, sir."

Hamilton could only watch as three two-man teams of uniforms swarmed the beach and took the gang member escorts into custody. He immediately saw someone dressed in black enter the water, swim to the bodies, and pull them to shore. Two other plainclothesmen with raid jackets could be seen using CPR to resuscitate.

"Damn it," Hamilton said in frustration. "We're sitting up here watching people die. Can you believe it?"

"Calm down, HH. We don't know if they're dead yet."

"They couldn't last that long in the cold water. One of them was small. It could have been a kid."

"I see it all the time from up here, Detective. I've seen officers shot because they were in the wrong position, and I couldn't move fast enough to communicate." Broderick tried to add calm in the cabin. "I think that's part of the frustration we feel up here sometimes. But we have a job from here, so let's concentrate on that, OK?"

"It doesn't make it any easier being up here, sir. If I were down there, maybe the same thing would happen." There was resignation in his voice.

"Let's concentrate on what we can impact up here." Broderick was giving Hamilton a lecture he would remember for a long time.

"Got it, Sarge. Sorry to get caught up in all of that. It's just very frustrating."

The silence was a tacit agreement to move on.

The Eurocopter continued hovering at high altitude over the La Jolla pickup spot. Hamilton could see the planning and coordination were paying off, as the van and driver were taken into custody along with the gang members and migrants.

"SD 45 to the airship. We have things under control down here. We'll impound the van, separate the gang members from their clients, seize their radios, get the wristbands as ordered, and bring the bodies to Anaheim Stadium. Unfortunately, we have one dead body here—a nine-year-old boy. The mother survived. We also recovered three suitcases. I think it's all contraband. Thanks for the assist up there." It was the voice of the SDSO supervisor.

All but two would never see the America they desperately desired.

He signed off with "Go Padres. You can't change that."

Everyone in the airship tried to smile to release the tension and the sadness.

110

All arrestees were to be transported to the Anaheim Stadium staging area, where a mobile mass booking facility had been established. As part of the overall plan, the migrants were transported to the local INS office in Santa Ana for processing.

Hamilton was concerned that somehow, the first group may have been able to communicate to the rest of the cartel that something had gone wrong in La Jolla. He listened to the radio chatter, and it did not sound like they were panicking or concerned with the La Jolla site.

The caravan of boats had moved north to San Clemente Beach, so the Eurocopter with Sergeant Dan and the crew did the same. Neither the task force nor the cartel had planned for rough seas, high winds, or a stormy beach. The only people to benefit from the massive waves were the Trestles and Old Man's Beach surfers just outside the United States Marine Corps Camp Pendleton gate on Basilone Road.

San Clemente Beach had the distinct advantage of having a pier and easy access to the beach by car or on foot. The pangas would land their clients in the downtown area of that incredible beach community, where they could quickly disappear into the woodwork. It was critical to the operation that the OCSD move quickly once the passengers could be seen heading to shore.

Broderick put his radio frequency to the Orange County frequency so Hamilton could communicate with the supervisor. The OCSD supervisor advised Hamilton she had a team on the pier with a direct line of sight of the caravan as they approached the area just south of the pier. It only took fifteen minutes to scoop up the gang members, separate the migrants, and gather the evidence from the beach. The suspects had tried to land the boat on the beach with what appeared to be suitcases or boxes. OCSD personnel confiscated all containers, and two additional suspects were taken into custody.

This part of the operation went much more smoothly than the La Jolla event. There were no casualties or altercations, and no one living near downtown or San Clemente Beach knew what had happened.

By then, the command post had announced the success of sites one and two but stressed the urgency to get to sites three and four, Monarch Beach and Laguna Beach. The cartel might have gotten wind of something that had happened at the previous locations, so wrapping this part of the operation was critical to the next phase: taking down their headquarters in Garden Grove.

Hamilton and Wolford watched as the Monarch Beach site was secured. This spot was a bit more complicated because it was between the Ritz-Carlton Hotel and a group of homes on a hill overlooking the ocean. Last week, the gang members had picked up the migrants just below the hotel and walked up a long pathway to a tunnel and into a parking lot used during the day by surfers and beachgoers. Because of the ocean surge and big waves, surfers were starting to show up, which would make for a more difficult takedown.

Hamilton saw three pangas pass the hotel location and continue north to a small cove just north of the dump spot used last week. "Aero 1 to CP. It looks like they will drop off away from the hotel and farther north. Can we move our teams on Pacific Coast Highway to accommodate?"

The CP said, "Roger that. Can you bring up site three's supervisor on your scanner?"

Broderick found what he was looking for, and Hamilton communicated what was happening from an aerial view.

Hamilton called down to the ground unit supervisor. "Sir, it looks like they'll drop off at the beach north of the hotel about two hundred yards. It looks like a walkway up to the homes, but isn't that a gated community?"

"Roger. It is, Aero 1. I've got a unit dispatched to the guard gate so we can gain access. There's also a locked gate from the beach side. Unless they force it open, they'll have a hell of a time getting their people to walk the stairs and climb over a gate. We've got it covered by the water as well. Just in case they try to boogie. Will keep you posted."

Site four, Laguna Beach, was close to site three, Monarch Beach. The

Eurocopter could see both locations simultaneously. Hamilton could see one of the vans, with the roof marking of *OCMB*, in a parking lot across the street from the gated Monarch Beach entrance. He could hear the radio chatter, and it sounded as if they were either panicking or wanting to shut things down.

"I think we should take both sites at the same time," Hamilton radioed to the OCSD ground supervisor.

"Ten-four on that, sir. Will do."

The movements could not have been choreographed much better, and the Monarch Beach and Laguna Beach locations were over in twenty-three minutes.

Just then, a familiar voice came over the airwaves. "Victor 11, this is Victor 7. Do you read me?"

Hamilton knew the voice of Phil of the Everlys and jumped on the mic. "Roger, Victor 7. What do you have down there?"

"We have a fleet of Mercedes sedans in the parking lot, waiting for the passengers from site four to load into the van. When they saw what happened, they took out of there like a bat out of hell, if I could quote Meat Loaf. I think they're spooked and headed to their HQ in Garden Grove."

Hamilton acknowledged. "Command post, did you monitor?"

"Roger. We did, and our next part of the operation is already in play."

111
CHAPTER

Daylight had broken, but the vans still lit up with the now familiar *OHMB* and *OHPD* as they exited the freeway and took surface streets to their destination.

Three LASD SWAT teams had been assigned to Operation Torment and were staging at Anaheim Stadium. As soon as they heard that all vans were headed to the Garden Grove industrial park where the cartel had taken up occupancy, they rendezvoused at a secondary staging location to await the arrival of the sedans and vans.

Hamilton was still up in the Eurocopter, and they were following the vans at a safe altitude up the I-5 freeway to the cartel headquarters.

"Sergeant Broderick, sir, we can stay as high as we need to, because we have two separate units tracking the suspects. We think we know where they're going, so I'll keep you posted when I hear anything on my end. SWAT sent out a scout, and we have a GPS device on several of the cars, plus a loose tail."

Broderick moved the airship to see the industrial park where the caravan would finally stop.

Hamilton used his high-powered binoculars to zoom in on the entrance gate. He peered through his binoculars and announced, "Looks like the gates are manned by two males with automatic weapons waiting for the cars to arrive." He tuned in to the suspects' frequency and heard Spanglish chatter. "They're five minutes out."

That information was relayed to the command post and SWAT commander.

Just before the gates were opened, the command post dispatcher said, "All units, be advised that we have one undercover and a CI in one of the follow vehicles, and we do not know which one. Our information indicates the UC is costumed as a one-legged man on crutches. A young Hispanic female will accompany him. They should be close together. SWAT commander, please acknowledge."

"Roger. That's all we need."

Hamilton was livid. "What the? Disney did it again and tried to get too deep into this operation, and now he's jeopardizing this whole fuckin' thing."

Wolford tried to calm him down. "Garcia can take care of himself, HH. And the CI. But they should have told us this before the operation. Because we're up here in an airship, maybe they thought we didn't need to know or couldn't communicate with us."

Hamilton grabbed his radio. "Can I get the SWAT commander on a simplex channel by himself?" he asked the command post.

"Roger that."

Hamilton waited until the CP had completed the transfer of frequencies. "SWAT commander, this is Victor 11 of Orchard Hill PD. The UC is one of ours. He should be easy to spot with one leg, but he will probably also wear an eye patch and headscarf. I don't know if he is armed. Repeat: I do not know if he is armed. Copy that?"

"Roger, Victor 11. Does he only have one leg?"

"No, he wraps it up behind him. He's double-jointed and does this all the time."

"Got it. Thanks for the heads-up. Any information on the female?"

"No, but I'll try to find out what she is wearing."

Wolford interrupted. "I contacted Hernandez. She's wearing jeans and a white hooded sweatshirt with *Peace and Love* across the front."

Hamilton relayed the information to the SWAT commander.

The SWAT commander said within thirty seconds, "We're going in."

112

CHAPTER

Hamilton's frustration was mounting. "Damn it, I should be down there," he said to no one in particular. Tapping his fingers on his laptop only heightened his emotion.

"Me too," Wolford said.

"Me too," Broderick added, "but we have our job up here, so let's do it." He then told his observer to keep track of the vans and the SWAT teams' locations at each building.

Then the fateful words came over the frequency: "Shots fired."

Hamilton heard the broadcast from the SWAT commander. "Can you take us down and land, Sarge?"

"Not advisable, Detective. Not until they secure the scene. After this is over, I'll take you back to the staging area, and you can drive to the location. There's nowhere to land this ship here, and we must keep tabs on what's happening on the ground."

"I understand," Hamilton said after resigning himself to do what needed to be done.

Don and Phil asked to be patched into the airship Hamilton was flying.

"Victor 11, be advised we stayed back, and three Mercedes vehicles circled the area after SWAT went in. They could be trouble."

"Roger that, Victor 7. I'll get the CP to dispatch some units to intercept. CP, did you copy?"

"Already in progress, Victor 11. We're deploying our backup detail just for such an occasion."

Broderick jumped in. "Let's advise the SWAT commander so he can deploy at the gate until the backups arrive."

Hamilton took care of the request and watched as SWAT secured the entrance. "Victor 7, what is your location?"

"We are still on the I-5, at the 55. It'll take these guys another twenty minutes to get to the Garden Grove location."

"Roger. We're deploying some units to box them in as they try to enter the gated area. It could call for trouble, so be on the alert."

Hamilton watched as the black-and-whites moved toward the industrial park and lined the side streets to ensure the suspects had no escape route. It was still early, and the morning rush-hour traffic was building.

Broderick spoke up again. "Tell those units they may box them in, but if they're armed, the uniforms could get caught in a crossfire."

Hamilton passed the information to the CP.

"We've not heard anything since the last shots fired. What's going on inside?" Wolford was trying to find someone on her frequency who could give an update.

Hamilton monitored the suspects' walkie-talkie frequency. "The suspects Victor 7 are following are in communication with their headquarters. I doubt they would head toward their home base, knowing SWAT is there."

"Victor 11, this is Victor 7. My suspects continued northbound on the freeway and passed the off-ramp to reach the target location. Not sure where they are going."

Hamilton jumped in. "We'll have the other airship go with them. You stay back and do a follow. I will patch you into the frequency for the Sikorsky. Their radio designation is Aero 10. Keep us posted."

Broderick heard the conversation and made the radio connection.

"Command post to Victor 11. Do you need units deployed for the follow being done by Victor 7?"

"Yes, we need at least three two-man teams in black-and-whites to connect with Victor 7 for an eventual takedown. Right now, we don't know where they're headed."

Hamilton relayed the information to the CP to coordinate the takedown with Victor 7.

The Eurocopter stayed over the target headquarters, where SWAT made entry. Then the SWAT commander broadcasted: "All units, we are code four here. We have two deputy-involved shootings. The suspects are down, and there are no injuries on our side. We have a lot of bodies in custody. Notifications were sent to the DA shooting team, and our detectives and I could use a paramedic unit and the coroner. I need a jail bus and some logistics. We need some intel units to come over and sift through what we've found."

113

CHAPTER

The CP acknowledged the request from the SWAT commander. Hamilton jumped on a side frequency to the CP and asked if he could go to ground and be one of the intel officers assigned to the target site.

"Sergeant Broderick, sir, I just got approval to be part of the inspection team down there. Can you take us back to the staging area so I can get there?"

"Roger. I need another airship to relieve me here. Stand by." He turned the ship south to Anaheim Stadium.

Wolford made eye contact with Hamilton, indicating she was going as well.

They landed, thanked Broderick for his expertise, and went directly to their car. They drove fifteen minutes to the Garden Grove location. While en route, they heard one of the units following the Mercedes caravan advise they were going into a residential neighborhood near the cartel headquarters. Then another shocking broadcast came over the airwaves.

"CP, be advised the suspects we've been following just dumped a body on the side of the road and kept going. Looks like a female with a white top. I'll assign a unit to stay with the body but need additional units to code two and a half at our location." It was apparent assistance was needed immediately. "Looks like they are going to a safe house in addition to the industrial park location."

The CP responded, "Backup units are already on the way. Hold back, and give us a location for them to rally with you."

Hamilton turned to Wolford. "We're not going there, Pat. I don't know who was shot, but I can only guess. I have a horrible feeling it may have been our CI. They need uniforms, not plain clothes. Even with raid jackets, we'd get our collective asses shot."

290

"Got it," Wolford said without hesitation as she took a deep breath. "I'm worried about Garcia because he was with our CI. I hope somebody is keeping tabs on him. If the body is our CI, Hernandez will go batshit crazy. She got too close to her. And maybe I did too."

They arrived at the industrial park site, identified themselves to the two deputies at the gate, and were escorted into the building.

It looked like a regular business office, with a reception area and a few offices off to the side. They were led through a door that opened to a cavernous hangar with tables, file cabinets, desks, and papers strewn all over the floor and on top of a series of eight-foot beige tables that looked like they had come from Costco.

Several Mercedes vans were parked toward the back of the warehouse, blocking an area from sight.

The SWAT commander approached Hamilton and Wolford. "Let me give you a quick tour here, detectives. Behind these vans is a narcotics packaging setup. And by the way, Detective Hamilton, your request for drug dogs has paid off. They are getting positive hits on every vehicle in the fleet we seized, even those that only carried the migrants. They use these things to move drugs when not moving people."

He pointed to an area with boxes and brown industrial wrapping machines with utensils that cut drugs into packageable form. "We have cocaine, fentanyl, marijuana, tar heroin, and ecstasy manufacturing."

Hamilton saw boxes, kilos, ziplock bags, and cutting tools to package almost any illicit drug imaginable.

"We've got the clandestine lab team responding to handle this. That's not what we need you guys for." He walked HH and the Wolf to the tables and file cabinets. "Tell me what you see."

Hamilton picked up some of the papers on the tables, opened the file cabinets, and took his time to absorb the data before him. Wolford did the same.

Hamilton spoke first. "From what I can see, sir, these guys were manufacturing fake or counterfeit Social Security cards and driver's licenses. They were undoubtedly providing them to the migrants smuggled into our country. I also see records that indicate various payments made, obviously money that was paid to be smuggled into the States."

"You're a quick study, Hamilton. Let me show you this setup over here." The commander moved to another office-type arrangement with partitions, computers, and additional file cabinets.

Wolford looked around, grabbed several files, sifted through them, and set them back down. "These fuckin' guys were filing for COVID relief funds for all the migrants they had processed through here. So the government sends the checks made out to whomever, and they cash them somewhere. Fuck me."

Hamilton laughed at the last statement. "I think Donny's got you off the market, Pat. But I get it. Look here. I found another file cabinet where they filed for unemployment insurance for all the females they had provided with phony socials and DLs. They also had phony LLCs and filed for federal funds because they claimed to have lost income due to COVID-19. They had them working the streets to pay off their smuggling debt while using them to siphon funds from the government. I don't know how many ways. Doesn't anybody track this shit? Millions of our tax dollars are being siphoned through here. It's an intel treasure trove that will take months to sort through."

Wolford held up another file. "Here's a list of obituaries from all over Southern California. It looks like they used recently deceased people's names, got their socials, and applied for unemployment or COVID relief. This is bullshit."

Then Howard spotted a file he was familiar with.

114

The label on the file was *Rod Dot*. It was a list of all the accounts of Mexican Mafia cartel members who were imprisoned within the state. A name corresponded to an account number where money could be transferred from the site to any prison in the state that housed their members.

Hamilton choked when he saw the number of accounts being tracked. Wolf shouted, "Hey, HH, look at this! This is un-fucking-believable. They kept a file of letters requesting COVID relief for all their Mafia buddies in prison. It's right here on the computer. They tracked the money, put it into the Red Dot accounts the state set up in the prisons for the benefit of their bullshit welfare, and bingo—millions of dollars from us taxpayers went to guys who may never see the light of day. And the state is acting like a bank account for these guys. And they don't even know it."

Hamilton was getting pissed. "I can't believe what I'm seeing. According to my sources at the CDCR, they have no clue they're sitting on millions of dollars from our government. But they will when I get through with this."

The acrid smell of gunfire still permeated the air. Hamilton could smell and taste it. But it didn't faze him as he sat down to review the various treasures of evidence. He glanced at the officer-involved shooting teams surrounding them, the presence of the coroner, and the multiple forensic teams working in every corner of the warehouse except the domain they had staked out. He noted that Wolford didn't even look up.

The SWAT commander came by to give an update. "Can I show you something else, Detective?" Without asking, he continued walking to the far rear of the warehouse. "Look at this."

The commander pointed to a chain-link fence with a locking mechanism that had been broken open. Every kind of merchandise someone could have picked up at a Costco, Walmart, or other convenience market was displayed. Liquor, paper goods, food, and soft goods were stacked about ten feet high.

"The best we can figure out is that these items are taken as part of the cartel's organized retail theft operation. They sell these items on the black market after sending teams to pillage stores all over the area. We'll have our detectives take this over, but I wanted you to see the extent of this operation. It just keeps on fuckin' expanding."

Hamilton and the Wolf returned to their tasks, shaking their heads at the enormity of their find.

Wolford found some empty boxes outside next to the trash bins and brought them in. "Let's box up all this and take it to our offices. It'll be easier to sort through there. I'm done for the day."

"Great idea, Pat." Just then, Hamilton's cell phone rang. He saw it was Barber. "Yes, sir, what's up? We're at the warehouse in Garden Grove. Wait till I tell you what we've found here."

"Hold on, HH. I've got some bad news." Barber took a deep breath that could be heard over the phone line. "Disney was taken hostage after they figured out our CI was the snitch. They killed her and dumped her body on the street. We're tracking them, but they're holed up in one of their safe houses in Garden Grove with Garcia. He may have been shot, but they want something to release him. I'm not sure what their demands are going to be. SWAT's on the scene, along with a bunch of uniforms. I wanted to keep you in the loop."

"Thanks, Sarge. I'll fill you in on what we have here later. It's nothing compared to what you guys have going on. Boy, these guys don't play games, do they? It's a fucking war. Is Detective Hernandez with you?"

"Roger that, and she's not doing well. I had her partner, DeLeon, take her back to the station. We'll deal with that later. These guys are playing for keeps, HH. I'll get back to you later."

Hamilton filled Wolford in on what Barber had told him.

She said, "This thing is so out of control. I don't know how we can get our arms around this, HH. I'm a bit scared."

"You and me both, Pat. I think we stay here and wrap up what we have. We started this thing, but it has so many tentacles now that I don't know if we'll ever recover. I'm just agonizing over wanting to be at that scene to rescue Al, but everybody has a different job here, and I guess we hope and pray things work out. Sergeant Dan was right. We gotta do our job, and it's here."

Hamilton took a moment to photograph the office area they were working before any files were boxed and labeled. He also took time to photograph the warehoused goods shown by the SWAT commander. He ran back to his car, obtained all his evidence-marking equipment from the trunk, and returned to the office area of the warehouse.

Computers and hard drives were boxed and sealed with evidence tags. File folders, computers, and three-ring binders were boxed by category. The Red Dot files were separated from the records for COVID relief, migrant payment records, and other items used to maintain records. It was painstaking and labor-intensive work that would only pay off when they were challenged in court regarding the seizure of files.

The packaging of the evidence continued until a broadcast from the CP advised, "SWAT just made forced entry into the safe house to rescue the hostage. We have another OIS, and the hostage officer is down. Paramedics are already on the scene."

Hamilton continued to listen to the frequency and heard Rikelman's voice say, "OHPD Victor 10 and 20 are at the scene. Be advised we are wearing raid jackets."

There was radio silence, but that didn't mean business wasn't being conducted. HH knew that with Rikelman in charge, everything that needed to be done would get done. He and Pat would have to wait until the dust settled. Barber would call him back for the update—no matter what.

115

CHAPTER

Hamilton could not concentrate on what was in front of him. He flashed back eight years, when his life with Clare and the kids had been simple. He'd patrolled a city with minor violent crime, almost no major drug problem other than weed in the high schools, and never the contentious issues he had been involved in since being assigned to N&V. Chaos seemed to reign outside the city limits of Orchard Hill. Inside Orchard Hill was just fantasy land now.

Garcia is one of us. He is part of our unit and a fellow partner protecting Orchard Hill. Whether in uniform or plain clothes, he is part of OHPD, which cares for the city. Our city.

Do we need to go out of the city to protect our city, or do we patrol the perimeter to ensure evil doesn't enter? The former chief talked about the department's ability to police the city, catch the bad guys, and ensure that outside elements were not welcomed. For that, he was taken to task by the media. Maybe he knew what lurked outside the city boundaries. But now that I've spent time outside Orchard Hill with these recent investigations, I'm unsure I could protect the home turf.

His thoughts were interrupted.

"Penny for your thoughts, HH." The Wolf could sense he had drifted from his tasks. "Hey, why don't we just bundle this stuff up, pack it in our car, and, after getting an update on Al, go back to the station?"

"That's just what I was thinking. Good grief, do you read minds too?"

"Just yours, HH. I see what's happening, and Al takes precedence right now. Let's get the fuck out of here."

Hamilton got permission from the SWAT commander to move his car closer to the entrance for loading purposes. With forensics, the DA, and other LASO investigators and lab people working feverishly, he needed to get out of their way and protect his precious cargo. They carefully marked each box appropriately and found a hand truck to trolley the boxes to their car parked about fifty feet from the entrance.

After loading the boxes into the trunk and backseat, he got on his cell phone to raise Barber. "Victor 20, what is your location?"

"We're with the Garcia family at UC Irvine Hospital in Orange."

"Can we come by to see you on the way back to the station?"

"Not much to see. He's in surgery right now."

"Well, keep us posted. Pat and I are headed back to the station. You will not believe what we have."

*   *   *

The ride back to Orchard Hill was somewhat somber. The cloud cover had not lifted even inland from the coast. A casual conversation between the Wolf and Hamilton centered on how they would divide the workload regarding the files confiscated as evidence. They both longed for the tranquility of Orchard Hill.

Hamilton exited the freeway and found his way to a familiar Orchard Hill street, heading toward the station. "Look at these streets, Pat. They're clean, with no graffiti. People care for their homes, and the businesses we see thrive. I think I just want to get back to policing our city."

They pulled into the station parking lot.

"Let's get a dolly and unload this stuff. I'll notify the boss, and we can go EOW. Better yet, I have an idea."

Hamilton ran into the office and was met by Don, Phil, Scotty, Billy, Tony, Johnny, and Louie Graham.

"I guess you know about Al, huh?" Scotty asked.

"Yes, we heard," Hamilton said, a bit winded.

"Hey, if we wanted that kind of action, we would have gone to LAPD," Billy said to no one. "This is bullshit."

Howard corrected him. "Hey, Billy, look at us here. We lost A. J. Johnson and others by other means. It happens everywhere. We're not immune. Get over it. We signed up for this to take out the bad guys, and we did. Can you guys help Pat and me unload some evidence from our car?"

Everybody jumped at once.

116

CHAPTER

As they started figuring out where to store their seizures, Rikelman and Barber showed up.

Hamilton said, "Any chance you have Garcia's wife's number? I'd like to talk to her."

Barber wrote her number on a scratch pad. "She's on the fifth floor, in the waiting room. But here is her number."

Wolf added, "Make it quick, HH. I'll guard the evidence."

Wolford walked Barber and Rikelman over to the boxes of evidence they would be sifting through for weeks. She explained in precise detail what they'd found. That move gave Hamilton the time to make his phone call.

He had experienced too many deaths of his fellow officers. Having Garcia survive made it vital that he convey his sentiments to his wife. And he did.

In less than ten minutes, Hamilton returned and thanked Rikelman and Barber for their indulgence. "I just needed to do that, sirs. Being in the chopper all that time, sifting through papers, and not having boots on the ground virtually killed me. At least I could get some closure here, find out Al would pull through eventually, and connect with the wife. It made a difference. Now I can go back, pray for him, and do my job."

"You're an interesting, complex guy, Hamilton." Barber grabbed him by the shoulders.

"Not really, sir. I'm just concerned with a fellow officer. Can you tell me how this all went down?"

"All we know right now is they figured out they had a snitch in Hernandez's CI, Gina. Somewhere along their travels, they shot her and dumped the body near their safe house. They weren't sure about Garcia,

298

so they started asking him questions. They didn't get the answers they wanted." Barber's words slowed as he dwelled on the enormity of the situation and how it affected him.

Barber collected his thoughts and continued. "They got to the safe house, muscled him into a room, and started pushing him around. He pulled his backup piece. He shot one, and the other suspect shot him. It looks like he took a round in the abdomen. All that roly-poly gut probably saved his life. We have to let the OIS team and the doctors sort things out. These fucking guys play for keeps."

"No shit."

Hamilton surveyed the mounds of evidence before them and told Wolford, "I think we take this all back to the office, inventory everything, book and seal everything as evidence, and store it in our James Bond room. It will probably take us a few hours, but it's got to be done. We go EOW and can come in tomorrow ready to rumble. It will probably take us all day tomorrow and Monday, but we can finish it. I'll let the lieutenant and Barber know."

"Sounds good, HH. I think we both need a break from all of this. Don't you have something special going on this weekend anyway?"

"Oh my gosh. I almost forgot. We're going to the Super Bowl. We fly out tomorrow morning and have two days before the big game. I can't believe it's here already."

Compartmentalize, Howard. You have to break away from this shit and live your life. Do not let the Phantom get you, at least not yet. Be with Lori and the kids. Is that so hard?

He took a deep breath. "Yes, it is," HH said spontaneously.

"What do you mean, Howard?" Wolford didn't understand.

"Nothing. Just thinking to myself. Mind if I make a call?"

"Go ahead; be my guest."

Howard hit his speed dial for Lori. "Hey, what time is our flight tomorrow? I just got a few things going and lost track."

There was a pause.

"Thanks. We'll talk later."

After he hung up, Wolf said, "That wasn't too lovey-dovey, HH."

"No, I guess it wasn't. Too much shit on my mind. I'll make it up to her later."

They packed all the boxes into two cars, drove to the station, and worked until midnight to inventory everything they had. Howard knew the continuity of the chain of custody of the evidence was important. But so was the Super Bowl.

117

Howard slept on the plane, exhausted from the previous week's activities. After their plane landed at Sky Harbor Airport, Geoff and Marty escorted Howard, Lori, and Marcia to the Scottsdale area.

Lori and Marty hit it off right away. Howard was impressed with Marty, or Martha, as she was sometimes called. She was mature for her age and appeared to come from a solid family background.

Lori gave Geoff the address to her condominium.

"Lori, you know how to do it right. That area of Scottsdale is nothing short of spectacular."

And it was. It was in the Kierland district, five stories above a golf course, with breathtaking views of Superstition Mountain, and furnished as only Lori could have.

"Marcia, let me show you your rooms." Lori calmly directed her down the hallway, raising her voice a few levels. "Here is your room, and here is Brandon's." She smiled at Marcia to make her point and ensure Howard overheard the conversation.

Nothing was ever mentioned after that.

They dined at several restaurants around Arizona State University, but all agreed their favorite was Olive and Ivy in Scottsdale, near the old town.

The big game lived up to everyone's expectations—it was a nail-biter to the end, with Kansas City pulling out the win. By late Sunday night, everyone was exhausted.

Despite the game activities, Lori and Howard had time, while Marcia and Brandon were out with Geoff, to discuss items that needed to be resolved. Lori's home was in escrow, and she still had not found her special place to downsize. Howard decided to take a big step forward in their relationship.

"How about when escrow closes, you move into my place until you can find the home you want?"

"Do you mean that, Howard? I mean, do you really mean that?"

"Yes, I do." He walked closer and put his arms around her shoulders. "I don't want you homeless." He laughed.

He kissed her forehead as she buried her face in his shoulder. She let some silence strengthen her for her subsequent response.

"I've been thinking about asking you, but Marcia—"

Howard interjected. "I'll talk to her. You don't have to." He smiled in an attempt to convey sincerity.

"Well, I was going to say she mentioned it to me. I shrugged it off because I felt it had to come from you. Did she say anything to you?"

"Not one word. This is my idea, Lori. Mine. I want you to be a bigger part of our lives, and I can't think of a better way than to take this next step."

Lori walked him to the couch facing the golf course window and let some silence pass. "Here are my conditions. I don't want to sound demanding, but ..."

They watched a foursome of golfers make their way on the fairway.

"That's OK. It's also a big step for you." Howard wanted to give her space for whatever she was about to propose.

"You must help me purge all the stuff I have to sell, give away, or consign. I won't need much, but I still have a storage unit. I can move the items I want to keep until we—I mean I—find a new place to live."

"I can do that."

"Second and most importantly, I want to bring my bedroom set to yours. All my lovemaking memories with you are in that bed, and I want to continue making those memories. Perhaps you can give yours to Marcia. She's due for a big girl's room."

"You think of everything, don't you?"

"If you want to know the truth, this was Marcia's idea, not mine."

"Really?"

"Yes, my dear, really."

It was all a conspiracy, and he was along for the ride. And he loved it.

"I think I'd better call in and ask for tomorrow off. I'm not sure I'm up to working right now."

"Well, that's good, Howard, because our flight isn't until tomorrow afternoon."

Howard took a step back, somewhat perplexed. "I don't know what I was thinking." He shook his head, trying to collect his thoughts. "I was thinking we would be flying out tonight. I'd better call Pat."

"I don't know what you have going on at work, my dear, but I guess I didn't communicate well on our plans. Sorry."

"Not your fault, Lori. We've been so wrapped up in this case. I guess I assumed too much."

He had not mentioned anything about the investigation he had been conducting for several months.

Why should I?

Both his kids were becoming mature adults right before his eyes. Geoff talked about getting an internship at an accounting firm in downtown Phoenix over the summer, so he would not be home during the summer break. Maybe he would never return to Southern California. The conversation regarding his plans was on Howard's list. But not for that weekend.

Another conversation needed to be had. Marcia was finishing her second year of college. Would she go to a four-year institution or go right to work for Lori? What about her relationship with Brandon? Were they serious, or was it a relationship that would transition to something or someone else?

And what about Lori? She had become the family matriarch without even being a family member—yet. She was intertwined in his kids' lives and seemed to relish her new role. He loved it, and he believed Clare would approve.

Wouldn't she?

118

CHAPTER

After returning from the Super Bowl and settling into his routine again, Howard, with the Wolf, completed the inventory of everything seized at the warehouse.

"Guess what," Barber said. "I just got off the phone with Captain Dial. Now that we have this done, the HURT task force has decided to take it over. Several agencies, including DOJ, DHS, DEA, and the FBI, will do the follow-up. Our job is done."

"You mean we spent two days inventorying everything, when they could have done it?" Howard sat back in feigned disgust.

"Look at it this way: we will take the credit for getting the ball rolling and passing it on so we can go back to taking care of our city."

"Sarge, you do have a way of sugarcoating everything. Here—you need to call this person."

Clearly, the case was much bigger than anything OHPD could do alone. The task force would bring all the information to the forefront for prosecution.

Hamilton contacted their HURT task force counterpart, Detective Shiela Jackson, to review everything they had.

"Shiela, I'll send over the inventory in a few minutes, but you have to keep us in the loop on all of the prosecution. I just got through asset forfeiture school, so I can help with the paperwork on everything else the task force seized."

"Hey, Howard, if it weren't for you and OHPD, we never would have gotten this case off the ground. You're not the only one with expertise, but I will pass along the offer to help. Be careful what you volunteer for."

Even though he had all the data, he knew he needed the help, even though the school had taught him the basics.

Working with Jackson and the task force would be critical. He would get a lot of experience in this area, because the only experience OHPD had with asset forfeiture was completing the forms necessary to seize funds or small assets. Hamilton would learn this part of the investigation on the job. It would be overwhelming, with more than twenty vehicles, financial documents, large sums of money, guns, and grocery goods stockpiled in the warehouse. And who knew what else they'd uncovered?

One of his first steps was to freeze all bank accounts seized, including checking & savings, deposit boxes, and prison accounts. This process would require a state Adverse Claim Report, which freezes the accounts for ten days while search warrants are obtained. He knew that much.

DEA would assign a team to assist, but the bulk of the work would fall on Jackson. The search warrants Hamilton and the task force had developed for Operation Torment would require follow-up reports to the court that approved them. He would need some advice from the district attorney on how to proceed with this part of the investigation. They estimated this process would take a few weeks to a month. Hamilton knew he still had much to learn about this part of the investigation and decided to take the time to be coached by the DEA, the feds, and the district attorney.

Where is Packer when I need him?

The tenuous relationship with the supervisor from the California Department of Corrections and Rehabilitation needed attention. Rikelman volunteered to review all Red Dot files with CDCR and relieve Hamilton of the responsibility. That was the least they could do under the circumstances. CDCR needed to take over responsibility for that part of the investigation but would need assistance from the California State Department of Justice.

That left the voluminous files associated with counterfeit Social Security numbers and driver's licenses, files on the fraudulent extortion of funds from the federal government regarding COVID-19, and unemployment reimbursements. In consultation with Captain Dial and his contact point at HURT, it was agreed Dial would contact the FBI and the Department of Homeland Security for advice, guidance, and direction. Everyone agreed that area of the investigation should not fall on either the task force or OHPD.

Wolford was attending the intel school the following week and, on her return, would be ready to work side by side in the intelligence position within the next few months.

For Howard, the biggest surprise came from an unexpected source. Donny entered his office with a file and set it on the desk.

"Thought I would add to your stack, HH. Pat asked me to do this, so I hope that's OK. For me, it was easy, so take a look. I did an extensive investigative report with the aid of Carfax for Police. I looked at all vehicles seized, including their plate numbers, vehicle identification numbers, and secondary VINs, and thoroughly analyzed their history."

He opened the file for Howard's benefit. "I identified counterfeit VINs, swapped VINs, and a crash history for each. It turned out that four of the Mercedes sedans had been used for fraudulent insurance claims, staged traffic accidents, and fraudulent stolen vehicle reports, all done to bilk the insurance companies. I also included all modifications to the Sprinter vans. I tied each car to a specific arrestee, because there were no ownership changes. They weren't that smart. What do you think?" Donny puffed out his chest a bit, obviously proud of his work.

"I think I owe you a drink or two."

* * *

Howard attended the swearing-in ceremony for the new chief, Rose Tustin. It was a lavish event that only an appreciative city council could have put on. The city manager was praised for his selection, and everyone was ecstatic to have a Hispanic female police chief. A select few knew the drama behind her selection, with her being chosen over Chief Melendrez and two OHPD captains. Only Howard knew of her relationship with Guy Coyle, and his lips were sealed.

The Chief clarified that she would not make any changes immediately. That statement ensured Howard that the process currently in place would remain. He would devote as much time as possible, on and off duty, to getting through the latest new laws, search and seizure, and department policies needed to pass the test.

* * *

And Howard did pass. He was unsure of his score on the written exam, as it was not revealed, but he was notified his oral exam was on April 15—coincidentally, Tax Day.

His studies did not take away from his relationship with Lori. They saw each other as much as time permitted, but busy lives made for busy people. Her business required more time, even with Marcia taking a more active role. She was close to closing escrow on her home. She had not found a new place yet, so he would have a new roommate when escrow did close. Was he ready for this?

His oral board was highly stressful. He didn't expect it to be, but it was. He returned to the office exhausted. The only one in the office was Barber.

"How'd it go, HH? Looks like they kicked your ass."

"I feel like they did, sir. I would have rather been in a shootout than go through that."

"Well, maybe you'll feel better if you tell me a little about it. Who was on it?"

"Well, I guess the new chief decided to have just one captain from OHPD, Pierson. She brought in a civilian member of the community. Somebody you know. The president of the chamber of commerce, Jeff Dryer, owner of the Orchard Hill Mercedes dealership."

"That should have been good for you."

"I couldn't get a good read on him. He asked questions, but they had nothing to do with what we did. The other member was the new chief from Redondo PD, who was appointed after Tustin left for Orchard Hill."

Howard knew this was the guy Mel Flowers was having an affair with, but he would not tell Barber anything about that tidbit of information.

"You know me; I can read people pretty well, but I couldn't get a handle on Dryer or that chief. As for Pierson, well, I don't know what he thinks. Never did. I don't know if it was good or bad. Honest to God, it was the worst forty-five minutes of my life."

Barber continued to console him, but his pessimism was overtaking him.

Mr. Dryer knows me as a tenacious investigator, but does that make me good supervisory material? The chief from Redondo doesn't know me, unless Flowers has talked about me. All I know is that Flowers has been fucking him for over a year.

"Hey, Sarge, it is what it is. I answered their hypothetical questions with as much detail as I could. It seemed they had already decided before I entered the room. I'm just glad it's over. I walked out of the room sweating bullets."

119

CHAPTER

On Monday, May 1, Howard reported for duty in the N&V office. A note on the board read, "Staff meeting at nine."

He went to the workout room to push around some light weights because he had almost two hours before the meeting.

He returned to his office, cleaned up some emails, and grabbed a notebook for the staff meeting. Everyone was in attendance but Garcia.

"The first item on the agenda is an update on Garcia." Rikelman provided details that assured everyone he was in full recovery mode. "Here is the problem." Rikelman looked around the room to make sure he had everyone's attention. "Disney will not be returning to the unit."

"Why?" Shotgun Morgan asked with his deep voice. "Why the fuck not?"

"His choice. He'll be moving to detectives when he comes back. And that creates some problems here. We're already short with Bowers's passing and Wolford taking over for Hamilton. So we have some vacancies to fill."

"Where's Hamilton going?" Morgan continued to lead the charge.

"Well, Wolford is going to intelligence school next week, and I think our man Hamilton will have a new job by then."

"I will?" Howard was as confused as anyone.

Rikelman shuffled some papers and produced a one-page memorandum from the new chief. "It seems the sergeant's list came out, and there are three bands. There is one name in band one, with three in band two and three in band three. The one name in band one is our own Howard Hamilton, so congratulations, Sergeant Howard Hamilton."

Was that a smile on Howard's face?

AUTHOR'S NOTE

Passing by a city or town hall complex can reveal many things. The fortification of public-sector buildings started in the late 1980s and continued into the twenty-first century's first decade. Concrete posts and balusters were placed as aesthetically as possible with designs to hide the real reason: to defend against terrorism. Police stations and city halls were at the top of the list for protection as the world started to change. In the late 1990s and early 2000s, bulletproof glass was installed in many municipal police departments as protection from snipers and other nefarious attacks on public buildings.

For many cities, policing the streets is less precarious than the intrigue and drama behind the balusters and bulletproof glass. The public want their governmental services to be protected. They do not know, or could not fathom, that those same safety precautions also protect secrets inside the hallowed halls. Police departments, public works, city councils, libraries, and parks and recreation hold secrets beyond policing, sweeping the streets, checking out books, and maintaining the beauty of our public parks.

The smiles you may see on public-sector employees when they diligently serve their communities belie the drama they face when returning to the office. Interaction with the public can be civil servants' escape to avoid the administrative bureaucracy that controls their actions and often dictates what they can and cannot do.

Police officers also have lives that may intersect with the work on the street. Relationships with coworkers, supervisors, management, and politicians affect what happens on the street. Their off-duty relationships are even more intertwined. Spouses, significant others, kids, neighbors, and friends impact service delivery in every community nationwide.

The Orchard Hill Police Department is not immune to disorders that put a claim on a municipality. Most officers go about their business because they feel they have a calling to serve. However, not every employee is affected or aware of what occurs within his or her organization. There are two things that police officers hate. The first is the way things are. The second is change.

Some are oblivious to the political intrigue because they hide on a night or graveyard shift, stay in the field at all costs, or rarely attend meetings that promote efforts to control behavior.

Lastly, there is not that much mystery in police work. There are thrills, but tenacious work results in incredible job satisfaction that makes mystery novels pale in comparison. There are no real Dirty Harrys, Jack Ryans, or Jack Reachers in police work—only Howard Hamiltons.

What occurs outside does not necessarily translate to what goes on inside.

ACKNOWLEDGMENTS

Writing a book of any length is a solitary effort, but that does not mean there are not many people behind the scenes who provide input and support. It is just the writing that only one person can do.

There are several people to thank as book four of the Howard Hamilton Ride-Along series is brought to life. Sandra D., my wife of more than twenty-five years, permits me solitude without interruption. She has been an invaluable mirror to bounce ideas off and periodically makes a startling recommendation that changes the course of the text.

There is also Dennis Packer. He is one of the best intelligence officers in the country, which is why I used his real name. He introduced me to Michael Bazzell, the best resource for searching and analyzing online open-source intelligence.

The primary inspiration for the Howard Hamilton series is the phenomenal work that countless law enforcement officers do throughout the country daily. Howard Hamilton is a composite of all those who serve. They perform extraordinary work under the most ardent of conditions. Factor in the number of contacts (an estimated ten per day) made by the men and women in blue, brown, and khaki daily (approximately two hundred thousand), and the incidents that may be seen on the nightly news pale.

Why do we cheer the Dirty Harrys, Jack Ryans, and Mitch Rapps of the fictional world and chastise a forceful takedown from an incomplete video that saved injury or death to innocent people not seen by the viewer?

The best surgeons commit more errors in their practice than law enforcement. Yet we see the magnification of law enforcement's action, with its blemishes and attempts to maintain public order, almost daily. Inhumanity can only be explained by experiencing it. Granted, police work is not always pretty, but decisions are required in seconds to gain control of a situation. Yet courts, the legacy, and news media take months to show whether those decisions were accurate and within legal bounds.

I thank my colleagues over the years for giving me the experiences of a lifetime on a 24-7 merry-go-round that never stops, 365 days a year, year after year. We all want to be like Howard Hamilton: we want to do our job, go home every night in one piece, keep our uniform clean, stay out of the rain, and never go hungry. Is that too much to ask?

Howard Hamilton represents the best in law enforcement, who protect communities from themselves. Our frustrations come when we try to balance the community's needs against the perils of evil. I will continue to extoll the virtues of good, solid police work done every day. We all need to appreciate the efforts of the Howard Hamiltons out there.

Please take the time to visit my website, jcdeladurantey.com. If you enjoyed this book, please go to my page on Amazon and complete a review. Your review will ensure that someone else will have the opportunity to ride along with Howard Hamilton.

Five stars would be nice.

ABOUT THE AUTHOR

With over 40 years of law enforcement experience, J. C. De Ladurantey combines street savvy and police department intrigue based upon true stories from a varied career. His previous books, COWARDS, CROOKS, AND WARRIORS, TWENTY-THREE MINUTES, and AVAILABLE TIME, were fast-paced page-turners that received 5-star ratings.

Visit: www.jcdeladurantey.com

Printed in the United States
by Baker & Taylor Publisher Services